Mo

Blood in Mio

written by

Curtis A. Deeter

OF RUST AND GLASS

Morning Blood in Mio

by Curtis A. Deeter

Published by:
Of Rust and Glass
607 River Road
Maumee, OH 43537

Typesetting: Curtis A. Deeter

Cover Art: Xero-Gee Comix
https://www.instagram.com/xero_gee/

ISBN: 978-1-7367728-3-6

To my wife, Danielle,
for bringing me back to Funny.
And to my parents, Beth and Dan,
for bringing me to Mio.

Prologue

In the beginning, there was Nothing. When Nothing got bored, it started mingling with all the empty space in between which led to Stuff in unfathomable amounts.

A lot of that Stuff became stars—not the red-carpet walking, jewel-studded, peacocking, Hollywood type of star but the red dwarf, blue giant, and yes, even the elusive neutron type of star. The bright, flickering kind that helped people realize we were never alone.

With space as their hangout, and nothing but dark matter impeding their dance floor, the planets got together and decided it would be pretty cool—or hot, depending on who you asked—to hang out with all those stars. "You weren't hip," they said, "until you found your own star to orbit."

Of particular interest: Earth.

Once Earth wised up and lassoed itself an atmosphere, interesting things happened with a swirling butt-load of the aforementioned Stuff.

The oceans filled, the mountains peaked, the forests plumed, all creating the precise amount of oxygen and other sciencey goodness that made the planet come *alive*.[1] There

---

[1] While this is not a lesson in astrophysics, it is a lesson about serendipity. As such, it would be irresponsible not to mention the fact that life, as we know it, shouldn't exist. The odds, in fact, are so stacked against life (stacked even higher than the odds of Rodney from down the street *ever* moving out of his mother's garage), it's almost irrational to believe humankind hasn't been put here for some divine purpose. Instead, we squander. But it's understandable; *The Office isn't going to watch itself.*

was room for fish and mountain lions, snakes and eagles, and—to everyone's chagrin—country-western singers.

Then, keeping in order with life's natural progression, anglers came for the fish, poachers for the lions, and when they realized the lavish lifestyles of the country-western singers—admiring their passion for life and their utter lack of concern for personal hygiene—pop singers joined the mix. They tip-tapped their designer, snakeskin boots to the beat of everyone else's own drum. It wasn't very complex or even in time, but that's a story for another day.

At last, there was God.

The brightest minds often overlook the most important question: which came first, the chicken or the egg? God or humanity? The best philosophical approaches to answering this question, as with other controversial inquiries, led down many-pronged paths of intellectual enlightenment to one ultimate answer. It was also a decent answer anytime the philosopher's wives asked them to do something unpleasant around the house.

Yes. Or, in the most desperate of times, *Yes, ma'am. Would you also like me to clean out the garage?*

The other questions weren't so simple. Why are we here? What's our purpose on Earth? Is our universe real or are we living in the Matrix?[2] What time of day does Burger King actually have fresh French fries? A large subsect of

---

[2] While one might assume the movie starring Keanu Reeves and Gloria Foster, this theory actually suggests we are spiraling down the dusty roads of the American southwest in a Toyota Matrix hatchback, with the windows down and the Grateful Dead blaring across the desert sands. No one has yet to provide solid evidence supporting the Matrix Theory; no one has refuted it, either.

humanity needed deeper meaning beyond the fact they were alive in the first place.

God anticipated these questions. Even though she prepared answers for herself during the early stages of creation, she remained silent on the major issues. Instead, she wrote a book. She threw in some parts about treating thy neighbors with kindness; entering loving, committed relationships with our spouses; not lying; doing unto others as others should do unto you, and so forth. She also threw in some parts about burning witches, selling daughters as sex slaves, and purchasing women you've raped. But let's face it: in today's market, fluffy rainbows don't sell books.

Besides, the one time we became too unruly, she drowned the whole of existence. Don't worry, though. She made up for it with, you guessed it, a rainbow. Oh, and there was that other time when she had to give those pesky Egyptians a stern talking to, but they deserved every plague of their punishment. If you asked her, she'd say they got off easy.

"I'd do it again, too," she said in an interview about her book release. "Might move some furniture around, keep it fresh for the kids, you know. Make everyone wear brighter colors. But, yeah, I'd do it again. Why not? I'm mother-freakin' God."[3]

---

[3] Before you judge God too harshly, we all go through phases. God has experimented for a *long* time. Here, she was test-driving the "Bad Boy Thrown into Sudden Fame" phase. She wouldn't intervene; she'd focus on her art. Major self-success comes with massive pressures from critics and fans alike. People expect more. They ask, "What's next?" Given enough time, they wonder if the first one might have been a fluke. There's nothing like a hobby—painting or sculpting or semi-professional beatboxing, for example—to relieve the stress of expectation. When it comes to God, there have been expectations a-plenty.

Since then, God made a conscious decision to stay out of humanity's business.

In the long run, her blasé approach to raising her children was in everyone's best interest. No one liked a helicopter parent.

Still, there were extenuating circumstances when God ought to have stepped in. Sometimes events played out in inadmissible ways. Sometimes the Others—her son, the Adversary, lesser gods, yadda yadda—forced her hand. When one of *them* got involved, she was compelled to strap on her Wolverines and pull up her shirtsleeves.

Which brings us to our story.

This isn't divine doctrine or pretentious commentary. It's not a clever means at making you, our dear reader, a believer or otherwise. It's not even a great document to pop on the back of your toilet seat; though, you might find it useful for beating clear a drain clog if you roll it tight enough or as a mediocre TP replacement during times of scarcity.

Nay, this is *Morning Blood in Mio.*

Chapter 1:

The Followers of Not

But this is not Mio. Not yet.

This is the utopia of utter devastation known as Detroit, Michigan.

From high above—below the clouds, but higher than the smog—observe the Great City: a patchwork of urban farms, city slickers on horseback, trashcan fires warming dirt-caked hands, high-rise hotels, and empty ballparks. It used to be the City. Some call it Hockey Town. Others—for reasons beyond the comprehension of the world's greatest dendrologists—call it the City of Trees. Its stubborn inhabitants still call it Motor City, but the engine is rusted through and the pistons no longer fire.

A few people claimed places like Detroit were dead, dying, old news, and forgotten. They were wrong; they'd never met The Followers of Not, who were more alive than anyone else. Overlooked, sure. They smelled like moldy cheese and bleach, but they were *alive*.

Their continued existence relied on a three key factors—puzzle pieces aligned in perfect harmony to provide them a habitable ecosystem. When these aligned, the Followers thrived. If broken into their original pieces, the whole delicate system would collapse.

Step one, for health reasons, involved mass quantities of booze and drugs housed close enough where they could haul their caches back to their hideout.

But people, even the Followers, couldn't survive on artificial dopamine alone. Luckily, in accordance with step two, the alleyways and abandoned hovels of Detroit supplied plenty of plump rats and lame-winged carrier pigeons to fuel their exploits.

Step three, they needed faith. Without faith, the rest was meaningless.

As it turned out, the Followers of Not weren't so different from everybody else. Booze, shelter, and faith. Sustenance, home, and purpose.

While they had those threefold things, they'd be okay. The fact they worshipped the Devil incarnate and Death in all her glory was neither here nor there. No one was ever perfect, after all.

Upon arrival to Detroit, they found the glory of all three in appropriate abundance. Their journey long, their travels arduous, they'd Arrived. What a place to settle!

With their niche in the world carved, they were free to pretend they had it all figured out. They'd pretended for so long they became their own fantasies. No one— themselves included—remembered who the Followers of Not used to be. Doctors? Teachers? Sons and daughters, though human-spawn was a stretch. Faith only went so far; few had active enough imaginations to believe *that*.

This sect, a trinity of three of the most devout Followers in recent history, included "Rascally" Randy, "Randy" Wilson—confusing, but well-suited to their personalities—and "Repugnant" Rachel.

Rascally Randy, the self-declared, undisputed Champion of Saboteur, Cunning Artifices, and Room-clearing Flatulence—the latter of which was not included in his official title, rather added as a footnote in the book of his supreme awesomeness—considered himself quite enigmatic. He also played the part of leader for the small, rogue group. They looked up to him for one reason or another: They didn't dare stand *down*wind for fear of malodorous demise, and, at seven-feet-tall, he happened to tower over them. So, they had no other choice.

Randy Wilson was second-in-command by default because (as was common knowledge) you couldn't trust women with leadership roles in devil-worshipping cults. They tended to do too good of a job and, in the end, skewed the core values of the group. As a result, he was the exact opposite of his "superior." Short, stumpy, well-kempt, and stupid, he liked what he liked and pursued it with single-minded brutishness. He'd earned his nickname—which was not, in fact, the same semantically as Randy's first name, but much more sinister. He rose every night to ask the world how it planned to get him laid, and every night the world responded by giving him the finger. Not a beast to scoff at, the "Tragedy of Randy Wilson" wrote itself into obscurity before he even found a pen to draft it.

Repugnant Rachel, the last Follower of Not—and, in the boys' eyes, the least—was childishly named because of her constant refusal of Wilson's many advances. She got the short end of the bargain. In Wilson's mind, she only denied his advances because she was "a filthy, raging lesbian with irreparable mental issues."[1] In reality, she was the only one in the ragtag group with her head screwed on even remotely straight. She wasn't repugnant at all. She was dignified. Several cuts above the rest.

She had goals, dreams beyond the Not. She had Hope, a dangerous thing for someone in her unfortunate position. Forget that she combed her hair with pinecones, using excess sap to fix the split ends, and foraged for their food on her knees in Detroit's numerous gutters. She did what she must for her companions, despite their delusional

---

[1] "Filthy", "raging", and "irreparable mental issues" are by no means descriptors specific to lesbians, rather applicable to all walks of human life. See King Herod, Cain, Bill Cosby, Harvey Weinstein, Jeffrey Dahmer, the Muffin Man, etcetera. An eye-opening commentary on human nature and far too extensive to include here. See also the current senatorial/congressional rosters for further reading.

superiority. Without her urban resourcefulness, the Followers of Not would've perished long before they had a chance to give her a nickname.

They sat around a dumpster fire in the bowels of the abandoned Michigan Central, eating a light "breakfast."

Randy licked the remnants of a discarded, moldy McFlurry cup and belched. His fondness for the gelatinous, slightly hazardous foodstuffs stuck at the bottom of such items made the exhausting effort of extraction worthwhile. Broken skylights on the vaulted ceiling above let pale, dawn light in, illuminating his face in all the wrong places as he chomped a moldy peanut.

"Not bad, really. But if *someone* had caught that big, furry bastard earlier, we'd be eatin' like bloody kings."

Rachel lowered her head. She'd failed. Again. It didn't happen often. When it did, Randy shamed her to tears for her shortcomings.

"Sorry." She picked a scab off her forearm.

Wilson watched her like a cat in heat while he waited for the boss to say something important; Randy always said something "important" if you gave him long enough.

Right on cue, he said, "Well then…" He stopped and, after performing a series of yawns and stretches like a malnourished contortionist, he got right down to business. "We all know what needs done."

"We do?" Rachel asked.

"Yes, we do."

"I know what *I* want to do." Wilson sidled closer to the woman he refused to let get away.

Rachel elbowed him in the gut, and he slid as far as the tethers of his hormones would allow.

Randy laughed, his own gut twisting as his slender body writhed with amusement. "I knew I kept you all around for a reason. Remind me to remember that next time you disappoint me."

After recovery, Wilson said, "What *exactly* is it that we need to do…er, sir."

"They need to be coaxed—courted, one might venture—with a fun-spirited sacrifice. Or serenaded with a throaty, Gregorian chant of sorts." Randy rattled his Adam's apple and gurgled. "That oughta do it."

"We should draw some pentagrams. Or burn some candles."

"Hum a hymn or two."

"Can we draw the pentagrams with Wilson's blood?"

Randy glared at Rachel. Geometry had never been his best subject, but he was certain a stop sign was the last thing they needed. If anything, they needed a go sign. He picked gum off the bottom of his shoe, popped it in his mouth, and asked, "What shape means go?"

The Followers ignored him. Brilliant questions deserved brilliant responses.

"Where we supposed to do these things? It's not like we runneth over with options here." Wilson spread his arms to draw attention to their current circumstances. Walking on thin ice always cooled him off.

"There aren't go signs; there'd just be no sign to begin with. You don't see a thousand signs a mile down the highway telling you 'It's okay, keep it up kid. You're doing great'—do ya?"

Randy considered this. He wasn't in the habit of considering the advice of *underlings*, especially Rachel, but this made sense. While he never understood much of what people said to him, he'd gotten good at faking cognizance, which gave him a chance to process his own feeble thoughts one independent clause at a time.

To establish dominance, he made the other Followers squirm. He could pee on them or hump their leg to convey the same message, but that was too messy. Uncomfortable Silence worked better.

When he was good and ready, Randy said, "It doesn't matter *where*, Wilson. They're everywhere and nowhere. It's our jobs—nay, our purpose—to find them." He kicked over a crate and stood on it as he spoke. "The Followers of Not go wherever we're needed. When darkness whispers, we answer. We follow the shadows to find the light. If it takes a year, a decade, or even lifetime, we'll keep on this unrighteous path. Our masters will bless us with their presence when they deem us worthy. Not a moment sooner."

"Patience, then." Wilson rolled his eyes. He'd heard it all before. Still, he liked Michigan Central; he liked Rachel. One day, with enough coercion, she might like him back. Or at least tolerate him. "If we must wait it out, so be it. At least we have each other."

"And leftover cup sludge," Randy added.

"Three months!" Rachel tossed her red hair and scratched at her lice. "Three months we've been here eating rats and sleeping on old newspapers. I used a dead raccoon as a pillow last night. It woke up halfway through, puked on me, and bit my hand. I probably have rabies now, for Not's sake. You want me to just...wait?"

She kicked the crate out from under Randy, flourished, and swatted the air. This was unfortunate for her old pillow, who had recently scurried back for round two. She caught it square in the ribs and sent it flying. It soared across the station and landed with a *zap* on the still-active tracks.

"Whoops." She clapped her hands over her mouth.

"Lunch is served." Randy picked himself off the ground. "For that insubordination, Rachel, you get to go peel it off. Better hurry, it's getting toasty."

"But I need a real meal. One that doesn't squeak before I bite into it."

Randy glanced at the charred remains of the rodent. "I don't think you'll have to worry about any squealing this time."

"You seem cranky," Wilson offered, taking the opportunity to scoot closer to her. "A nice shoulder massage might—"

Rachel brandished a jagged piece of glass. "Touch me one more time, man, and I swear to Not I'll slice you up and have *you* for lunch. Capeesh?"

Arms raised, Wilson backed away, nodding. "Don't blame me for trying."

"We'll eat like kings and queens when *they* come. Those of us who remain gracious, at least. You, *you'll* be eating out of the gutter unless you shape up. One of these days, as you're cutting into steak at a fancy, hoity-toity downtown steakhouse—one with artisan ice cubes and thirty varieties of flan—you'll wake up and realize we're gone. You'll be eating a nice candlelit meal, wiping your face with a cloth napkin, and wishing you woulda stayed true to the Not."

Rachel smiled. She liked cloth napkins. They held in juices better than paper ones. Like the cast iron pan her grandmother used to cook with—the one only washed clean when Hell froze over—a good cloth napkin added delicate yet refined flavors to any meal.

Randy despised her obvious joy. He wouldn't allow it. "*Clean* cloth napkins. Silken ones with gold embroidery and a monogram reminding you of your posh, seafaring family lineage."

She gagged. It was too much to stomach. "You've gone too far, Randy."

Suddenly, before the argument could escalate any further, the whole station quaked. They braced themselves against whatever was closest. Chunks of glass fell from the ceiling, popping like water balloons with tacks in them as

11

they hit the floor. A chunk of concrete broke loose and smacked Wilson on the head. He floundered before buckling at the knees.

All life inside Michigan Central, save the three Followers of Not, hightailed it for the exit. Those that couldn't find the doors threw themselves ritualistically onto the tracks.

"Is that…a train?"

"Don't be an idiot. These tracks haven't run in months."

"Maybe it's *them*," Rachel suggested.

A sound like scraping ice, nails on a chalkboard, open-mouthed chewing, and a dozen colicky babies all thrown together and agitated with a stick cut Randy off before he could interject. It rushed them, developing a life of its own—this noise had *form*—and kicked them square in the chops.

Then, it stopped, and silence reigned.

Randy wheezed. "It *is* them. They're finally here."

Wilson, who'd distracted himself from terror by sucking his thumb behind their fire barrel, peeked out.

"Oh my goodness," Rachel said. "How does my hair look? Oh my, oh my, oh my. I'm not ready for this. I need more time!"

"Urgggh," Wilson said, still hidden. "What a horrible time to need a dump!" Why had he said that out loud? Had he no dignity left?

A sharp pang shot through his body. He clenched his chest with one hand and his stomach with the other. The pain inside of him was like a woodpecker tearing its way out of his body. He doubled over, teeth clenched and eyes bulging. Sweat formed in swaths along his forehead. Whatever was playing power chords on his organs was coming out, one way or another.

Rachel rushed to his aid and lifted him to his knees. Despite his perversions, he was a Follower of Not. That made him family, and you didn't choose family.

Randy was there before she stood Wilson up. He wrenched her away from Wilson and slapped her across the face.

"It's supposed to happen this way. Don't you get it? They're here. If they want Wilson dead, they can have him. If they give him diarrhea, even better."

Wilson continued to writhe in agony. Michigan Central shook and moaned. The steel beams above them bent like paper clips. A meteor shower of glass and concrete fell all around them.

"He's going to die," she said. "We have to do something."

"He's been chosen," Randy snapped. "He's to be their vessel. I'd be *honored* if I were in his place. Now silence, woman. Let them come in discord."

The chaos ended like it had never begun. Stillness blanketed the interior of the station, leaving the Followers of Not in suspense.

Wilson rocked, uneasy on weak legs, pale and sweaty, murmuring something incoherent about rats and second helpings. His stomach gurgled and his muscles ached, but he was nonetheless alive.

"Must have been something you ate," Randy said, stating the obvious.

"I told ya not to cook it so damn well-done. Rat meat's always better raw. This is culinary basics, ya know?"

"Doy," Randy added, helpfully.

Footsteps approached. Randy checked on his companions, both present and accounted for, then focused on the noise. There was no other explanation at this point; no mortal dared intrude on the Follower's territory. They were actually coming. He quivered with anticipation.

13

A shadow rounded the corner, stretching and distorting as it got closer, before snapping to its original, amorphous state. It became a man, shapely and bald, dressed as if ready to go fly fishing in the King's moat. He faded in and out as he transitioned into being.

Riding a primal twinge of manliness, Wilson stepped between the newcomer and Rachel. He held her behind him with one arm and puffed out his stomach. He'd have done the same with his chest, but Wilson had been born with a rare condition much worse than pigeon chest: egg belly. Or, as it was known in certain scientific circles, Humpty-Dumpty Syndrome. His biggest fall? Too much high-cholesterol garbage.

"Stay back, foul beast. Not one step closer," he said.

Randy moved forward to greet the man. "Please excuse my colleague. Can we be of assistance, m'lord?" He bowed low, touching his toes with his pointy nose. "We are but humble servants, ready to do thy bidding."

"Like Hell we are," Wilson said.

"That's a kind offer." The stranger waved off Wilson's outburst with a faint smirk. "I think I'll take you up on it."

He phased out of existence, reappearing within kissing distance of the fattest member of the Not. His outfit changed, too, transitioning in cascading pixels to a black tuxedo and a red, feathered fedora.[2]

"Hm. That never works first try. Hoped it would this time." He shrugged. "You were *so* ready for it, too. Damn. What's your name, my child?"

"Erm, Wilson."

---

[2] An underappreciated fashion that will outlive time itself, second only to jorts.

"Wilson, eh? Great English name. How faux-Medieval of you. Did you know your ancestors were kings?" Wilson shook his head. "And look at *you*. What a shame..."

"Who do you think you are, mister?" Rachel interjected for the speechless and star-struck Wilson. She had to be certain; she needed to hear it from the Devil, himself.

"I'm..." He stopped to ponder. "Call me Stan. And I am *everything*, young lady. Everything and more."

Rachel hid behind Wilson, white knuckling the loose, pungent tatters of his button-down.

Randy fell to his knees with tears streaked across his face, chanting and bowing in prayer. He paid no attention to what happened next.

Stan smiled, his breath reeking of sulfur and heat emanating from his eyes. Gently, almost courteously, he laid a hand on Wilson's shoulder. In an archaic, serpentine tongue, he whispered the answer to the meaning of life in Wilson's ear. Like a lightning bolt on a clear day, Stan plunged an ethereal dagger into Wilson's stomach, slid it up through his heart, and let him go. He sighed, having taken no pleasure in the deed.

Wilson fell like a sack of dead perverts. Stan squatted by him and brought Wilson's agonized face to meet his own.

"Shh, shh, shh," he said. "It's okay, now. You're free. Easy, there you go. I'm sorry we had to go through this charade a second time. You should've been dead upon our arrival. I'll work on that next time, just for you."

Wilson gagged, sputtering blood onto the concrete. He gasped for air but found little. What he took in escaped from his open torso. Blind, he pawed towards his killer, trying to find a handhold—something to grab and bring the villain down to his level.

He died without retribution.

Wilson lay on the ground, twisted and motionless. However, his shadow danced as if it were a mime freeing itself from an invisible box. After jerking and snapping, it broke away and stood—an exact figure of the man. It curtsied to Stan, who bowed. Then, they did a celebratory jig together before embracing for a long, passionate kiss.

Rachel looked away. What was happening, if it was real, disturbed her far too much to process. Nothing made any sense. This wasn't at all how she envisioned their arrival.

"You've been a doll," Stan said to Wilson's shadow, before banishing it from this mortal plane. In its stead, a beautiful young woman with long black hair and pale cheeks appeared. "So happy to see you, apple of my eye."[3]

"Glad to be here, dark of my night.[4] But did you have to do that?" She turned to the Followers. "I apologize, he's always been one for theatrics. We're working on it, I assure you."

"Ah, but theatrics are the only way to exist. We can't be here if we can't break through mundanity. I thought I told you that, dear."

"You did. I just didn't think it would be so messy."

"Ah, my apologies. I suppose I could have been a bit more forthright with some of the finer details. None as fine as you, of course."

"Oh, stop it, you."

"Ahem," Randy said.

"Yes, dear?"

---

[3] Since his fall, the devil has gleaned an odd perspective on the way humans operate based on his unsavory clientele. He's convinced we speak in clichés, one of the few things he's gotten right.

[4] Death is the most ubiquitous cliché of them all.

Randy forgot everything he'd planned on saying. He was unworthy, standing with his masters in the flesh. Both of them! In all honesty, he never expected to meet either one. How had he gotten so lucky? What had he done to earn their favor?

"Ah, yes. This is my dear wife, Anaya. Perhaps you've met her before?" Stan said, seeing the man's dumbfounded expression and the drool pooling at the corner of his lips.

"Charmed." Anaya kissed the space around Randy's cheeks. His skin sizzled.

He nearly passed out, growing red in the face and shrinking to about three-feet-tall. Nothing prepared him for this. Pursuit alone had kept him a Follower for most of his life, but he hadn't worked out what to do when he arrived at his final destination.

"These humans look like hell," Stan said, growing weary of the silence.

"No, you look like Hell, honey."

He put his arm around his wife, smooching her on the nose. "I believe that's the kindest thing anyone's ever said to me."

"Shall we?"

They hooked arms and turned to leave, but Anaya spun around to Randy.

"Ever been to Jamaica?" He shook his head. "What about Cancun? I hear it's nice this time of year."

Randy mumbled, "Too hot, madam. Always been a snow dog myself."

Stan, tapping his foot, harrumphed. "See, I told you. Too hot. I'm ready for a break from fire. Michigan is the perfect place, you'll see."

She shrugged, gave a cute little groan, and tapped Randy on the neck. He buckled at the knees and fell down dead.

"At least we won't have to deal with all those tourists," she said, focusing on the bright side. "Just no more work, okay? The office stays at the office. You said so yourself."

"Deal," Stan said. "Why'd you do him in, though?"

"He was *begging* for it."

"True."

"One more thing, dear."

"What's that?"

"We need a car with a drop-top. It's been *too* long since I've felt the wind through my hair."

Their conversation trailed off as they walked away, leaving Rachel all by her lonesome.

She cowered and rocked, cradled in her own warmth, wishing away the events of the last few minutes. If she wished hard enough, if she kept her faith, Rachel might erase the loss of the two people closest to anything resembling family. If not, maybe she'd just wither away.

She didn't want to face the harsh realities of the world alone, but she had to. She couldn't be done yet. There was so much she hadn't seen.

But first, there was a raccoon to prepare. One couldn't answer the call to adventure on an empty stomach.

Chapter 2:

Death Comes to a Shrine in Mio

Our story continues in the unincorporated community of Mio, Michigan. "Unincorporated" doesn't ring as self-satisfying as village or kingdom or even town, but facts remain facts.

For the first time in decades—since the mysterious deaths of Brian Ognjan of St. Clair Shores and David Tyll of Troy—the Sabbath day was not only a celebration but also a day of mourning and, to a lesser extent, reckoning. While they celebrated the life and accomplishments of their Lord and Savior, the Mionites wept the brutal passing of two of the congregation's own: Mr. and Mrs. Stillman.

By the light of the moon, someone murdered them. In the morning, Dolores Delilah D'Bouvier found their bodies lobbed over the top of the Our Lady of the Woods shrine. The culprits had vanished without a trace. A testament to the people's devotion had been defiled, converted into a pillar of evil. Historically, Mionites hid from the sins of the outside world, but an atrocity so vile and senseless deserved that reckoning.

Despite the darkness within the human heart, love conquered. Mr. and Mrs. Stillman died holding hands at the apex of the shrine. *Rigor Mortis Amore*, everlasting.

"It's almost sweet," a volunteer firefighter said to herself.

"Even in death, Mary and Dave give us hope," said another, who'd fawned after his female counterpart for far too long to still be considered "just a healthy crush." He winked and put his arm around her, hoping for the best. His eyes watered when he did—not from sadness but from where she punched him in the nose.

The people observed the gruesome scene, some crying, others holding their loved ones, or whomever they could get their stubby arms around without earning a swift right-hook of their own.

Amid the sheep, Mio's sheriff ran her fingers through graying hair. She moaned as her cracked nails drug across her scalp. Itch scratched, she got to work. She cocked her head and grumbled, shifting her weight between her feet. Preoccupied with the susurrus of confusion, no one was paying enough attention to notice her moment of indecisiveness. Murder was new to her *and* everyone else. The only place she'd seen a dead body before, outside old western films and daytime soap operas, had been a mercy in a nursing home.

Mionites didn't kill. They weren't capable of such a heinous crime. Her whole world would be turned upside-down if they were. Hell, Mionites didn't as much as cheat on their taxes or swear at their neighbors.[1] They lived full, uneventful lives close to their families until they died in their sleep from heart attacks or from getting hit by a drunk teenager on a snowmobile. There *was* that one time with the opossum—poor, sweet Rico—but that sort of thing seldom happened.

But they didn't kill.

"No," Sheriff Grace said. "Not like this. Never like this."

"What was that, ma'am?" Her lapdog, Deputy Lawson, rose his voice over the *berp, berp, berp* of the rusty, old cherry-picker.

It hadn't taken long to realize no one in town owned a ladder tall enough to reach the loving, dead couple; if they did, they sure as God's good grace weren't willing to lend it

---

[1] Although, they wouldn't hesitate to run over a household pet if they were late for B.I.N.G.O night.

out. In Mio, if you weren't vigilant, "lend" turned to "borrowed indefinitely" which inevitably led to bad neighbors. There was no bad neighboring in Mio. Not with Sheriff Grace running the show.

To add to the woes of the situation, the town's only fire truck lay dormant in a mossy grave at the local State Farm Insurance office. A relic at the best of times, it boasted being one of the few operational hand tubs left. Until the incident, of course. Like a lot of things in Mio, it appeared one day and became an integral part of the landscape. A beauty mark on the cheek of Mio's hottest downtown strip…Mio's only downtown strip.

Fortunately, the electric company had been working a blown fuse down the street. Sheriff Grace "borrowed" their rig "indefinitely." When they asked for compensation for their time, she paid them by not shooting them in the feet with her ivory, throwback 36-caliber revolver—complete with gold-brush plating. They obliged, throwing in a couple cups of cold, black coffee as a consolation.

Unfortunately, the arm snapped at half its maximum reach, a few feet shy of the Stillmans. The machinations within the vehicle sputtered, smoked, and screeched to a grinding halt. Flummoxed, the driver reversed and hightailed it the hell out of there, hoping no one noticed. His colleague, cowering in the bucket, hoped the sheriff's aim wasn't half as accurate as her threats were terrifying. He sucked his thumb as they drove off towards the sunrise.

"Now what?" Deputy Lawson asked.

Sheriff Grace massaged her jaw. She scratched the nape of her neck where nervous sweat beaded, dripping down the small of her back to leave a nice puddle above her buttocks, and swore.

Clueless—his usual state of existence—Deputy Lawson mimicked his superior's actions. He squinted hard in her direction, studying her every move with ape-like determination. He'd long since perfected her dumbfounded expression and summoned pure rote memory. He'd spent years mimicking the sheriff, yet still had a job—even earned himself a fat living-wage raise or two along the way—and saw no reason to suddenly start pursuing his own thing.

As his mother used to say, *If it ain't quite fixed, don't break it.*

A shrill, elongated scream—reminiscent of a 1970s science-fiction vixen tied as an offering to one island monster or another—broke both his concentration and the glass of Sheriff Grace's shades. She removed them, inspected the lens, and tossed them into the grass before pulling another pair out of her shirt pocket.

Members of the congregation fought to restrain the newcomer, but the young woman's grief proved stronger than their brawn. Tears streamed down her puffy cheeks. The jostling crowd bunched the back of her dress, but she either hadn't noticed or didn't care. Her disheveled hair made her look like a mix between a banshee and a mad scientist. She'd have been a handsome woman under better circumstances.

"Oh, good Lord," Sheriff Grace said. "Go deal with the loon, kid. I think that's Ms. Margaret Stillman. The granddaughter if memory serves."

Distracted, Deputy Lawson "heard" the sheriff's orders. His gaze followed the flight of a solitary black-and-white bird. It called to the crowd, *haaaaa-oooh, haaaaa-oooh*—an inappropriate response, considering the circumstances. The loon wanted people to acknowledge its presence. Satisfied, it alighted on the surface of the Au Sable River basin, using the bridge over the river as shelter from the sun.

"But, ma'am," the deputy said, diverting the last sliver of his attention span back to his superior. "That loon ain't botherin' nobody. Just looking for a mate, I suspect.

Like us all," he added under his breath. "Besides, I can't swim."

"You're kidding."

"Nah. Never had lessons. I reckon we should focus on the Stillmans, though."

Sheriff Grace smacked him upside the head. "The girl, you damned fool. Go check on the girl. She's liable to start a riot."

"*Oh*, that loon. I was gonna say..." he trailed off, knowing what was good for him.

"Say what, Deputy?"

"Nothing, ma'am. Yes, ma'am. Sorry, ma'am. Off I go."

He scuttled off toward Ms. Stillman before the sheriff could reprimand him again. The fires of her wrath spread across the glossy surface of her eyes, fogging her aviators, and he refused to let her gaze burn him.

Sheriff Grace addressed the nearest poor sap who'd listen. "Where's the damn mayor? What about Tony Dietrich? That S.O.B. said he wanted a more proactive role in this town! Well, here's his chance. And somebody get a tall enough bloody ladder or there's gonna be hell to pay. Does anyone have an aspirin? Where'd the deputy go?"

"Er, you just sent him off, Sheriff," a fresh-out-of-training officer said, flinching as she turned her wrath on him.

"Yes, good observation. What's your name, kid? Ever think of being a cop?"

"Miles, I'm in your depart—"

"Miles? Right, good name. Sign on with me, kid. You'll go far."

"Yes, ma'am."

Sheriff Grace tipped her hat to the poor redhead. "Miles, go get me a coffee. None of this cold brew, hipster stuff they got at the Snowshoe. Folgers. Black. And kid?

Keep up the good work. There might be a badge in it for you."

"But, ma'am, I'm already—"

She held a finger to his lips. "Step on it, Miles. I need someone…er, something dark and strong to help me figure this one out. Those bodies will start stinkin' soon."

Officer Miles nodded and sprinted off. Several citizens and other anonymous police officers glanced from each other to the disappearing figure before running off with purpose in half a dozen directions. They'd heard the sheriff and wanted to avoid her wrath. Too bad the ladder guy ran off towards the coffee house, the mayor's assistant ran towards Mackinaw Island, and Officer Miles ran straight home to his roommate (his mother).

At least they all ran; that was the important part.

Meanwhile, a group of surly, burly, sun-soaked men reeking of cigarette smoke and whiskey were struggling to hold Margaret. They were henchmen at Henchman's Acres, a local tourist attraction and kayak launch settled on the bank of the Au Sable River. Thanks to a recent sewage spill of over 80,000 gallons of refuse, they hadn't seen action in days. Surprise, surprise, this spill deterred the bulk of the recreational tourists. The henchmen spent the greater portion of last month swatting flies the size of finches and banging their heads to Five Finger Death Punch.

They looked like henchmen waiting for the right super villain to come along and bend them to his will. In reality, they weren't much more than bald teddy bears. Their soft demeanors weren't enough to console the disconsolate young woman. One of them had a black eye and a bloody nose. Another wore scratch marks across his cheek where she'd clawed him with her Dollar General talons. The third pretended to help the other two restrain her, working himself into near cardiac arrest. He came out of the ordeal unscathed, save the rolled ankle from sidling away from the scuffle.

All three flushed with relief when Deputy Lawson came to their rescue.

The deputy took young Ms. Stillman under his protective wing, whispered something to her, and they hobbled to the nearest curb. The henchmen watched, dumbfounded, as he calmed her with nothing but silken words and his charming, Northern grin.

"Was that a smile?"

"She laughed at *that* joke?"

"Can we get a burger yet?"

"S'only just after nine, ya great buffoon. Ten's when the menu switches over."

"Think they pushed it back to eleven."

"Son of a…"

They argued as they disappeared into the crowd, leaving the deputy, the shrine, and their failures behind to swat more flies and wait for the lunch menu.

"My heart goes out to you," Deputy Lawson said. "It really does. Sheriff Grace will do whatever's in her power to find out who did this. I'll do what I can to see you taken care of in your time of grief. If you need anything at all…"

"Thank you. That means so much to me," Ms. Margaret Stillman said, allowing a faint smile to cross her face. She leaned towards him. "They were all I had here. Now, I don't know why I'd stay."

"Well, here's my personal number. Call me anytime you need."

The rest of the conversation trailed off as they spoke more intimately and as the crowd's dull murmur grew into more of a riotous racket.

Even if the deputy was slow, even if he didn't possess what most people considered common sense, he understood the ladies. They flocked to him. They swooned at the sight of him, melted at the slightest whiff of his princely halitosis. At the sound of his voice, women told him things—their life stories, their deepest regrets, the size of their...shoes. His innate talent saved what little dignity remained of the deputy's day.

I'd be lost without him, Sheriff Grace admitted to herself. *Lost, but saving a fortune on Advil...* She resisted his charms, so far. She played a dangerous game keeping him around, so she kept her cards—and hands—to herself.

She sighed as the young woman giggled and rested her head on the deputy's shoulder. He winked at the sheriff for validation. She waved him off; feeding the ambitious young man's ego would make him weak. It was a risk she couldn't afford.

The riotous racket erupted into a full-blown cacophony. Large crowds were always the best and most accurate predictors of disaster. She hoped they were wrong just this once. *For the love of God, please be wrong.*

The tires of a split-pea green, wood-paneled woody squealed around the corner, burning rubber across the pavement. The driver had seen too many Hollywood chase scenes. A trail of smog followed in its wake. The distorted wail of Swedish metal blared from the speakers, and cigar smoke seeped from cracked windows.

Nearby, a baby cried because its mother had seen the split-pea abomination tearing down M-33 and was in the fetal position, sobbing. Relentless, the woody barreled towards the crowd of people, none of which were gawking at the dead bodies hanging from the shrine anymore. 25 miles per hour. 30. 35.[2]

Time stood still in Mio; the crowd stood stiller.

---

[2] This, of course, being the max speed of any station wagon we encounter until it's coming right for us in the wrong lane.

Ms. Stillman peeled her gaze from Deputy Lawson's long enough for her eyes to widen and her inflamed lips to drop. She stood, dusted the dirt off her dress, wiped the saliva off her face, and screamed. She quivered, clenched her fists, and gritted her teeth as the car rushed towards them.

In slow motion, Deputy Lawson stood, hands buried in his pockets, his stupid grin suspended in time. He looked around, trying to plan a good old-fashioned Great Escape, but only got as far as covering as much of himself with his arms as physically possible. Picture your grandmother that one time you accidently walked in on her in the shower, and you've about got it. Less wrinkles, but equal parts vulnerability and shame.

Sheriff Grace took off her new aviators in slow motion—one of her signature moves—and scrunched her upper lip. She'd seen it in a movie once—Dirty Harry or the Blues Brothers, she couldn't remember which—and it stuck. She pointed at the station wagon in case anyone had missed it.

The crowd pointed with her. Mesmerized, the entire town of Mio held their collective breath. Their mouths dropped; their hearts pounded in their chests. Someone swooned. Someone else wet themselves, and it wasn't the crying baby. Resigned to their fate, they left their lives in the hands of God. She hadn't failed them, yet.

Mr. and Mrs. Stillman held their ground from the apex of the Our Lady of the Woods shrine, remaining as dead as before. The trifles of the living bothered them even less than the flies buzzing around their bodies. They were already dead, after all. How much worse could life get?

Father Time released Mio from its shackles. Lost seconds rushed back like water through a broken dam.

The woody became a green and brown streak. It jumped the curb, missing Ms. Stillman and Deputy Lawson by inches, slid and skidded through the stunned crowd, barreling sidelong up the concrete steps of the shrine. The shrine itself was there to bring its rampage to a swift and noisy end.

The Stillmans slid from their resting place like melted butter off the edge of a plate, landing with a thud on the roof of the woody.

The collection gasped.

Mr. Stillman let out a long, raspy wheeze before flopping off the car and onto the pavement.

The collection said, "Ope."

Mrs. Stillman slipped after him and barrel-rolled onto the ground.

The collection said, "Oooh."

Sheriff Grace sighed. She picked the wrong week to quit smoking. A slew of the usual woe-is-me-isms darted through her mind. *Why's this happening to me? How can this get any worse? When will I catch a break?*

Aloud, she said, "At least the bodies are down."

After what felt like a decade—the 2000s perhaps, or maybe the 80s—the driver's door, rusted through in at least a dozen spots, swung open on creaky hinges. An avalanche of pop cans and greasy fast-food wrappers cascaded onto the concrete, burying the Stillmans. A can bounced down each individual step before coming to rest in the grass. Mildew from inside the car danced from nostril to nostril.

An enormous man got out, belly first. He wore a tweed jacket two sizes too small; his hair was slick and matted to his forehead. The presumed Evel Knievel of *My 600 Pound Life* rolled his neck from side to side, managed a few half-hearted jumping jacks, causing a small earthquake in China, and cracked his bulbous knuckles.

He beamed at the people staring at him. They beamed back. When he waved, they waved too. No one was sure why, but the newcomer captivated them.

Sheriff Grace and Deputy Lawson snapped free of his hypnotic grasp and drew their revolvers. Hunched in the proper cop-position, both holding their weapons with locked arms, they stared him down with cop-intimidation. Someone in the crowd played the *Cops* theme song on their phone and held it over their head. In unison, everyone started humming. You couldn't not. It defeated the auditory laws of earworm physics.

"Hello, everyone," the fat man said, nonplussed. "It's nice to see so many new friends."

"Get on the ground." Sheriff Grace menaced him with her weapon.

She pulled back the firing pin and let it make that wonderfully unnecessary *click* sound they always made in the movies. Bad guys needed to hear it.

"Keep your hands where we can see 'em," the deputy added.

"No funny business. I *will* shoot you, *new friend*."

"Do what she says," Deputy Lawson said, as the fat man slid to his stomach.

The deputy fought the urge to drop to the ground himself. He knew what sort of justice the sheriff dished out in moments like these. It involved thresholds and pain and lots of extra paperwork.

The fat man wiggled into the sea of trash and put his hands on his head, once again causing minor seismic activity. He strained to look once more upon the crowd of gawkers and then down the barrels of two revolvers. Acquiescence was his best play here, so he put his head back down and kept quiet except for the faint whimpering. He couldn't seem to help that part.

With cop-speed[3], the sheriff and her deputy tackled him, bouncing around as if he were a Magic Castle Bounce House, before getting him in handcuffs. They used zip ties to extend the range of the cuffs and grunted with effort until they clasped shut.

"I'm sure all of this isn't necessary," he said. "The brake pedal just moved on me."

"Shut up."

"If it's all the trash, I'll clean it up."

"Shut up, please?" Deputy Lawson asked, reinforcing the sheriff's command.

"Fine, fine. No worries. Name's Chase Cross, by the way."

"Good for you," the sheriff said, roughing him up enough to get her point across while avoiding unwanted attention from citizen's rights activists.

"Sheriff said 'shaddup.'"

"I heard," Chase said, dejected. His frown added three more chins to the three already there. "Just trying a bit of diplomacy. Might give it a try yourselves."

Before they squeezed him into the backseat of their squad car, he mustered one last act of defiance. He expanded his chest, grasped the frame of the door in his pudgy hands, and pressed against the sheriff's weight.

Chase saw the bodies of the Stillmans out of the corner of his eye. He'd first heard them as they collided with the roof of his car, but he wasn't sure what—or who—the impactees had been. Chase Cross wasn't one to squander an opportunity.

"Don't you want to know why I'm here?"

---

[3] In most cases, 2.7 miles per hour. In Sheriff Grace's case, 27.3 miles per hour, just shy of Usain Bolt's 2009 record. But, unlike the sheriff, Bolt didn't do it in full gear with a loaded gun in his hand.

"Nope." Sheriff Grace threw her shoulder at his mass with all her strength, but she was met with an unopposable force.

"Not even a little bit?"

She sighed. "Fine. Why are you here?"

She didn't care, but people were getting restless. She had a precedence to set. If she couldn't get this man to cooperate with violence, she'd be forced to use—*gag*—Diplomacy.

"I'm, uh, here to solve the case. I'm one of those...whatchamacallit guys."

"Case solvers?" someone offered, helpfully.

"Car crashers?"

"Pizza eaters?"

"Shower avoiders?"

"Shrine desecrators?"

"No, not that." He nodded toward the Stillmans. The word hit him in the face, along with a set of car keys someone had thrown; that last accusation had struck some nerves. "No, none of that. I'm a...detective. That's right. *Detective* Chase Cross, at your service."

He extended a hand to the sheriff, flapping it like a seal's flipper. She took it and used it to leverage him into the backseat.

"You're under arrest, *Detective*."

Chapter 3:

Repugnant Rachel Lives

Repugnant Rachel crawled out from her hiding place behind a stack of rotten pallets. The last thing she remembered was Wilson convulsing on the ground, his stomach on the brink of exploding. She'd gone to help, but Randy shoved her away and refused to allow any interference. That's when she hid, and when she started contemplating her revenge.

Why had Randy let one of his own die? Why hadn't he done anything to stop it? They'd signed up to embrace the Devil and Death, not *die*.

She vowed to take her revenge. She vowed to—*gasp*—leave his side for good. To never look back at life as a Follower. If she had known he was such a monster, she'd have never thrown in with him to begin with. Being accepted...with other *people*! What a thrill that had been. She had her ant farm to keep her company as a kid and a couple of online chat rooms,[1] but her bond with Randy and Wilson was *real*. Or at least she thought it had been.

With their deaths, Rachel was alone again.

Randy had embraced Death; she remembered it through the haze of her thoughts, denying her the revenge she'd plotted for those long minutes after he'd betrayed them. His exit seemed so wonderful, so fulfilling, so *right*. If she had the courage, she'd have followed him in a heartbeat. That's what they were always meant to be: Followers.

Now I'm alone with all this...silence.

---

[1] These are the best places to make horrible decisions without facing any lasting, real-world consequences. They're also the best places to poach desperate, lonely girls like Rachel—and where she'd first met Wilson. Coincidence? Only if you still use your Myspace account.

"Hello?" Her voice trembled, echoing across the abandoned tracks of Michigan Central. "Mr. Man? Mrs. Death? Are you still here?" She waited. "I'm ready to go, now."

No response. She missed the train and another one wasn't scheduled to arrive until last Monday.

"Shit." She kicked rocks. One kicked back, bounding off a crack in the concrete and careening into her forehead. "Ouch!"

Rachel balanced alongside the tracks, teetering on the edge. She cursed the loneliness. She cursed Randy and Wilson. Most of all, she cursed herself for lacking courage.

After a series of harrumphs and dramatic arm waves, she flopped onto the hard ground. She sought affirmation; if no one saw her dramatics, their effect would be null and void. A temper-tantrum didn't count if it fell on deaf ears. When she remembered how utterly alone she was, the sense of isolation struck her like the desert floor.

"Hello, Death. It's me, Rachel."

Squeak, squeak, answered her would-be supper.

"No, thanks. I'm not hungry anymore. Have you seen a pretty lady and a big man wearing a fanny pack?" She hadn't seen Stan in his tuxedo. It wouldn't have changed anything if she had. "Touristy, passed through not too long ago?"

The rat appraised her, decided he'd better count his whiskers while they were still under his snout, and scurried off to the train station's darkest recesses.

Rachel missed the others. Sure, the Followers had their flaws, but there was no one else in the world she'd rather spend her misery with. She had a hard time making friends and never knew her family, so she settled for the next-to-last best thing: Randy and Wilson.

Besides, she always thought she'd be the one to kill horny ole Wilson. He'd chug too many White Claws, then pull out his willy when she was in a Mood. Rachel would have no choice but to ring his flaccid neck. Someone needed to set an example or men would never learn. It should have been her; she could have changed the world.

She leaned against their fire barrel, its paper bag flames providing her little warmth, and plopped her face in her hands. Tears streamed down her cheeks. The rat returned with renewed bravery, nibbling on her bony ankle, and it dawned on her. Death no longer seemed frightening. It almost felt like a gift. If the others had made the ultimate sacrifice, found their promised paradise, why couldn't she? Abandoned, she deserved as much. She deserved the storybook ending Randy had promised them.

Rachel sifted through a rubbish pile until she found a menacing shard of glass rounded on the outside edge like a tiger's tooth. Several minutes of messy work later, Rachel fell back, lightheaded and exasperated but still alive. Her arm throbbed; the smell and taste of iron overpowered her senses. She was lighter by several pints, but she'd needed to shed a few pounds anyway.

"Well, cripes," she said, unsure where she learned such colorful language. "That's not supposed to happen. Might have to rethink this. What do you think, buddy?"

The rat paused from lapping her ichor and answered with a *squeak*.

"You're a bloody genius, kid! Thanks. I owe you one."

After a considerable amount of mental strain, and stopping for a wee break in the corner, Rachel found the perfect place to execute what she had in mind. She slid several abandoned benches and trashcans together to build a mock-staircase, which proved difficult with only half of her blood in her body, but her magnum opus was complete.

She stood amongst the pigeons in the rafters, psyching herself up. This was the only option. She was ready, even though her brain screamed she wasn't.

Don't do it. You have too much to live for...well, you have some stuff to live for...Like, uh, erm...Mushrooms are nice. And those fine, upstanding lads who play the bongos on the corner of Griswold and Congress. Not to mention the "free smells" from the corner sub shop. What else could a girl want?

She shrugged. Even free smells weren't enough.

"Here we go."

Rachel swung her arms like a skier preparing for the gate lift, aiming for the tracks below, and launched herself from her perch. She somersaulted and twisted, only balking a bit on her third full rotation before making herself needle-straight. The freefall pushed her greasy bangs from her forehead and flapped her eyelids. Adrenaline surged through her body. She squealed in delight at the rush, until she met the ground.

There should have been a *splat*. Rachel should have been *gone*. She missed by "just this much."

Bruised, battered, and dragging herself on a broken leg, she heaved herself onto the platform and struck a pose like a seal on an iceberg. Agitated, she cried until her eyes hurt. Then, without a second thought, she left Michigan Central in search of other ways to join the other Followers of Not.

Somewhere out in the big, bad world her Maker awaited. It would've been a shame to make him wait any longer than he had to, not to mention totally against her selfless nature.

Chapter 4:
The Cell

Chase Cross, Detective Ordinaire, flopped with a *kerplunk*, a *thud*, and a *bo-oo-oo-oing*. He aimed for his bunk but missed by a mile, smacking his tailbone on the corner of the steel cot's frame and flipping face-first onto the sticky, concrete floor. The charade ended with the bile-inducing *splash* of his feet landing in the toilet. A panel of cockroaches held up tiny signs. It was tens across the board.

He turtled around more than the average terrapin, kicking his stubby legs and flailing his arms, but somehow managed to re-capsize himself. He scrambled to his feet, banging his head on the way up.

Mio is not treating me well... His car was likely totaled, they'd pointed guns at him, and no one had bothered to feed him yet. ...*Not treating me well at all.*

Outside the bars of his cell, Deputy Lawson licked his finger and changed the page of a book he may or may not have been able to read. The way the bridge of his nose scrunched made it clear he was concentrating, but that's all Chase could say for certain. Chase squinted to read the title—*Taking up Space: A Man's Guide to Manliness*—and chuckled.

The deputy peered over the book, rolled his eyes, and spat chew into an old, glass Coke bottle.

Chase Cross and Deputy Lawson were two bulls in a china shop, circling each other. Round and round, like scum in a sink drain, it was only a matter of time before they collided, clogging the whole system.

"You're some kinda idiot, ain't ya boy?" The deputy tried on the persona he'd been practicing in the mirror for years.

Chase rubbed his egg noodle and raised an eyebrow. "No, sir. Mother always told me I was just gifted with two right feet."

"Don't you mean two *left* feet? Doesn't the saying go, 'He's got two left—'"

"All due respect, I know my own feet. Haven't seen 'em in a while, but they're there.[1] Besides, if I had two left ones, I'd walk counterclockwise everywhere. How could I ever move forward?"

Deputy Lawson wiggled his mustache, or the little scruff his genes allowed, and considered Chase's logic. He'd grown up knowing two things: *survival* depended on physical prowess, and *living* depended on hard work. His father was a lumberjack, complete with a chest-length beard, an all-flannel wardrobe, and a faithful wolf-dog companion. He had a mutt named Brutus, too. The deputy's four older brothers were the cruelest Gringos south of the Canadian border. His mother, the only person meaner or tougher than the Lawson Boys, was always too busy to step in.

"The chickens ain't bringin' themselves home," she'd say. She was right. Left to their own devices, the chickens took to pecking each other and—to Block Watch's dismay—wandering the neighborhood like ruffians out for a fight.

Logic and cleverness were not part of his skillset. Chase's logic seemed sound, though. Walking in circles around each other accomplished nothing but dizziness; there wasn't enough Dramamine in the world to relieve the symptoms of catching a bad case of Chase Cross.

They stared at each other for a few minutes, then looked away, doing everything in their individual powers not to remake eye contact. Deputy Lawson attempted to whistle

---

[1] Chase's feet aren't the only extremities to go the way of the Bermuda Triangle. There are his knees, too.

but failed. Spittle splashed the pages of his book. Chase Cross returned to pacing; his options were rather limited.

Chase broke the silence. "I'm sorry about the...er..." He dug deep into the archives of his auditory memory. There was a lot of digging through piles of two-note commercial jingles and obscure movie quotes, but he found what he sought through perseverance and no shortage of dumb luck. "Sorry about the Stillwells. I didn't know them, but I bet they were good neighbors. It's a shame what happened."

"Man," the deputy said.

"What?"

"*Man.*"

"I mean, now's not the right time, is it? It's just the two of us." Chase paused, pointing to the cell across the way. "And him. There's already more than enough men in here."

"Still-man."

Chase scratched his head, showering the cell floor in dust. "Well, yeah. I suppose you're right. One of them was a man. A dead one, but same difference, I guess. The other one was a woman. *Wo*-man. They had a cute little granddaughter who's certainly not a man. I'm sure you'd attest to that. Eh, Deputy? Eh, eh?"

"They're the Stillmans. Not *well.*"

"Another fine point. They're not well at all. You don't need to be a detective to see they're dead, Deputy."

Deputy Lawson inhaled—dreamed of the waves lapping against the hull of his fishing boat on a slow, Saturday morning while counting to ten—and exhaled his frustrations. Though satisfying, it wouldn't be professional to break a detainee's face. Instead, he returned to his book, hoping his 400-pound problem would somehow become someone else's problem.

It didn't.

"I can help, you know. It's kind of what I do now?" *For the past 24 hours at least,* Chase thought, after vocalizing it with an extra emphasis on *kind of, now,* and the question mark at the end. For good measure and self-reassurance, he added, "I'm a detec—"

"Yeah, you've said so already." Deputy Lawson kicked the underside of his desk. "You're a 'detective.'"

"It's true. You need help finding this bastard before someone else gets hurt. I'm assuming this whole murder-y thing is new territory for y'all. I can help. Pleeease let me help."

The deputy grunted, ruffled some pages, and cleared his throat. Anything to drown out the "detective."

"Any leads? Fingerprints? Torn bits of fabric or shoe prints? Any ole swoosh might do. Always evidence at a crime scene. You just have to know where to look."

"Nope."

"Nothing at all? Did you harangue the witnesses? Interrogate the groundskeeper?"

"Nope. Willy's harmless, anyway."

"Did you at least find a cigarette butt or *anything* for DINNA? There's always good DINNA on a wet butt."

"Dinner? You're disgusting."

"A well-educated man like yourself should know DINNA. Dioxy…er…Dioxy ribbons something or another. Genetic makeup."

"I'll make you up," Deputy Lawson mumbled. "All black and blue."

"What's that, *sir?*" Chase held up his dukes and shuffled his feet.

Impatient, Deputy Lawson set down his book, brought his fingers to his temples, and thumped his forehead onto his desk so hard it rocked his pen carrier off the corner and onto the floor.

Smugness became Chase's countenance. "S'what I thought. You need me. I bet you didn't even bother to check the scene for hair or skin cells. So amateur. God dammit, Deputy. Come on, now. Get it together."

***

Far off—somewhere beyond the stars, and beyond even them—a long-haired woman perked up. She appeared to be in her twenties, but she was older than time itself.

She swore she heard her name. This kept happening to her, no matter where she was or what she happened to be doing. It was always a different voice, too. At first, she thought it was self-flattery. Everyone wanted to think everyone else was always thinking about them. Alas, it was more than the echo of her own egotism she heard on the wind. Vaguely familiar—as if she'd experienced similar occurrences in her childhood but blocked them out of her memory for sanity's sake—she recognized she'd have to answer.

Hers was a name evoked for all the wrong reasons. One day, sooner than she'd like, they'd evoke it for the right reason.

The only reason.

For now, dejected at being unable to locate the source of the utterance, she returned to her work. It was big, important work she couldn't afford to procrastinate. Bigger than gardening. Bigger than Jesus. There was a storm coming; she'd bring a rain jacket, this time. Maybe even an umbrella. But that still wouldn't be enough.

***

Chase Cross and Deputy Lawson stared at each other, confused. Something stripped away a split-second of their life, suspended it in the void, and thrust it back upon them in a single heartbeat. They both struggled to remember where they were. The deputy got their first.

"D'NA stick your nose in other people's business," he retorted, unable to come up with anything cleverer. "And you should'na use His name in vain."

"Who's to say He's a he? Either way, I wish my nose was elsewhere, or I wouldn't be sticking it anywhere near you. It smells like baby farts and brimstone in this cell. Can you at least spray some Airwick or something?" He gagged a bit, trying without success to ignore the overflowing steel toilet behind him. "I saw what you did there, by the way. S'a good joke. Color me impressed."

A sudden wave of high-fructose-hunger washed over Chase. His tummy grumbled, and he let out one of those empty-stomach burps people claim, like many other bodily functions, they never have. Face it, you've had them. We all have them. Toots, too. Well-known scientific fact, we'd explode otherwise.

Deputy Lawson grimaced and held his breath.

"What's your favorite food, Deputy?"

"Piss off."

"Never heard of it. Delicacy of France, I assume?"

"I'm serious."

"I can tell we're going to be best friends, you and I. There's a real connection between us. I feel I can tell you anything, without judgment; confide any secret to you, without worry. It's a rare bond, Deputy. How did I get so lucky?"

Tired of the "detective's" verbal upchuck, Deputy Lawson returned to his book. He'd lost his place; but, as we so cleverly deducted before, he hadn't been reading to begin with. There weren't enough pictures to keep his attention. Saccadicly, he stumbled through a chapter about luck. He stopped to find the "recipe for luck, a delicacy many don't realize is a sprinkle of zest away" in the appendix. If all it took was a pinch of pepper and a spritz of lemon, he might be alright. A Luck Casserole was exactly what he needed.

He flipped the page.

"God only knows…"

***

"*I know* what?"

No answer.

She brushed the dirt from the knees of her jeans and looked all around her. Her jeans were pulled halfway above her belly button. She'd been a mom and knew the drill.

I shouldn't have gotten off my meds, *she thought.* Are the voices getting louder?

"Hmph. Whatever."

She returned to her garden. The daisies wouldn't push themselves.

***

Chase, forgetting the hunger pangs racking his body, took a leak in what he had assumed was the toilet. Parts of it looked like a toilet. It smelled like a toilet, but it sounded like a boiling volcano caldera—gave off enough heat, too. The dampness soaking into his sock *felt* like toilet water. Not wanting to disturb the small utopia of sentient bacteria growing on the handle, he opted out of flushing—as the last three thousand people apparently had—and returned to doing jail things. Pacing, mostly.

The cramped cell was bigger than the inside of his woody, which had been his prison the last few months. The cell also contained fewer soda bottles and wasps, smelled a little better despite Mount Vepoovius, and wasn't half as sticky. Even so, the gray walls closed in on him from all angles. His skin crawled. *Those final seconds when they tighten around me forever. What a way to go, huh?*

He could almost squeeze through the bars. Two years ago, Chase had been half the man he was now—in more ways than one come to think. In his youth, he could have shimmied his way to freedom without as much as a light greasing.

But those days were well behind him. He just couldn't see around his massive torso to find them.

"Damn you, royal heir to the burger throne."[2] He shook his fists at the sky. His life would've been better if it weren't for aggressive marketing campaigns and Trans fats.

Since there was little else to occupy his time, Chase stared through the bars, thinking about escape and drooling on cold iron. *Good guys don't break out of jail,* he reminded himself. *Not even when we're hungry.*

Good guys stayed up all night, compiling their defense. They flipped through old textbooks, digested the minutes of case after case, and ingested vast amounts of toilet-hooch until they found a defining moment in law's triumphant history that earned them their God-given right to walk the earth as a free man. The camera cut out, panned to them writing by candlelight; they're doing push-ups or putting in the last layup to win the game for the Shirts team. In the nick of time, they drafted an irrefutable letter of proof—a document that became paramount for all unjustly caged innocents to proceed—and they saw the light of day right before their mother passed away. But they attended her funeral free. Absolved.

In short, they montaged, and it worked every time.

He was lost in yet another 90s movie fantasy. Chase placed his hands on his hips, stood straight with his nose towards the ceiling, and shouted, "Justice will prevail," in his most heroic voice.

"Shut up." The deputy brought him back to reality. "And sit your ass down."

"Yes, sir." Chase kicked the air in Deputy Lawson's direction and stuck out his tongue.

---

2 This "sly" omission of trademarked materials is not to avoid legal trouble. It's because Chase Cross can never remember whether the burger throne is sat by a king, an emperor, a friendly despot, or a power-hungry vizier. It's the calories that count, not the facts.

Regardless, he obeyed. There was Innocence to prove; he didn't have time to row. That ship had sailed.

Chase wasn't alone; an older man—by the sound and smell of him, with a full, silver-fox head of hair—existed in a world of his own. It was a world of throaty sounds and deviated septums. He wore a gray bathrobe that helped him blend with his environs. The old man rolled, every joint popping. He grunted like a deaf cow prodded with a brand, let out a mushroom-cloud fart, and smacked his lips together. All the while, his arms twitched under the pressure of whatever nightmares he was having. For good measure, he groaned, giving the Sydney Opera House a run for its money. His subconscious bodily effects, playing to a crowd of one, were quite the bedtime symphony to behold.

"Some dream you're having," Chase said.

When he leaned into the bars his face oozed through the gaps. He scrutinized the man he'd spend the rest of the night with. A normal person would've felt creepy, but Chase learned at an early age that modesty was a dangerous game. Besides, everyone was a suspect until proven innocent. Even though this man slept as sound as a babe—with cheeks as red and turnipy as one—he might've been the story's villain.

A second fugue of snores began, composed by Deputy Lawson. It looked like learning to be a man had worn him out. Chase couldn't help but wonder if these skills impressed the sheriff. Was her protégé reading to win her heart? Did she like a man that took charge? One with intellect and confidence? One with his own gravity? If so, Chase had a belly start.

I need that book…any book, really. Anything to end this horrendous boredom.

Speaking of the sheriff, where was she? He hadn't laid eyes on her since she shoved him in the backseat of her cruiser, one glorious, dark-skinned breast bashing him upside the head. It wasn't much, enough to daze him; but,

44

in conjunction with her domineering disposition and take-no-prisoners (figuratively, as it turned out) attitude, he'd fallen flab-over-cankles for her. Not like with the others. No, he was having what he assumed were feelings for the woman. She was powerful; powerful women attracted men like Chase Cross.

The drive to the station was pleasant enough. She had him, so he kicked his feet up and enjoyed the ride. One right turn from the church, a quick left, and—*poof*—they were there. It wasn't his first time in a police car, and it probably wouldn't be his last. He wasn't a criminal, per se. Chase just had an innate ability to rub people the wrong way, particularly authority.

His dad had been a cop, and a sad sack of a failure to boot. Not all cops were like Pops (if they were, half the population would either be behind bars or dead), but it was hard not to see his face behind every black uniform. The face of intimidation, of violent totalitarianism. A face that said, "I'm in charge, and I don't care where I have to shove this billy club for you to understand."

When he met Sheriff Grace, all of that had changed.

He couldn't resist a bit of light-hearted anarchy, though. It went against his nature. In the sheriff's case, it came in the form of awkward flirting. Viva la Revolucion.

They drove down Main Street, Mio in a flash. Even though she'd been driving twenty-miles-an-hour, it was there one second and in the rearview the next.

His first impressions of the town—those he'd forgotten to have while speeding through, under the influence of a heavy dose of caffeine and a heavier dose of divine intervention—were mostly good. Not fancy, but far from drab. What one might expect of an unincorporated town in Middle-of-Nowhere-Michigan. Plus, quilts—loads and loads of quilts.

There was an antique shop with a single dusty window. Behind the glass, nightmare-inducing antique dolls, broken archery sets, rusty kitchenware (oops, sorry, "rustic" kitchenware), dull hunting knives, water-stained, spine-cracked paperbacks nobody would ever read again, and a plethora of other fine garbage—er, treasures—filled the store. Out front sat a row of red wagons and technicolor tricycles with flat wheels, twisted spokes, and bells that went *wah, wah, wah* instead of *ding, ding*. They were all waiting for a gang of pop-cap collecting teenagers from the 50s to rescue them from obscurity. A hand-woven rug, a tapestry of blues and greens, hung above the door. Adults came here to bargain and gossip; kids came to ogle the backlit pin-up girl on the wall.

Down an alleyway across the street, between the local government building and the Black Bear Real Estate office, was a place where the same kids broke bottles and antagonized feral cats. Like a lot of other small towns, Mio provided opportunity for everyone. You had to but squint to see it.

Outside the real estate office, in stark contrast to the pin-up girl inside the antique shop, a middle-aged woman labored away. She busied herself de-weeding the large brick planters lining Main Street, from the top of the hill all the way to the bottom where the river began. Blissfully unaware of the murders, she worked as if it were the most important work in all the universe. If she didn't pull every weed, life as we knew it would cease to exist in a shower of anticlimactic sparks.

Chase and the Gardener caught eyes for a moment; she wiped sweat from her brow, and he sped up the hill in the back of a police car. She gave no thought to him, and he gave only one thought to her: *Dear diary, suspect number one.* He ended the thought with a special footnote, though. He recognized a potential red herring when he smelled one. He'd read all the books.

One of Mio's finer establishments drew his attention from her almost as soon as he noticed how strange she was. At the end of the block stood his knight in shining armor, a fine establishment dubbed: "Walker's Fine Foods, Spirits, Bowling, Billiards, Dry Cleaning, and Tax Consulting."

His eyes lit up. "Care for a game of pool, Sheriff?"

"Nah."

"Afraid you might lose? I'm a shark, wouldn't want to embarrass you in front of all your fine folk here. Oh, and I don't believe in letting ladies win just because they're ladies. Or kids, for that matter. All that equal rights jazz, am I right?"

"Eh? Is that so? That's not it at all, 'detective.' I'd hate to embarrass *you* any further. Considering I'm throwing you behind bars, afterwards... Doesn't seem courteous."

She couldn't help herself. She knew better. Really, she did. It wasn't proper to bait detainees. It wasn't protocol to give in to their goading, either. She shouldn't give the "detective" the time of day. His personality...it had to be his personality. She couldn't allow anything else to distract from her work. Especially him. Not with that belly. Hell, she struggled to get him in her car. How could she let him suck her into his games? She'd play for now, see what cards he held, and trump them with her own.

And why am I making all these card game references? I really must get out more often. Video poker and spider solitaire only went so far.

"Fair enough," he said. "How 'bout we stop in for a pint, at least? What could go wrong? Give a man his last meal. Or maybe you have a few shirts you need starched and pressed? We could review our W-4s together while we wait."

"How romantic." The sheriff blushed, despite herself.

"You haven't seen nothin' yet, baby."

She slammed on the breaks and jerked the car into park. Chase's head slammed against the window.

"Shut up, already. We're here."

The Mio Sheriff's Department—which was an L-shaped, brick farmhouse set back from the road—loomed. Chase didn't see it coming. He had been sightseeing, forgetting the destination while enjoying the journey. The building was old and weather-worn with several mismatched vinyl additions. Around back, a wooden ramp wrapped around a staircase leading to the second story. Where there must have once been a screen, there was a thick door with security bars and bullet-proof glass, giving the farmhouse more of a fortressy vibe than a home-sweet-home vibe. An antenna—larger than it had any right to be—protruded from the top, parallel to dual chimneys. The police force was either trying to contact Mars or catch the Lions game in HD.

Another deputy—not the one at the shrine, but his much cuter counterpart—appeared from inside the station. Armed to the teeth, she was clearly not there to greet new arrivals. Stopping halfway down the stairs, she lit a cigar and risked a glance towards Chase and the sheriff. She nodded, flicking her match onto the lawn, and continued about her business. She didn't seem encumbered by her body armor or the combat shotgun slung over her shoulder.

She made her way around the corner of the house to a large tool shed within eyeshot. Deputy Lawson sat on the stoop, reading a book. They fist bumped as she approached, moving in close for conversation. Chase tried to read their lips but couldn't quite make out words through the haze of smoke billowing from the woman's nostrils like dragon's breath.

The treasure she guarded inside the shed soon became apparent. A third officer exited, this one wearing a white t-shirt and holding a rifle against one shoulder. Chase caught a quick glimpse inside. They were hoarding enough weapons to provide a small village the means to overthrow a ruthless dictator. Viva La Revolucion, indeed.

To Chase's amusement, they were watching the Lion's game inside on an old television set. Smugness washed over him. *Maybe this whole detective thing is my calling after all.*

When the first officer caught him staring, she hurried to shut the door. Stillmans aside, Mio was preparing for war. Whether the two scenarios were related had yet to reveal itself. He made another mental note to follow up on this new clue. Unfortunately, his mental repository was filling up fast.

He cleared his throat. "What are you doing with all those g—"

"None'ya…I mean, it's nothing." Sheriff Grace corrected herself. "I'm sure I don't know what you're talking about. Now, watch your head, 'Detective.'"

She helped him out of the car, handed him off to Deputy Lawson, who jostled him to a holding cell, and sped off in the opposite direction away from town. When he concentrated, Chase smelled the sweet scent of pheromones over her cheap perfume.

A smile crept over his face that made his neighbor and Deputy Lawson's symphony tolerable. Thinking about the sheriff somehow made this whole predicament worthwhile.

***

It wasn't a dream. *It couldn't have been…*

Dreams are dreamy enough; you know they're not real. There's a haze around the edge of the picture. Faces blend together. People from the past, ones you haven't seen for decades, take the place of your closest relations.

No, it wasn't a dream; but it wasn't real, either.
Was it?

49

The ever-present roar of his companions' disruptive wheezing continued to assault his ear drums. The reek of their semi-conscious bodies was jarring. Still, he couldn't be in the same place he'd fallen asleep in.

Could he?

Despite the purplish haze and star-like material floating all around him, he remained confined to the same jail cell. The same clogged toilet harassed him from the far wall, flies buzzing and dying as they alighted on the molten mass oozing within. His imagination was better than this. *If this is a dream, I should be on a beach somewhere sipping a mojito or at a buffet in Wisconsin polishing off a third plate of fried cheese curds.* Hell, he'd settle for a harem in the desert at this point.

He had a hard time believing his senses. They enjoyed lying to him and, if they lied once, they'd lie again.

In a trance, he rolled off the cot and waddled to *them*, his back aching, knees popping. He slept better on the cot than in his car, but neither were a five-star with a California king. He played it as cool as leftover porridge. Chase Cross *always* played it cool in front of the ladies. As a kid, he didn't. He had the scars to prove it, too. Emotional and physical.

So, he half-waddled, half-swaggered his way to where he'd stood for so long earlier in the day. He exaggerated each step to a comical effect, holding his chest up and letting his shoulders sway further than they had any right. His joints complained, but who cared what they had to say?

"Evenin' ladies. Deputy Dimwit know you're here?"

The four women beyond his grasp giggled and tossed their hair, one right after another. Their synchronicity would've alarmed anyone in their right mind, but they already had Chase under their spell.

Confidence. It was all about confidence. Act the alpha dog, the pack would follow. Fed up with years of bullying, Chase taught himself how to walk the walk. Now people, especially women, gravitated towards him. It helped that he'd let himself get large enough to develop his own little gravitational field, but that was neither here nor there. He needed to figure out how to keep them longer than five minutes, as if his life depended on it.

In this case, it might.

"What do I owe this pleasure?" he asked.

"The pleasure is all mine," they said in unison. The timbre of their individual voices joined in a sexy, demonic way, and sent shivers dancing down his spine.

One of them stepped forward. The other three stepped back, their boots sounded like an army moving into formation on the concrete floor.

Her pale skin and sapphire eyes lulled him into mesmerized fascination. He longed to reach out and smell her golden hair. Her slender, witch-like fingers wrapped around the bars and she leaned in, drawing him to her with sheer force of will. They kissed, long and deep, leaving Chase in a light-headed stupor. He nearly fell but managed to keep upright.

"Are you Mr. Cross?"

"Uh huh."

"*The* Mr. Cross? Who drove across country to save us?"

"Well, I wouldn't say acro—"

"So, you *are* the great detective mastermind. By my heart and eyes, you are."

He blushed. "Suppose so. I'm whoever you want me to be." Dumbly, he added, "Just say the word, and I'm yours."

A sinister smile. A coy tilt of her head. She had him where she wanted, and he'd never know it. Not even after it was too late.

"The word is, Mr. Cross Super-Detective, that the new man in town—most handsome and suave, deeply intelligent, and unmatched in the art of lovemaking—is a real problem-solver. He's a shark in a sea of guppies, if you catch my drift. Is he here for his own benefit? Or to do some actual good? I'm not too sure, but dammit if he's caught *my* attention."

"I follow ya," he said. He didn't. None of that sounded like the real him, but he would not look a gift whore in the mouth. He growled a little. "Sharks bite, though."

They shifted formation again, the redhead was now in front. She wore more freckles than there were waves on the ocean's surface.

"You won't be the one biting, Mr. Cross." She bit her lip, drawing blood, and ran her foot up his leg.

He shivered. "I hope you're right."

Stomp. Switch. Back to attention. Now a set of twins stood front and center. They spoke as one, their two voices indistinguishable, their individual features blending and shifting.

"We hope so, too. We'd hate to be wrong. We're never wrong—are we, ladies? But how rude of us. I'm Lily."

"And I'm Amelia."

"This is Eisa and Naomi."

"Pleased to meet you, Mr. Cross."

"Er, pleased to be met," he managed, drooling.

Again, Chase tried to ooze his way out of the cell. This time not towards freedom, rather towards a different kind of servitude. A sexier kind. He wished he could turn into pudding and then back into a man, sail on the trail of a shooting star with them, split his veins to give them the blood of his life—anything to spend eternity at their side. Instead, he found himself stuck, panting like a lost puppy dog.

Eisa, with hair black as night, helped him wriggle free. She shoved him back, the warmth from the palm of her hand radiating on his forehead.

"No need to be hasty, Detective." She didn't even bother with quotation marks. "You'll be out soon enough. When you are, we'll be waiting."

One last shift. Naomi, the redhead, knelt before him. She ran a single fingernail down his cheek. "The rumors were true. You truly are quite the specimen. We're going to have fun playing with you."

At once, as if Chase was God among men, the women feigned fainting, one hand over their hearts and the other facing outward on their foreheads. They acted as if they stood on weakened knees, awed by his presence, shaking at the mere sight of his man-splendor. The desired effect—to set his false confidence through the roof—was immediate. He tripped over his own ego and fell backwards onto the floor.

"Silly, clumsy, little man."

"Yes, we're going to have fun with you."

He scrambled to his feet—circumventing the upturned turtle routine and pretending he hadn't fallen—and looked around to see if anyone had noticed. Ordinary people often didn't notice much, but these weren't ordinary people. Still, one was allowed Hope, no matter how futile.

"I'm all about fun," he said. "I'm the funnest guy around. You'll see."

"Most fun. And it's too bad, you seem preoccupied. Can't do much with you with these horrible, awful bars between us. We're patient, though. Oh so patient."

"Good for me," he said, a ray of hope alighting on the bleakness of his situation.

"We'll see about that."

Desperate, Chase stooped to begging. "You could just let me out. Slip the keys from our sleeping Deputy over there."

"But if he wakes up—"

"But nothing. He's a jerk. I'm betting any one of you could, you know, seduce him into turning the other heel while the rest of you bust me out of here."

"It's turning the other cheek," Naomi said.

"Now, *that's* silly. You can turn your head, but your cheek stays right where it is. Duh. *Everyone* knows that."

"Either way, Mr. Cross, we just couldn't. Could we, girls?" Lily and Amelia looked at each other, licking their lips and shrugging. "No. We couldn't," they said in their shared voice.

"You get yourself out; we'll take care of the rest. For now, we like you exactly where you are."

He liked the sound of that, at least.

"Where can I find you?"

"You won't. We'll find you."

They didn't leave; they were gone. They vanished, the faint shimmer of their memory twinkling in the empty space before him like they had never been there in the first place.

Ice settled in his veins. His whole body, to the most miniscule molecule, throbbed. The darkness of his cell collapsed in on him. He staggered to find a wall, slid to his butt, and shut his eyes. He wanted to die. *What is happiness? Will I ever find it again?*

***

Chase fell headlong into reality. Once again, he found himself on the floor. Maybe it *had* been a dream.

In the world of the waking, his neighbor screamed in his sleep, wrenching the whole universe out of its own peaceful snooze. Chase waddled to the bars to check on him. When he got there, he still smelled *them* on the air. It was a fleeting whiff, enough to give him hope of finding happiness again.

"Er, howdy neighbor." Chase tried waking him, and it worked. The man answered with a blank stare. "You okay?"

The older man's glare wasn't directed at him. Instead, it was directed over his shoulder as if he watched a terrible monster coming around the corner. Chase turned to see hints of dancing shadows.

"Well, what do I call you?"

"Bob," the man answered.

"Bob?"

"Yes. Bob."

"Got a last name, Bob, short for Robert?"

"No, it's Bob, not Robert."

Chase stood back to appraise both the situation and this man with the odd name. He squinted hard, scanning, and found him featureless save his flushed, grizzly face and gray hair. What he lacked in physical features, he managed to make worse with his "dynamic" personality.

"Nice to meet you, Bob Not Robert. Odd name, but who am I to judge?" Another grunt in response. "Anyways, what are you in for? And don't lie. I'll know it if you try to lie. I'm a detective. It's what I do."

"I can't remember."

"Whaddya mean you can't remember? Were you drunk or something?"

"Nope. Just can't remember."

"How long have you been here?"

"It's hard to tell," Bob Not Robert answered.

All prisoners had pseudo-scientific ways to measure the passing of time. No matter how bleak their sentence, no matter how isolated their existence, they ticked off the days of their incarceration.[3]

---

[3] Incidentally, prisoners are the fourth largest consumer of chalk, after elementary teachers, coroners, and Pica sufferers.

It was early and, despite the clear gap in understanding between the two, Chase returned to his bunk to attempt rest. He tripped over one of his two right feet on the way. He recovered gracefully, slowing his descent to the rock-hard mattress with his face before anything embarrassing could happen.

After gaining his composure for the first time in his life, he snuggled under the single, thin blanket. Even though he was short, his feet stuck out the other end. From tip to tip, the blanket didn't even cover his bulging stomach; but, it was better than nothing.

"I can tell we're going to be friends. Oh, yeah. Best friends. Goodnight, Bob Not Robert."

"I told you, it's just Bob."

"*Oh*, I think I get it now," Chase said, exasperated. "Sorry. Goodnight, Just Bob."

"G'night."

"I'm gonna get us both out of here in the morning. Just you wait. How does that sound, buddy?"

By the sound of Bob's snoring, he didn't care either way.

Chase shrugged, resigning himself to a few more hours of uninterrupted, unsexy, and unfulfilling rest. In the morning, he'd make all the friends. He'd become the hero Mio didn't know it needed. They wouldn't remember the murders of the poor Stillmans. Nay, they'd remember the broad shouldered, well-loved—if not slightly goofy—detective who'd rode in out of the sunrise to save the day.

They'd remember it was *him*.

And then, they'd lay tacos and pizza at his feet.

Chapter 5:

Follow the Red-Toyed Road

Rachel had acquired a bicycle somewhere. One of those little numbers with pom-poms dangling from the handles and a horn between the handlebars. The rusted chain popped every third rotation or so. As a mode of transportation, it was better than walking.

That bicycle laid in the center of the road, mangled and unrecognizable as said means of transportation. It looked like a kindergartner's rendition of John Carpenter's *The Thing* but with more spokes.

M-33, a two-lane route leading from Interstate 75 to the edge of Grayling State Forest, was more treacherous than meets the eye. People were lulled into a false sense of security by its rolling hills and serene forestscapes. Then, when they least expected, a convoy of lumber trucks would appear at the top of the hill or a family of deer might flounce across the road (it was *their* country, after all).

It was common to notice vultures overhead—vultures that often mistook midsize sedans for large carrion. They swooped, lashed with their powerful talons, and met the eyes of drivers—their victims—before flying off in the opposite direction. All the while, the hapless motorist—screaming and swerving, scarred by the image of a great golden eye appraising their worth as a meal—jumped the shoulder, careening into a pine tree.

Not one scavenger from those skies could process what had happened. It was infuriating. They found no death. No dinner. Only confusion and disappointment.

The road, paved overnight and reeking of asphalt, resembled something straight out of a bad 80s apocalypse film. For a three-mile stretch, the contents of a toddler's toy room—tragic in its own right—littered the road. Motorists pulled to the side of the road to avoid teddies and Beanie Babies. They stood on the shoulder, scratching their heads.

A red SUV slammed into a water truck after running over a life-sized doll. The driver thought he'd hit a teenager and, after twenty minutes of losing his lunch in the ditch, called everyone important in his life to tell them how much he loved them.

A rocket-shaped lamp knocked out a motorcyclist taking his sweetie out for the first time. He spun out, and the two of them slid sideways into an Astrovan.

A police officer, already at the scene of the accident, was building a castle out of Legos in the middle of the road. He giggled in delight every time a difficult piece fit. Though he'd seen everything in his day from horrific farming accidents to live births, seeing his childhood memories strewn across a bloody highway was too much to process. The disfigured GI Joes sent him beyond his breaking point.

Repugnant Rachel, dazed but still alive, sat Indian style with her chin resting in her palms. She watched the wheel of her stolen bicycle as it spun, creaking with every rotation. It was the only indication the twisted metal had once functioned as something other than modern art.

"Ma'am? Ma'am?!" A man rushed towards her. "Ma'am, are you okay?"

He was the most recent victim of the hypnotic roll of hills and passing blur of green forest.

She ignored him. Her body throbbed. Her brain screamed that her spine should be broken. *You should be dead and off to join the Followers.* Alas, she was alive; a fact she couldn't cope with no matter how many times she went over it.

Nor could the vulture that flapped its wings twenty feet away. It pecked at the dirt and squawked in frustration. In cases like these, nature was supposed to take its due course. When it didn't, everything spiraled into chaos.

The man, bleeding from a gash beneath his hairline, knelt beside Rachel. He put a hand on her shoulder. Even though she watched his mouth move, saw the palpable concern in his eyes, all she heard was a ringing in her ears and the howl of wind. He seemed too far away to touch her, but the sensation was undeniable.

She asked, "Am I dead?"

The question took him by surprise. His own mortality never even dawned on him. He'd checked on his wife and daughter, took stock of the contents of the vehicle, and took inventory of his life and accomplishments—all before maneuvering off the road to let traffic pass.

But nobody wanted to pass. They couldn't bring themselves to, not when it meant flattening Curious George under their tires. They all gawked instead, creating a motionless line of traffic all the way to the golden gates of Ohio.[1]

"I think you should be." He put no tact into his response. "I was going pretty fast there. Are you okay?"

"Frickin' A-plus." Rachel spit black onto the pavement.

"You look like hell."

"That's where I am. I'm dead, and this is Hell. We've all made our way there, and it turned out to be exactly like our lives on Earth. What do you think? Could we have been wrong about everything? Is this crappy stretch of highway the River Styx? Are you, sir, Charon?"

---

[1] The gates are tarnished and a bit lopsided. For outsiders unfamiliar with the region, this is because the Ohio Department of Transportation has been busy doing everything besides finishing projects. A golden gate, sponsored by McDonalds, was brought up in a board meeting, but no one outlined a strategy to actually complete the ambitious project. Once the free nuggets ran out, it was all but abandoned.

He considered his family, his beautiful, virile wife and sweet, intelligent daughter. If his life was Hell, let him burn.

A large beetle passed between them. Rachel grabbed a piece of broken bike pedal and smashed it. It continued on its path, waddling like an uneven disc across a tabletop.

"Hmm," the man said. "That's not right."

The vulture guffawed. That was it, last straw. It got a running start, took flight, and left its home skies forever. Sometimes things were too good to be true. The veritable buffet it had enjoyed all its life had finally dried up. It was time to move on to meatier pastures.

Across the world, people encountered similar head-scratchers and faith-rockers. Some just rocked.

In Switzerland, for instance, in the Engadin Valley, a young couple celebrating a successful first year of marriage were given even more to celebrate. Hans, a financial planner by trade and a daredevil once those tights came on, had taken a plummet down the rocky side of a mountain while skiing. His wife looked on in horror. At the end of his comical, ski-over-head descent, he stood, shook the snow off his outfit, and thanked his maker.

A rope bridge in China snapped, releasing its two travelers into the misty depths below. They fell, they collided with hard earth, and they broke bones. The knee of the eldest was pulverized to mush on impact, but they survived. Emergency teams rescued them in time for their afternoon oolong.

A son pulled the plug on his mother. She begged him. She had the right to choose. But someone had other plans for her. She got up, gathered her belongings, and walked away, her exposed backside telling her son exactly how she felt about him.

Someone started the hashtag *#notdeadyet*. Someone else followed up with *#stillatentdead*—not because they couldn't spell, but because it was the right thing to say, once said by someone much, much cleverer than they would ever be. That was just how these things went sometimes.

The list went on and on, ranging from the outrageously violent to the mundanely natural.

People caught on at their own pace—whether they didn't want to admit to certain truths, or they couldn't. But, when they did, word traveled fast: Earth was immortal. And her people were free from Death's scythe.

Rachel stood, checked her limbs from neck to toe, and sighed. She helped the stranger to his feet, hugged him, and said, "Thank you, for trying. I think I'll be off now."

He held one finger out as he watched her walk away, but he couldn't find the right words to say because there weren't any.

Chapter 6:

Two Men and a Motel

Sheriff Grace handed Chase the contents of his pockets, holding them out as far away from her as possible, nose scrunched. Advanced civilizations of microorganisms took residence on some of them. If you listened close enough, you could hear them scream for mercy as she passed them back to him.

She didn't want to return anything but protocol insisted. He'd destroyed a piece of the town when he'd crashed into the Our Lady of the Woods shrine. He'd taken their sense of security and squished it under his boot. She wanted to take something from him. Even if it was only empty food wrappers and sticky pocket lint.

Deputy Lawson checked off each item on a clipboard as the sheriff passed them over.

"A, uh, wad of receipts, mostly Burger King. A gift card to Applebee's. A picture of...er...a rodeo clown?"

"Excuse me, madam, but that's my mother, thank you very much."

"You're welcome," the sheriff said, moving on. "One Danger Dog wallet. One paperback book: *Detectiveing 101*." Deputy Lawson snorted at this. Sheriff Grace rolled her eyes. "Why am I not surprised?"

Chase snatched the book from her and shoved it into his pocket, knocking her coffee over in the process.

Watching coffee spill onto the beige carpet, Deputy Lawson dropped the clipboard and went for his billy club. Sheriff Grace, much more patient than her young protégé— she had to put up with him, after all—stayed his hand.

"A bit of light reading," Chase mumbled. "It's, er, good to check on the competition. See what works, what doesn't. There's always room for improveme—"

Deputy Lawson held a finger in his face. Chase took the hint.

Sheriff Grace rolled her eyes as she gave him the rest of his stuff.

Grateful he was out of the gray jumpsuit, he signed the document with a flourish. Dressed and reunited with all his earthly possessions, and within eyeshot of his beloved woody, Chase Cross felt whole again.

The officers herded him out the door.

"What about Just Bob? We can't leave him in there."

"Excuse me? Who?"

"Just Bob. I can't leave him. A man gets lonely stuck with his own company. He seems like a decent enough guy, too. We became such good friends in the clink. Besides, he doesn't even remember what he's in for."

To be fair, Chase's idea of friendship was skewed. Any time a fellow human being tolerated his ranting or acknowledged him with as much as a grunt, he latched on like scabies to the epidermis of their kindness.

Sheriff Grace hadn't considered the other prisoner. In fact, she'd forgotten all about him. She did her best to avoid the holding cells. They gave her the chills. She shot the deputy a look that said, "We've screwed the pooch on this one. But, if word gets out, our careers will be over before we can say 'woof.'"

Deputy Lawson nodded, understanding. "We don't remember what he's in for, either." Sheriff Grace elbowed him in the ribs. "What I mean to say is that nobody's lookin' for him, so what does it matter?"

Chase protested, but the sheriff grabbed him by the shoulders and brought him close to her. So close, they were practically mouth to mouth. *Yes! It's happing.*

"Bob is doing his time, Mr. Cross. There's something you need to understand about Mio law. I haven't figured out what it is yet, but you need to understand it. Do you understand?"

He thought about this for a moment, caught a whiff of her pheromones, and nodded his head. "Yes, ma'am. I think I do."

"Good."

Chase clung to a lot of people, both fictional and real. In dark times, he channeled them for inspiration. All the detectives he'd read about or seen on T.V.—all the heroes he'd pulled on his speedos to act like, all the dazzling sports stars he admired—they all had one thing in common: sidekicks. Left-hand mans. Or womans.

Holmes had Watson. Frank Hardy had Joe Hardy—though, in that case, he wasn't sure who was which. Jordan had Pippen. Xena had Gabrielle.

He needed a counterpart. He needed an accomplice to chime in with something clever every now and again, someone to ensure Chase he was doing a knock-up job.

"I'd like to post Just Bob's bail then."

Sheriff Grace huffed. The "detective" was grinding her gears. There was work to do. Time was too precious to trade words with this delicious idiot.

Delicious? Are you kidding? She shook her head in disbelief.

"You'll have to…pay me for his stay. Then I'll let him out."

"Well, how much is Just Bob's freedom worth to you?"

The sheriff and deputy exchanged glances, the former leaning to whisper into Deputy Lawson's ear. After a series of exaggerated facial expression changes and shoulder shrugs, they concluded their pow-wow.

Sheriff Grace counted on her fingers how much a nice steak dinner and a couple tumblers of whiskey would be at the Au Sable River Restaurant. Her mouth watered, but she couldn't come up with a conclusive figure. She took a stab in the sirloin.

"Oh, how about seventy-five dollars plus tax. That should cover it."

Chase produced his wallet and thumbed through its contents. His eyes turned puppy dogged as he began fidgeting through his other pockets. Desperate, he scanned his immediate surroundings until he found a penny, heads to heaven.

"How about this and a gift certificate to Applebee's? I think there's at least a soda-pop left on there."

"There ain't an Applebee's for at least an hour's drive away from the neighborhood. How you expect us to be eatin' good—"

Sheriff Grace put her hand over the deputy's mouth. The phantom smell of Edna's seductive cooking left her weak in the knees, but necessity overcame desire.

"Fine. Good. Whatever. Give it here and go away."

As Chase handed her the gift card he said, "When this is all said and done, Sheriff, I'll take you out for a real dinner. Something tells me that's exactly what you need right now."

"Release Bob," Sheriff Grace ordered. Deputy Lawson, eager to impress his superior with decisiveness, bowed and ran off. "And you, 'detective,' better not make promises you can't keep."

"I never do."

At that, the two—a gun-slinging sheriff and a burger-packing "detective"—parted ways.

Soon, Deputy Lawson returned with a zombie-like Just Bob. They approached, the stark contrast of naive youth versus resigned age.

In the parking lot, hidden between two old 1990s Chevy squad cars, Chase's dented woody awaited, keys in the ignition, doors unlocked. The thing about places like Mio was no one worried about grand theft auto. No one had anywhere to go, anyway.

Chase opened the door for his new companion, helped him into the car, and sprinted—which, in his case, meant moved at the regular pace of a saunter—to the driver's side. He ignored Just Bob's lack of gratitude as he wriggled into the crater of his seat.

"Where to, Just Bob?"

"For the last time, it's not Just Bob. It's just Bob."

"Ah, God," Chase said.

***

Fed up, the woman threw her popcorn bowl across the room.

"I can't even enjoy my soaps without interruption." She clicked a button on the remote. A porthole in the clouds overlooking a mid-sized town in New Jersey swirled shut. "Fine, fine, fine. I guess I'll get ready to intervene."

When you could no longer ignore your problems, sometimes action was the only choice that remained.

"But one more episode of Earth *before I do." She scrunched down into the couch cushions for the long haul. "This should be a good one."*

***

"I'm so sorry," Chase added. "Bob. Got it. I just get confused sometimes. No one bothers to correct me..."

He had thought the man's name was odd. It was the 21st Century, and he'd heard weirder names before. Ahmerical, Jermajesty, Ruffia. He'd even met an Orang'ello in school, and a Bacardi.

But *Just Bob?*

How embarrassing. The whole ordeal reminded him of the one time he'd gone an entire day with a booger stuck to his mustache. Not a single person had been kind enough to nudge him or scream in disgust or even bothered to point at him and laugh. You could wear your mistakes like a dunce

66

hat in the corner of your third-grade classroom, but no one took the time to properly ridicule you anymore.

Chase turned to his passenger before firing up the engine. "Bob, mind if I ask you a question?"

"Yes."

"You were there a while?" Bob said nothing. "Did anything weird ever happen?"

"It's not that sort of jail."

"No, I mean…well, I'm not sure what I mean. Ever been, like, visited by four gorgeous, scantily clad, eerily choreographed women? Anything like that?"

Bob focused on Chase. He scrunched his eyebrows, wrinkles moving like heat waves across his forehead. If he thought any harder, his head might pop.

Bob took a deep breath. "Sounds like succubae to me."

Chase started the car. "Yeah, sounds right. Thanks. Now, where to?"

"Don't know."

"Anywhere I can take you? Where do you live?"

"Can't remember where I'm from."

"I see." Chase put his arm around the headrest of Bob's seat and leaned towards him, face as serious as a concussion. "What happened to you, Bob?"

Sure, he forgot his wallet or his keys sometimes. He even forgot his pants before leaving his downtown apartment in Minneapolis. After the fourth time, people gave him a nickname. It wasn't flattering.

But forgetting his apartment all together? Forget about it. Even blind drunk, walking on his hands and juggling Dos Equis off the soles of his feet, he'd know how to get home. Even if the world ended. Home was the most sacred space on Earth. Home, wherever that was for you, was the only place you were free to be you. Whether a physical address, a state of mind, or even a measure in your favorite song, you wouldn't forget it. No matter what.

Bob relaxed his posture. Moisture formed under his eye. For a moment, he looked like a frightened child who had lost his mommy in the mall.

"I...don't know," he repeated. "Everything is hazy. I know there were things before. I had friends, a family. Then, as if someone took an eraser across the slate of my memory, I was trapped in that jail cell without a clue as to who I am."

"How far back can you remember?"

"Honestly, I opened my eyes and you were staring at me through the bars. I thought I was dead."

Chase shuddered. "I see how that could mess you up a bit."

Bob shrugged.

"All's well. We'll figure it out, you and me. I promise. In the meantime, I've got a room at the Au Sable River Motel.[1] You're more than welcome to crash with me until your memory comes back."

"Thanks."

"No worries. I don't know about you, but I could use a hot shower and a clean pillow to lay my head down. Well, mildly clean. A generation of bed bugs, at most."

As they left the station, Bob fiddled with the knobs on the dashboard. None of them worked. He moved on to the glove box. It was jammed, but with enough coercion it popped open. Empty soda cans spilled out onto the floor, becoming confused with the empty soda cans already there.

---

[1] Yes, everything in Mio *is* named after the Au Sable River. You've got the diner, the bar and grill, the canoe shop, the boat launch, the hotel, the motel, the check and loans, the burger joint, the three antique shops, and...well, you get the point. It's a popular page in the phone book.

He wriggled his feet down into the mess until he found solid floor.

Chase sideswiped Sheriff Grace's car. She watched out one of the farmhouse's many windows—certainly not checking out Chase—and rushed out waving her arms in a frenzy. The damage had already been done, and by the time she got to the parking lot Chase's woody was long gone.

Chase glanced at the Au Sable Bar-Laundromat-Tax Accounting Firm, or whatever it was called, one last time as they passed. It was cliché, but he needed a drink. His mind wandered to a frothy, heady beverage and a plate of chicken wings. It wandered so far he didn't see the red light until it was too late.

Chase slammed on the brakes and Bob's head hit the dashboard. Stuck in the middle of the intersection, people blared their horns and stuck their fingers up at them. Chase put the car into gear and rolled on through.

"Sorry 'bout that, Bobo, but you know what they say: 'seatbelts save lives. Click-it or ticket.' All that good stuff."

"It's just Bob."

"I know. We got there earlier. Anyway, see down that street there?" He pointed towards the Our Lady of the Woods shrine. "The scene of the crime. You're going to help me, Bob. We're going to solve the case."

Bob might have hazarded a glance, but it was hard to tell. If he bothered to look, he didn't bother to give a crap. The glaze over his eyes had returned. His mind was away, farther than far. He sat in the passenger seat still as stone. Stiller. Stone could at least roll given the right kind of encouragement.

Despite the two mom and pop diners across the street, the pizza shop at the far end of town with the giant pink elephant out front, and the fresh game sellers, a line of cars wrapped around the McDonald's drive-thru at the bottom of the valley. They honked at each other as if not getting their Big Mac in the next five seconds would herald the apocalypse. One car had a bumper sticker above its license plate that said, "Living the American Dream."

"God Bless the United States," Chase said, grinning ear to ear.

The Mio Dam sat in the valley beyond the fast-food frenzy. It was low for the time of year, but still attracted toothless fly-fishers and scandalous teenagers from across Oscoda County. The fishermen grumbled about "kids these days" and spit chewing tobacco into the river; the teenagers skipped stones, tagged giant penises on the underside of the bridge, and made out with their classmates. A condom stuck in the reeds bobbed beyond the mouth of the Au Sable River. Nearby, an empty Miller Lite case served as a nest to a family of Kirtland's warblers, or jack pines as known by the natives. Thick oil slicks slapped against the riverbank. An unrivaled, placid scene.

The motel itself was a cheap, vinyl-sided ranch with an unvarnished patio jutting off to one side. There was a fire pit with several lawn chairs circling it. Three pick-up trucks and a U-Haul from Utah packed the small, gravel lot.

Chase undercut the turn, bucked the curb, and careened through the establishment's lawn, leaving massive gouges in the grass. When he realized there weren't any spaces, despite the sign that stated, "Additional Parking in the Rear," he popped the woody into park right where it was.

"Sir! Sir!" an older woman wearing a turquoise visor called out. Like Sheriff Grace had done, she was running out of the building, waving her arms above her. Chase had that effect on people. "You need to move your car right now. You can't park there." When she saw her ruined lawn she added, "Dear Lord, look what you've done."

He acquiesced with a smile that could bring a fire to its knees. On his way, he drove over the fire pit, breaking several of the lawn chairs, and almost took out the patio's support beam. It clung nail and bracket to the building.

She cringed as metal cracked wood and bumper smacked ground. Each new collision sounded like a year added to her debts before she'd finally be able to retire. Which was just as well. If this maniac newcomer hit one more thing, she'd be spending the rest of her life in jail anyway.

On her way inside, the phone strapped to her belt rang.

"Hello? Mhm. Okay. You're not serious. Nooo. Yes, they were staying here. No. When shall I expect them?" She held the phone away from her ear, rubbed her eyes, and hung up.

It was about to get busier at the Au Sable River Motel.

***

Chase was rested for the first time in days. Despite Bob's best efforts to keep him awake and the sun sneaking between the broken slats of the window blinds, he managed an hour or two of undisturbed sleep. No nightmares. No sudden jolts. And most important, no sexually confusing visits from disturbing women.

To his surprise, he'd noticed a pool room when he'd checked in. By the motel's general disorder, it was a stretch to expect indoor plumbing. And they had a pool! Chlorine was just what he needed to get rid of the lingering smell from the jail cell which smelled like *that* friend in everyone's friend group. No amount of scrubbing in the shower would remove it. It would take a special sort of industrial chemical.

If there was a hot tub, a good pruning would top him off. His back was sore, and he needed to be limber for the challenges ahead.

The woman with the visor was gone. She'd seemed on edge when he arrived, but her compulsive twitching slowed as they drew nearer the end of their conversation. Instead, a much younger and homely woman sat behind the counter. Chewing bubble gum and reading the tabloids, she leaned back with her feet propped up on the desk. As she blew a bubble the size of her head—which wasn't large, in retrospect—Chase pretended to pop it with his finger. She huffed, ignoring him.

He turned towards the pool, colliding with a rack of travel brochures. The two fell, toppling together. He wrestled with the rack, scrambling to scoop as many brochures as he could and tripped backwards, throwing them over his shoulder and halfway down the hallway. Defeated, he picked himself up and dusted off his shirt.

"You've got a bit of a mess here. You should, uh, tend to that before someone slips and falls."

He snuck off to the pool before she could say anything.

The attendant twirled her gum on her finger, contemplated picking up the brochures—as her mother would expect—and buried her face in her magazine with renewed vigor. If you ignored your problems, they'd disappear. She didn't have time for mundanity; too many important celebrity things were happening.

The young woman's eyes rolled in their sockets. Her head tilted with them. A tightness came across the top of her skull, and her hair slithered like a hundred thousand garter snakes. From the follicles out, each strand transitioned into a deep-space black. She groaned, dropping her magazine to grip the arms of her chair, and quivered ever so slightly.

She stood, straightening her name tag that now read "Eisa," and unbuttoned the top three buttons of her shirt.

Eisa knew Mr. Cross. Weak, like every other man. Derailed by the lure of a woman. There was power in femininity. Sure, she could use her intellect, but why waste the effort when it'd go right over his dense head? No, Eisa had a plan. As long as her master got results, the process didn't matter.

He was already in the pool, wearing a tight-fitting t-shirt and shorts that sagged at his waist. Allowing his natural buoyancy to float him near the edge, he hummed what nobody would call a tune and tapped a "rhythm" on his belly. The tides created by his own gravity washed across the pool, crashing on the far corner to splash water onto the deck.

Eisa removed her blouse, let her pants drop to her ankles, and dove into the pool. She broke the surface like a needle, not even disturbing the tension, and harpooned toward the detective.

Chase Cross never saw her coming.

***

Safe behind a locked door, Bob sat on the edge of the twin bed. He was busy doing Bob things: staring at what appeared to be a bloodstain on the eggshell wall, sitting stock-straight, and hiding within the vast emptiness of his mind.

Bob wasn't stupid. At one point in his life, he might have been a genius. The problem was he didn't know, and that infuriated him beyond reason. Stupid was easy. Being utterly lost? Not so much.

He tried to remember who he was, who he had been before. The answer dangled in his face but out of reach. He cast into the ocean of uncertainty, only to reel the line in clean. There was something out there. It tugged at him. It toyed with him. Every time he thought he hooked it, it broke free. There was a vague sense of purpose somewhere out there. Someone, or something, much larger than Bob, but he needed clarity before braving that great, blue beyond.

There was this "detective," a bumbling idiot—like real-life, push-instead-of-pull, ignoramoose idiot. The man peacocked the spectrum of undesirable qualities a human could possess: a drunk, a womanizer, a gluttonous buffoon, you name it. Still, by the Grace of God—Allah, Vishnu, or whoever—they'd crossed paths at a most unlikely vertex of time and space in a small, middle-of-nowhere town. Bob couldn't pronounce it, but serendipity came to mind. Perhaps it was the fact Chase was the most obnoxious person in the world, bound to kill someone someday with his mere existence. But that was the essence of his irresistible charm. His clumsiness might become Bob's salvation in the end.

Because it would probably get him killed.

Still, any man capable of busting somebody out of jail with a penny and an Applebee's gift card was destined for great things. Before Chase, Bob would have died. He had no family or friends, no one to mourn his passing, and he couldn't even recollect how he came to be in Mio.

He owed the "detective" his life, and then some. He'd follow Chase Cross and hope it led him to a Promised Land filled with answers and explanations. If not, they'd end up somewhere different. God only knew where, but different sounded fantastic.

The door flung opened. Chase stood in the opening, sopping wet with a shrunken towel wrapped around his waist. It mostly covered him but stopped shy. His—*ahem*—manhood stuck out under his belly, begging for someone to come to its rescue before it got squished between his thighs. Chase held his clothes in one hand and the towel with the other, naked chest heaving.

"Are you alright?" Bob asked.

"You. Will. Not. Believe. What just happened. To me," Chase answered, exhaling between each word.

"What's that?"

"Remember our talk about succubae?" Bob nodded. "Well, you were right. I think they're out to get me."

"Ah, I see."

"But why?" Chase propped a leg on the bed, stretching.

Bob averted his eyes. "Maybe it's your charm and good looks."

Chase was pacing, his stuff swinging like a pendulum below towel level. Bob bobbed and weaved to keep as far away from it as possible.

"She *found* me. Like they said. I was just floatin' around the pool and, *bam*, there she was, naked and caressing my chest. I didn't even hear her jump in. She didn't even disrupt the surface of the water—not a ripple or splash. Ugh. It was terrifying, Bob."

"Sounds awful."

"Well, not entirely awful. I rather enjoyed myself, but that's not the point. The point is, how did she find me so fast? What could they possibly want? I'm nobody."

"I thought you were a detective?"

"Oh, yeah, Well, there is that."

Rap, rap, rap.

Both men stopped dead in their tracks and turned towards the door.

"Are you expecting company?"

"Nope."

Rap, rap, rap—louder now, with extra bass.

A million possibilities danced through Chase's mind, 999,999 of them dressed like succubae and twerking against the bed posts. The other one, strangely enough, was his mother, dressed in a beige pants suit, yelling at the 999,999 other possibilities to turn down their music.

"Mio Sheriff's Department. Open up."

Chase swore under his breath and peaked out the peephole.

Deputy Lawson stood out in the hallway, playing on his phone. Two non-distinct officers flanked him, both with the demeanor of someone waiting for something exciting to finally happen in their life. Chase unlatched the lock and opened the door.

"Sir, I have a few questions to…" Deputy Lawson began. "Ah, for Chrissakes. It just *had* to be you, didn't it?"

The two flankers tilted their heads.

"What's happenin', Deputy? Long time no see."

Deputy Lawson leaned in, saw Bob sitting on the bed, and tipped his hat. Wanting to be anywhere but with the "detective," he looked for a quick exit. When he realized there was none—that he was screwed—he sighed.

"See anything weird here last night?"

"Just got in this morning. Got held up last night and missed my check-in time if you recall. Who should I bill for that?"

"Am I to assume all the destruction out front is your doing?" Deputy Lawson reached around for his cuffs. "Ms. Gabberdeen is in a fury."

He caught his first glimpse of Chase hanging out below the towel and left the cuffs alone, going for his billy club instead.

"Now, now, now." Chase threw his arm around the deputy and grabbed his hand. "None of that is necessary. I'll put on some pants and pay the nice lady for the damage. Then, we can call any extra charges even between the two of us. Whaddya say?"

Deputy Lawson moved Chase back with a hand to his forehead. "Sure. Anything. But keep *that* away from me."

From inside the room, Bob took a sudden interest in the exchange. "What brings you here, Deputy? What weirdness were we supposed to have seen?"

"Well, the Stillmans were staying here. I think they died here, too. Right out in the hallway. Someone must have dragged them down the hill, to the shrine."

"Cameras?" Chase indicated to the watchdog bolted to the ceiling. "Did you check the footage yet?"

The two officers burst into side-splitting, knee-buckling laughter. Deputy Lawson struggled to suppress his own hysterical tears.

It was Bob's turn to tilt his head.

After they'd settled down, Deputy Lawson put his serious face on. "Ms. Gabberdeen barely keeps the lights on these days. Those cameras haven't worked for over a decade. Oh well. One way or another, we'll find who did it."

He glared at Chase with squinted, accusatory eyes. Chase shrunk into himself. He was guilty, but not of murder. If it came to it, he wouldn't even be able to hurt an inquisitive deputy.

"So, you've got nothing to go on?"

"Just hearsay. One of the guests saw two people in the parking lot, putting a couple hulks of…something in their trunk. Like rolled up carpet or a Christmas trees."

"Make? Model? Plate number?" Deputy Lawson shook his head. "Damn, so close."

"Don't worry, 'Detective.' We've got everything under control." He tipped his hat. "Have yourselves a nice day, boys."

Once the deputy and his henchmen were out of earshot, Chase said, "I'm going to clean up, Bob. Then, I think it's time to get to work."

"Okay," Bob said.

Chapter 7:

The Four Sisters

They were in a place beyond all other places—not a part of reality, but not exactly separate, either. It was their place. A place outside of time where no one could bother them while they hatched their devious schemes.

Each played her own role in the decorations. Even temporal sanctuaries needed a touch of home-sweet-home.

Amelia and Lily, always trying to one-up each other, sprawled upon lavish thrones. Amelia's was built of a dark, lustrous metal, lined with the finest velvet material, and accentuated with intricate molding. Each spiral told a story, each encrusted gem held the soul of a man who had fallen to her charms. Lily's was made of gold, simple yet queenly, and spit-shined daily by her harem of wayward soldiers.

Naomi, always one to let her personality speak for itself, sat cross-legged on the hardwood floor—which stretched far enough to encircle the entire floating space, ending in jagged, broken pieces. She gazed into a crystal ball, watching her third sister with care.

"She's here."

Eisa stepped through the fabrics of time and space, kicked off her boots, let down her hair, and shook water out of her ear.

"I hope you've brought us good news."

A wicked smile became Eisa's entire face. "Yes, sisters. Chase Cross will not be accomplishing what he's so set in doing. Thanks to our mortal friends in the Mio Police Department, he will be detained. Indefinitely. If not, I do believe he will be taking quite the nap after our brief encounter."

Naomi swirled her witch-like fingers around the crystal ball. The magnified images within swirled, too. She stopped with one nail resting on the center of the ball. She tapped, observing the scenes inside.

"It would seem you have failed, sister."

Eisa screeched like a banshee and swooped to her sisters' side. The crystal ball rocked under the force of her movement.

"How can that be?"

A scene unfolded. Three police officers outside a hotel room, rapping on the door. Chase Cross, mostly naked, answering their beck and call. Mute conversation. Tension. Patience about to break. The dramatic climax they expected petered without a bang. The officers left, a cloud of reluctance and disappointment settling in their wake.

From their thrones, the twins Amelia and Lily cackled in delight. They loved one-upping each other but loved watching others—especially humans, especially their sisters—fail more.

"I see," Eisa said, counting her toes. "I will do better next time."

Naomi rested her hand on her sister's shoulder. "We cannot control the actions of humans, dear. We can only set them in motion and hope they don't spin off in some other direction. But at least you had your fun. Girls?" Amelia and Lily were there, saluting. "It's your turn."

Chapter 8:

To the Shrine, Bobman

Showered, shaved, and less shaken than he had been after his encounter with Eisa, Chase met Bob outside by his woody. The interior reeked of charred wood from the bonfire he'd ran over. This was an improvement on what he'd grown used to. He grinned to his co-pilot, threw her in reverse, backed through the grass—leaving a second pair of deep tire-thick ruts—and hopped the curb again.

Returned from whatever fresh new hell she'd been dealing with, Ms. Gabberdeen charged out of the hotel, holding her visor on her head with one arm and waving with the other.

Chase waved back.

"It's nice to make so many friends."

Bob rolled his eyes.

Chase dug around for his CD case, first in the back seat and then between Bob's legs. Tunes always helped him concentrate, usually on something other than what he really needed to be doing at the moment. By the time he found it, along with his wad of emergency cash, they were already at the Our Lady of the Woods shrine.

Police tape encircled the whole area. Despite everything he'd ever seen in the movies, there wasn't a soul to greet him—no hustling mustachios or voyeuristic photographers flashing their cameras. To Chase's disappointment, the only person at the shrine was Deputy Lawson, leaning against his squad car and chewing on a toothpick.

After their most recent encounter, the deputy looked equally displeased.

"Fancy seein' you here," Chase called from inside the car.

"Chase. Bob." He tipped his hat in appropriate cowboy fashion. "You boys shouldn't be here."

Bob was already out. He shut the door and wandered off without a word.

Chase opened the trunk and fiddled around, tossing the eclectic contents held within over his shoulder, pushing aside layers of trash to get to the real treasure. A volley of old-timey relics soon littered the sidewalk behind him. Measuring tape. A corncob pipe. Broken pocket watches. It all had its use, but they weren't the right tools for this job.

"That's, what, thirty counts of littering? Best pick all that up, 'Detective.'"

"You see, Deputy, but you do not observe. I'm searching for something of no consequence to you." A black case came out and he rested it on the bumper of the woody. "Ah-hah! Here we are."

After undoing the latches of the case, Chase rubbed his fingers together and licked his lips.

Despite the loathing building inside of him like decongestion, Deputy Lawson watched in fascination. For a moment, he forgot to breathe.

Chase looked over his shoulder, moved his body to block the deputy's view, and strapped something to his neck. He snickered as he put the case in the trunk. Deputy Lawson about choked on his disappointment. The "detective" had produced a simple magnifying glass and a ten-year-old digital camera: hardly the equipment of a master sleuth.

"What's so funny?" Chase brought the magnifying glass to his eye. "I've been saying, I'm here to solve your case."

"Yes, I suppose you have."

"No one is above suspicion at this point. Even *you*, Deputy. An outsider's perspective is what you need. A third eye is exactly what the dentist ordered."

"Doctor," the deputy corrected.

"No, I'm a detective. Dee-tect-ive. Jeez, it's like you aren't even listening."

"I mean, the phrase is...never mind. This is a crime scene, 'Detective.' I can't let you interfere with the evidence. Now, kindly piss off."

While the deputy and Chase rowed, Bob ducked under the police tape, hands stuffed in his pockets, and shuffled his way up the steps towards the shrine. As he put more space between them, the argument grew distant. He tried to decide who annoyed him more: Deputy Lawson, who'd belittled him for months and ignored him for even longer, or Chase Cross, who was a good-intentioned fool and would be the death of them both.

Either way, he willed himself to tune them out as his feet compelled him towards the shrine.

The hill-like monument, built stone by stone at St Mary's Catholic Church, grew more impressive as he drew nearer. Off to one side, before the steps began, someone constructed a smaller secondary mound with two headstones affixed at the apex, each depicting half of God's Ten Commandments. A single ray of sunlight broke through the clouds above, alighting on a stone, highlighting the sixth.

Another ray of light graced a statue of Christ the King across the lawn, cutting a path to the Globus Cruciger—a cross-bearing orb representing Christ's dominion over the world—which he cradled in the crook of his arm.

Bob reflected on the symbolism of this. Though he wasn't a witness to the murders of Mr. and Mrs. Stillman, nor had he seen their bodies desecrating this holy place, he noticed the town moved quicker in the wake of tragedy. Heck, a blind man could see it with his nose pinned shut. They moved with a renewed sense of purpose. They were even cooperating, brought together by a power greater than themselves. The shrine embodied this, bringing both purpose and meaning to the world of Mio, holding the town's fate in its arms.

He followed a man-made babbling brook with crystal clear, blue-tinted water to the shrine proper. Small leaves like vessels floated atop the surface, unwithered by the passing of time. Marble fawns were nestled alongside the wall, covered by red begonias and baby's breath. Their mother sat at the highest point of the escarpment, at the threshold of a white-stone alcove, legs folded beneath her body. Inside the alcove, an orb weaver wove its web around the arms of a plain, wooden cross. Beyond that, in a second alcove housing Mary—her hands clasped and head bowed in solemnity—a buck stood tall and proud over his family.

Several other statues and outcroppings decorated the otherwise stark stone facade of the shrine itself. Three planters filled with shrubbery. A sandblasted lamb, water gushing out of its mouth and cascading into the brook, stood vigilant outside the lion's den. A series of tunnels wound through the shrine, each leading to distinct prayer chambers.

Overcome by serenity, Bob dropped to his knees, closed his eyes, and cleared his mind. Sensation flooded over him. The ambient tinkling of the waterfall, the chirping of the jack pines that had made their nests in the oak trees around the shrine, and the hushed whisper of far-off traffic. The intoxicating aroma of fresh cut grass and frankincense wafting out from the cavernous Undershrine. How could anyone commit violence in the shadow of such a wonderful place?

A warbler landed on his shoulder, bringing him out of supplication. It picked at his shirt, shook its wings, and tilted its head.

The bird spoke to him in voice larger than life, itself. "Go forth, Bob, and prosper. I've set you apart, appointed you as a prophet to the nation of Mio."

"Uh, what?" Bob asked.

The warbler hid its face in the crook of its wing. "Just follow your heart, Bob. I will never lead you astray again...er, it will never lead you astray. Now go."

Bob watched the bird take flight. *What a weird freakin' bird. I must need some serious sleep...*

It was either that or the universe was trying to tell him something. And *no one* ever told Bob *anything*.

He ran his fingers along the rough patchwork of stone that made up the shrine's outer wall, letting them fall into grooves that needed a good regrouting. Christ the King, holding the world in his palms, watched as Bob drank it all in.[1]

An invisible force had guided Bob through the last chapters of his life. Or so it had seemed. Now, in the shrine's presence, he *saw*. He'd cross unsteady waters wherever the light took him. It wasn't an invisible force; it was *destiny*.

After long deliberation with Deputy Lawson, and a few rounds of "I Know You Are, but What Am I?," Chase approached.

"Find any clues?" Chase asked.

Don't dignify that with a response, thought Bob. "Nope. No clues."

The "detective" rubbed the stubble on his chin, humming a dissonant note or two as he followed the same path Bob had taken to the shrine. There was something blasphemous about his pilgrimage. Insulting, almost.

Inside Chase's head, gears jolted and popped. He was working out a thought he couldn't get started. He examined a few things with his magnifying glass flipped around the wrong way and had an idea.

---

[1] Figuratively, of course. Drinking stone and mortar is discouraged by four out of five gastroenterologists. The fifth can't be found for questioning. They say he took the survey before an afternoon swim with the fishes.

"Deputy Lawson told me the Stillmans stopped going to church last month. Said they'd been attending services regularly for decades, helping with raffles and fundraisers. Never missed a day. Ever. Then they stopped. Know what I'm thinking, Bob?"

Chase walked towards a statue of Mary setback some twenty feet from the shrine wall, closed one eye, and used the magnifying glass to examine her chest. He giggled, turning to look where the Stillmans had been found, where he'd so graciously helped the townsfolk get their bodies down. He followed the arc of their descent all the way down the shrine, stopping to scrutinize specks of blood the local cleaning service had missed, until he arrived at a ten-time magnified version of Bob's left eye.

Bob was mortified by the whole charade.

"I'm thinking," Chase said. "I'm thinking I don't have a damn clue what happened, but I promise you I *will* find out. With the holy Mother Mary and all these petrified deer as my witness, even if it was God himself—" *Hey! Himself? You better get your facts straight, sonny boy—* "I will find out who did this, and they will pay. These people didn't deserve the fate that befell them. They didn't deserve to die."

"Be merciful, just as your Father is merciful," someone said through Bob's lips.

"My father was a prick. Are you still with me, Bob?"

Reluctant, despite his earlier decision, Bob nodded.

Chase Cross dropped to his knees, shook his fists at the sky, and cried out to the heavens. While Bob hadn't pegged him as pious, he admired how emotionally invested Chase was in solving the case to help the people of Mio. Especially when there was zero chance of those same people rewarding his efforts.

You had to respect someone who showed so much determination to solve a seemingly unsolvable mystery, even if that person didn't have a single clue to lean on.

Chase stood, brushed off his jeans, and took Bob under his own wing.

"Time to get a drink, Bob. I need to do some serious deducing."

So much for determination...

Chapter 9:

The Honeymooners

Stan, indifferent to having slept through most of the day—
it'd been a long, long night after all—laid in bed, covered to
the chin in the musty sheets provided by the Au Sable River
Motel. The events of the previous day—a day he'd rather
not remember—ran through his head. Sprinted was more
accurate. Despite cold sweats and fuzzy nightmares,
sprinkled with a dash of unabated panic, everything was
falling into perspective.

Today will be a good day.

It helped that Anaya, bushy-eyed and bright-tailed,
was awake and getting ready to the sounds of her own music.
Her melodious voice like silver honey echoed from the
bathroom. He craned his neck and admired the silhouette of
her legs through the door frame.

"Have you seen my Coach bag? It's pink, with little
bananas." She peeked around at him as he shook his head.
"Crud. Anyway, what do you want to do today, honey?"

"Anything, as long as I'm with you."

She feigned vomiting, smiled coyly, and charged the
bed. With one great, cat-like leap, she landed next to him,
dotting with her big eyes and dimpled cheeks.

"Anything?"

"Let's just stay away from people."

She slapped him on the shoulder. "Don't even think
about that. It's a great day! It *is* the first day of the rest of our
lives."

"You're right. I'm sorry. Forget I said anything."

"Well, we could go on a hike. We talked about
getting into shape before the wedding. It's now or never.
Whaddaya say?"

On the way, they stopped at Mac Donald's for a late breakfast—not to be confused with the popular chain, but rather a Ma and Pa greasy spoon ran by an Amish family who knew their way around a gas kitchen. After a meal of grits and eggs, plus too many cups of thick coffee, the newlyweds left the dining room of farmers and retirees—all proud NRA cardholders—for the open road.

They were glad to get away from Mio. Civilization had already gotten the best of them. A good, steady hike and breathtaking scenery would cleanse their thus far disastrous time on Earth. It would also help with the food babies now occupying their stomachs.

Neither Stan nor Anaya said much on the drive. They were too busy taking in the rambling forest all around them. Red oaks. Pines. An occasional hawk soaring high overhead. Road-nearly-killed everywhere, still moving at a crawling pace. The more-than-occasional scattering of brains and entrails reminded them they were never far enough from civilization.

Thick woods were interrupted by intravenous clear-cut patches where the rejects stood alone. Either too short or scraggly, too thin or too defected, the survivors weren't sure what had happened. One day, surrounded by siblings. The next, alone, swaying in the winds of human progress; thankful to be alive, but sad in their arboreal loneliness.

Humanity's uncanny ability to shape the world to their own desires amazed Stan. It took rivers centuries to cut through their environment; even then, they ebbed and flowed by the will of the land. The waterways cut their paths with a sense of purpose, to reach the oceans they paid tribute. Then roads came along almost overnight, reshaping the entire surface of the planet, bending the landscape to *their* will with no purpose other than to get elsewhere as fast as humanly possible. People built them, people used them, and people abandoned them with no regard for the roads' impact on the environment around them.

This was Pure Michigan; this was *humanity*.

A place where people, proud of their accomplishments as they ought to be, answered the primordial urge to scream their names out loud. They displayed their heraldry, the legacy of their family bloodline, at the end of their driveways with funky-colored mailboxes and miniaturized lighthouses. The fact the nearest coastline was a hundred miles away didn't matter. Pride couldn't be bothered with logic, yet alone geography.

Once the monotony of the drive kicked into full gear, Anaya thumbed through a brochure she'd found on the ground on their way out of the motel. Her tongue played at the corners of her mouth as she squinted to read, gasping "oooo" and "ahhh" as they drove on through the hills.

At first, the vocalization of her mannerisms drove Stan crazy. How could everything be *that* fascinating? Now, he lived for everything she did. She still drove him crazy, but good crazy. The kind that gave meaning to existence. He wouldn't give it up for anything.

"Honey, it says here one of the biggest industries of this area is logging, that deforestation in the United States has been a problem for a long time. Most of this area used to be white pines, sturdy and ancient compared to the scattering of lesser pines we see now. How can these people do such awful things?"

"They do what they want."

"Animals lived in those forests. Do you think they realize? No wonder I'm so busy all the time."

He put his hand on her knee and rubbed her thigh. "It's your turn not to think about it, babe. We're here to enjoy ourselves."

"One of the biggest industries," she repeated. "They're better at my job than I am."

"I see." He half-listened, pulling into a parking lot at the edge of one of the many trails leading through Huron National Forest. "We're here."

Two paths split: one for hikers and one for snowmobiles. The path for hiking was narrow and overgrown with poison ivy and thistle. Discarded Fanta bottles and cheeseburger wrappers clung to the fence posts as if they had abandonment issues.

Rubber testicles[1] dangled off the trailer hitch of a tank-sized truck parked next to them. Various tools, knives, and empty ammunition cases lined the truck's rusted bed. The owners were nowhere to be found, likely out in the wilderness killing small creatures with big guns[2], peeing on bushes, and chugging Bud Lights.

Human things. Stan cursed under his breath. *They used to be* so *interesting.*

"What's that, honey?"

"Imagine the world without people. It's unnatural what they do to the place. I mean, decorate, sure. Spruce the place up, but this is too much. They cut down trees, dam up rivers, pump chemicals into oceans, and pollute the air with their Bieber and Hip-Pops. How can the Big Lady let this happen? Remember when the world was a beautiful place?"

"Yes, I remember. I also remember we're supposed to be trying to enjoy our trip. Please, try not to get yourself so worked up."

---

[1] In some cultures, relics of this nature are associated with bravado and manliness. Used most often by beta males trying to be alpha males, they tend to have the opposite effect on females of the human species. They are also effective at distracting from other…shortcomings.

[2] See Footnote 1

Stan grunted. She was right, of course, but she wouldn't catch him dead admitting it. Humanity was already rubbing off on him.

A split-rail fence, intact but sagging in parts, surrounded the entrance. They followed it to the hiking trail. A Kirtland's warbler sat on a post, puffing out its yellow chest. When the couple walked by without acknowledging it, it sang for their attention. Its tail bobbed, keeping the beat as it crescendoed into the grand finale, at which point the people were long gone. Ignored, it took off to go find a juicy worm somewhere. Some people had no appreciation for fine art.

The autumnal wind nipped at their faces and blew Anaya's skirt in a wave around her. She hadn't dressed for the weather. Then again, she was used to cold bones. A little breeze didn't bother her. Embarrassed, she straightened her skirt and held it in place with the weight of one arm. For comfort rather than warmth, she took her husband's hand.

Each trail marker displayed a number, mileage, and a fun fact about the warbler, Mio's official symbolic bird.

Anaya read it out loud. "Outside of Mio, Michigan's courthouse, stands the world's first monument to a northern songbird. It's built into a stone cairn and represents the tenacity of Oscoda County's residence. 'Through rain and through shine, through fire and flood, we sing.'"

"That's tweet. Come on, I see something up ahead."

Before long, the forest path ended, and a shady beach began. "Beach" was a stretch, but there was sand—though, covered in rotting pine needles—and a small lake of sorts. Bearded men stood out several yards into the water, casting fly-fish lines and chugging Pabst Blue Ribbons. They waded up to their waists in muck, early-afternoon inebriation, and disappointment in their children.

Further down the beach, red and yellow tents jutted towards the forest canopy. If you squinted, they almost looked like Bart Simpson's hair. A sliver of smoke from a campfire curled up the side of one, dissipating into the leaves above.

The whole place—beardos and trees, alike—reeked of fish.

Stan noticed a bench built from the roots of a great oak. He motioned to his wife, and they made their way to it.

She nestled close to him, and he realized there was no greater joy than the warmth of someone else. In his line of work, he met a lot of people but never got close to anyone. He couldn't afford it. On the seldom occasions he let someone in, they inevitably turned out to be a criminal or a rapist. Sometimes, in the worst of cases, a corporate defense attorney.

Anaya couldn't allow attachment, either. Together, though, they could be whoever they liked. Do whatever they wanted to do.

They gazed upon the green waters of the lake and watched the day go by. When they were tired of gazing, they scrunched in close and smooched for hours. *Yuck.* We'll fast forward through that part if you don't mind. If you do mind, browse the romance section at your local bookstore. You'll find all the best kinds of hanky-panky there.

Anyway, by the time they'd wound their way around the hiking trails, the sun was already beginning its premature descent for the day.

"That was lovely," Anaya said.

Stan, despite his better nature, agreed.

A black bear appeared on the path—oblivious, at first, to their presence—and stopped, blocking their way out of the forest. If they knew anything about the fauna of the area, they'd have recognized her sudden appearance as an omen. Such a creature south of the Upper Peninsula was a rarity.

The bear crouched low, growling, the fur on her back sticking up in clumps. Spittle dribbled out of her pale, rubbery lips.

Anaya didn't even blink.

One second, she was leaning against her husband. The next, she was ahead of him, kneeled to eye level with the bear. Her Crocodile Dundee impression was uncanny.

"Today is not your day, girl." She reached toward the creature.

The black bear bared her teeth, stood tall on hind legs like tree trunks, and roared. Even the leaves on the trees shook, but Anaya stood fast.

"I'm telling you, it's not your time. It'll come, but not yet. Not today."

The bear whimpered, appearing to nod in agreement as if to say, "You're right, nice lady. It's not my time."

She dropped her front paws onto the ground, kicked dirt into the air, and licked Anaya's face before turning her lumbering body towards the woods and trotting out of sight.

The excitement in Huron National Forest didn't end there.

Half a mile later, with the rental in sight through a scattering of saplings, a group of hunters rode up to them on four wheelers. They circled them, hooting and hollering, smoking cigarettes, and showing the gaps in their teeth. Everyone took part in the ruckus, even the teenagers.

Once they were satisfied with their show of dominance, they stopped in formation, blocking Stan and Anaya's escape.

"Where y'all from?" the vilest of the troop asked, hawking a loogie onto the path between them.

"Far away," Stan answered.

"Well, we don't care for your kind here."

"Yeah," one of the teenagers said. "You ain't welcome round these parts."

"That's funny," Stan said. "We've been greeted with nothing but kindness and respect in town. Everyone's so welcoming and considerate, considering we're strangers and all. No telling what a stranger might do. Don't ya think?"

The troop considered his threat. One of them revved his engine. Another coughed.

"That's a pretty lady you got in your arm. Hey, pretty lady, you wanna' come off with a real man? I'll show you everything you need to see."

Anaya burst out laughing.

The man who'd said it didn't appreciate her response. With an exaggerated swoop of his leg, he got off his four-wheeler and right in their faces.

"I ain't jokin', lady. I ain't one to take gettin' made fun of lightly."

Anaya reached for him, but Stan stopped her, stepping in between his wife and the man who smelled of body odor and synthetic deer piss.

"Got a proposition for you," Stan said.

The man spit again.

This must be some sort of show of intimidation, Stan thought. He couldn't help but worry about the man's dental hygiene.

"Go on, then."

"There's a lake a few miles behind us, nice spot. I'm sure you fine gentleman know the lake I speak of."

"Uh-huh."

"Perfect. How 'bout, we race to the lake and back. Me on foot, you on your little bicycles there. If I win, you leave us alone, let us go about our business."

The troop grunted and wheezed. Shook their heads. They didn't like the idea of not being allowed the pleasure of bullying tourists. Nor did their leader like the idea of returning home to a lonely bed again.

"If I win?" the man asked, flexing his pecks.

"If you win, I'll let you take my wife out on a date. Who knows, maybe she'll fall in love with you, and *y'all* can ride out towards the sunset on the bed of 'yo daddy's pickup truck.'"

Smoke poured out of the man's ears as he thought about the challenge. He could simply take what he wanted, but the stranger was right. You never knew what people were capable of doing. Besides, his Yamaha topped out at what, twelve miles an hour? The stranger couldn't run faster n' like ten. He was never good at math, but those odds swung heavily in favor of a hot date.

"Deal," he said, mounting his glorified go-cart.

As the troop sped off towards the lake, Stan took his wife by the hand, and they ran towards the car.

"I wish we could stick around and give those bastards what they deserve," Anaya said, as Stan opened her door for her.

"We don't need any more attention, or I'd be okay with that."

"I'm just saying...what a bunch of 'ignant' assholes."

"Yup," he agreed, starting the car. "There's about seven-and-a-half billion of them and only two of us. I think they're coming back already." He heard go-kart engines nearby. "Huh. Surprised they caught on so fast. We gotta go."

They came pouring out of the woods, revving engines and doing burnouts in the grass. Fire flickered behind their eyes. It was the fire of embarrassment, fanned by a false sense of pride. They'd been made to look foolish. By an outsider, nonetheless.

"You can say that again," Anya said when the leader slung a shotgun he'd had stashed over his shoulder. "I *am* getting hungry."

The newlywed's rode off towards town, giggling like school children; the setting sun warmed the sky to their left with a wash of blood-orange paint. The effect it had on the puffs of blue clouds was breathtaking—like embers falling to the surface of Earth, cooled from the coldness of space above.

***

A multi-noted door chime, muffled after years of use, announced their arrival at the restaurant. For a weeknight, and since Mio boasted a population of about 2,000, the place was hopping.

It was a nice, small-town eatery. Wood paneling accented the sponge-painted walls was hidden by a variety of eclectic wall-hangings. Trophy bucks. Glistening fish mounted on plaques. Spice racks. Old black-and-white photos of Mio in its golden age. A taxidermy masterpiece graced the corner closest to the bathroom. A few black squirrels and what appeared to be the owner's old pet beagle locked in mortal combat with a cooper's hawk, its talons outstretched towards the pooch as it swooped from the popcorn ceiling.

It was Monday, so it was the restaurant's weekly fish fry. Coincidentally, every night was weekly fish fry night. Cheap, easy to cook, you could deep fry anything and it'd taste the same. Most people wouldn't notice the difference between a deep-fried boot and a deep-fried slab of cod. One was chewy, the other had more shoelace; in essence, they were the same meal and prompted the same heartburn.

Stan pulled a chair out for Anaya, helping her into it with a palm on the swell of her back, and kissed her on the forehead. She winked but was too busy attending to her skirt to properly appreciate his chivalry. An inch or two further and the whole town of Mio would've been privy to a free peep show.

Dinner was wonderful.

Anaya thanked the waitress every time she came by to fill her water glass or clear their plates. She dabbed at the corners of her lips with the dainty charm only she was capable, wiping clean nothing and everything.

Stan, in turn, entertained Anaya with jokes and bad puns. Her favorite came when the waitress asked if they wanted dessert. Stan replied with, "No, no, I cod hardly eat another pike." She laughed so hard she almost peed her pants.

When they were well-satisfied, she grabbed his wrist and pulled him out of his seat. Her touch sent a coldness through his veins he wouldn't wish on anyone else—a coldness only he could desire. He'd never be able to get over the feeling of eminent doom whenever they touched, but it no longer distressed him. He understood she took no pleasure in her work.

"Let's dance," she said.

"Here? But I don't—"

"Shut up. Just follow my lead. That's it. Now put your hand there. Nope. No. Right there. Good. With the other, just grab my—"

"In public?" She smacked his cheek. Then kissed him. "Okay, okay. In public."

He didn't recognize the song, but she danced as if it was her favorite song of all time, as if it was the only song that ever mattered in the history of music. As instructed, he followed her lead, losing himself in the curves of her body and the sway of her hips.

She twirled around him with ease as they moved between tables, using the whole dining room as their dance floor. He dipped her, tossed and caught her above him, and spun her on the tip of his finger. When the song ended, he dipped her one last time and stared into her eyes.

Captivated by the spectacle, the diners exploded in applause. Someone even whistled. Metaphoric rose petals fell all around them.

Over the next hour, Anaya salsa'd to country music, line-danced to Godsmack, bee-bopped to Hip-Hop, and did…something to a smooth jazz number that reminded Stan of dishes breaking. The whole restaurant watched them dance, but no one was as transfixed as Stan. Everything besides his wife moved around him in a blur of insignificance.

He grinned. *My weird but oh-so perfect wife.* She didn't care what people thought. Her beauty was in her lack of modesty and her carefree attitude. She had a different perspective on life than anyone else. A better one.

The only one. Because she understood it from the other side.

"Well aren't y'all just the funnest," a big man in overalls said when they stopped for a breather. He slapped Stan on the shoulder—hard, with a hand like a sledgehammer—and Stan nearly fell over, bracing himself on the edge of a table and disrupting the place settings. "Yeehaw!" the man yelled at the ceiling. "Sorry 'bout that. I get too excited sometimes. Don't be mindin' me, now."

"Where you folks from?" An imposing woman, presumably his wife, cha-cha'd in between them, popping her eyebrows up and down. She shimmied, slapping Stan with the insides of her arms.

"South," he said, exasperated and desperately trying to wiggle free.

Against their will, Stan and Anaya found themselves dance partners. Anaya didn't seem to mind the company, but Stan preferred to be elsewhere. They slammed him about the restaurant with their cellulite, slapped him across the face with their sweaty skin, and stepped on him more than once with their size sixteen boots.

Once everyone was worn out, their clothes soaked through with sweat, all four plopped around a random table.

Most of the diners had gone home. Only a few Ten O'clock Warriors remained.

"Whew, lordy," Paul Bunyan said, slamming his fists on the table. "What a dance."

"I'm Rhonda," Anna Haining Bates said, as if she'd been asked. "This is my husband, Dale. It's been a pleasure shakin' our booties with y'all."

The giant offered his hand. Stan reluctantly took it. Anaya pulled back, hiding her hands in the folds of her blouse.

"Dale Carter. Pleased to meet you," he said, not put out in the least.

Drinks were ordered and finished, only to be replaced by another round. They gabbed. Well, Dale, Rhonda, and Anaya gabbed. Stan listened and swirled around the ice in his cocktail. For the first time in a long time, he wished he hadn't stopped smoking to give him an excuse to excuse himself for a bit.

He wanted to go to the hotel to enjoy some sleep and other honeymoon-related activities. His feet ached, his head throbbed, and he was started to feel like they'd never consummate the damn thing.

Just as he hoped for sweet relief, the worst possible question dribbled out of Dale's mouth. It was worse than the wet peanut guts sticking to his beard.

"We got some box wine back at the cabin. Y'all interested in a night hat?"

"Nightcap?" Stan corrected. "No, I don't think we—"

"Hush, Stan. What my husband meant to say is we don't want to impose, but that does sound lovely."

"I wasn't gonna take no for an answer, anyway."

"It's settled, then." Rhonda stood so fast she knocked her chair over. "If you want to follow us on outta here, it ain't a far ways down the road."

The drive was farther than expected. Night gave the forests of northern Michigan a sinister vibe. At any moment, the trees might grab them by their throats and shake the money out of their pockets.

Their house was a green-roofed cabin. It looked like it had been built out of a box of Lincoln Logs. Still, Stan expected worse. He appreciated the high-vaulted ceilings, the open floor plan with a catwalk leading to the master bedroom upstairs, and the floor-to-ceiling windows in the back overlooking the dark waters of Perry Lake.

If only the rest of the interior matched the quality of the home's architecture. No amount of mock-grandeur concealed the piss smell from their eight cats or hid the poop gum-dropped across the bearskin carpet that dominated their living room. The fireplace would have been a nice touch if it weren't occupied by a dead rat.

"Lovely home." Stan gagged. Safety pinning his nostrils between thumb and forefinger, he lifted a wet newspaper off the couch and sat down, willing his butt to hover above the stained cushion. "It's very…homely."

"Drink?" Dale offered. His added weight all but tossed Stan across the room. "Wine for the ladies. Moonshine for us *men*."

"Great."

Dale stretched and groaned like a bear before excusing himself with another slap to Stan's back.

Anaya and Rhonda leaned in close to one another, whispering and occasionally pointing at their men. Every time they did, they giggled before returning to hushed gossip. She hadn't known what it was like to have a friend, and she was reveling in schoolgirl delight.

Dale returned with a box of wine in his armpit, two plastic glasses, and a brown jug containing fermented liquid of some sort. It was likely plain, run-of-the-mill poison.

They all raised their cups.

"To new friends."

"To good times."

"To easy lives."

"To blocked olfactory nerves."

Dale scrutinized Stan. He clearly heard the intent behind Stan's toast but didn't seem to understand the words.

"To... er, good times," Stan corrected. He downed his glass and gagged on the vile contents. "Holy shit, that's strong."

"Make it myself. Pappy's recipe, been passed down through my family from generation to generation."

"What's it made from?" Stan took another long draw, enjoying the drink much more after the initial shock settled.

"Pee."

He spit it out all over the floor.

"Are you messin' with me?"

"Nope. Made out the piss of diabetics.[3] Namely me. The sugars make for a real nice flavor."

The room spun. Stan felt impending sick, and then it came. Twice. After he finished clearing his system, he decided he was done drinking for the night.

Over the next few hours, several things happened.

First, the women took a tour of the house, downing the entire box of wine. They acted like long-lost sisters, laughing, crying, and squawking over one another, until moving their party of two to the back porch.

Their absence allowed Dale the opportunity to unload his burdens on an ill-prepared Stan.

"Marriage is great. Don't get me wrong," he began. Statements like these usually led to long-winded ventilations, but Stan saw no way out so he settled in for the ride. "But I

---

[3] Yes, this is a real thing. No, I don't want to try any, thank you very much

wish things were different sometimes. You know what I mean? Course ya don't. You two are young and in love. Things seem so perfect and blah, blah, blah. That'll change. Oh boy, will that change."

"Change is inevitable."

Dale scowled. "I see your lips movin' sometimes, hear ya talkin' words, but don't understand half a what you say to me."

"Sorry."

"No worries, my friend. Things and stuff. You're a pretty man, Stan."

Stan choked on his spit. His cheeks flushed with embarrassment.

"Not like that. I ain't gay, ask anybody. I'm like any other man. I hunt, shoot guns, go fishin', and like to build stuff. My truck's my baby and so is my boat. But sometimes I also like to go into town...not Mio. Never Mio. No, somewhere far, far down the road. A place called Lewiston. I go into town, get my eyebrows done, listen to classic music, and sometimes even join a yoga class or two. Those are *nice*. The guys I meet doing them are nice, too. Did you know you can drink wine *and* paint? Turns out I'm quite the art-teest."

Dale stood, stumbling a bit, and stretched his arms to bring attention to his collection on the wall. A vase with flowers, a table of fruit, a bridge over troubled water. They were all colors and brush strokes, contrast and texture. They were all terrible, like a five-year-old with palsy tried to color in the lines.

"Told Rhonda I got 'em at the Home Depot. Do you know how hard it is to live a life that no one understands? I feel constant shame. But, boy, dancing with you all? That was somethin' else."

"Strangely, yes. I do. It doesn't get easier, being misunderstood. I wish I could say it does."

"It's the absolute worst, Stan. Enough to drive a man insane."

"Life's short, Dale. At the end of the day, it's *you* that has to be happy with the choices you've made, the adventures you've had. When the sun goes down, *you* have to be content with the person you are. You can't let other people dictate how you live your life. Can't worry about the things they might say. That's the fastest way into an early, miserable grave. I've met too many people who ended it all because they didn't feel free to be themselves. Be unapologetically you, Dale. That's the best thing you'll ever do in your life."

Dale staggered and swayed, held up a finger, then let out a long, rumbling burp. "And these GODDAMN CATS, Stan."

The conversation clearly over, Dale threw the half-full bottle of alcoholic piss into the fireplace. Glass shattered outward. Two orange tabbies hiding within hissed and sprinted off to hide somewhere else.

Behind them, the screen door opened.

"Welcome back ladies," Stan said, relieved to see the beautiful face of his wife.

Rhonda winked at him with both eyes and belched, giving her husband's earlier ejaculation a run for its money. She mumbled, slurring and raspy, and threw her arms around Anaya. The women's cheeks touched, and Rhonda fell backwards through the screen door and onto the porch, deader than Dale's soul.

"What the fack!"

Dale stepped forward, leaned back, and took a swing at Stan, who sidestepped a knockout blow. Dale fell face first onto the couch. He lumbered to his feet and moved to grasp Stan in a hug with the sole intention to break every bone in his body. Again, Stan dodged the attack, leaping the back of the couch and straight onto a glass table. His leg shattered the glass, but he dislodged it before Dale could grab him, earning himself only minor abrasions.

Anaya, no longer petrified at the horror of her new friend's death, skipped to where the men were fighting. She took a deep breath and grabbed Dale's shoulder. He went limp and fell into the broken remnants of the table.

An eternity passed.

Neither Stan nor Anaya dared to move a muscle, both suddenly as sober as nuns on Sunday. The Carter's house was thick with silence and death.

Anaya looked at Stan with cute, puppy-dog-blue eyes and burped the prettiest little burp he'd ever heard.

"As suitable a eulogy as any," he said.

"Oops. I've done it again."

"*We've* done it." Stan buried his face in his palms. "We've done it again. We're a team, now. Through thick and thin."

"You're sweet."

"You're drunk." He put his arm around her and kissed her on the temple. "I'll pull the car around."

"I'll get our stuff."

Chapter 10:

Bowling for Solutions

The bowling alley on Main Street—also a dry cleaner, closed to the public due to overwhelming demand brought on by bedbugs—teemed with a lot of things, but life generally wasn't one of them. A dusty ceiling fan with blades like chrysanthemum petals stirred around cigarette smoke, creating a carcinogenic cyclone. Half-empty bottles of liquor lined the shelf behind the bar, reflecting off the floor-to-ceiling mirror. A rack of rank shoes dominated the rest of the bar space, standing ready for anyone brave enough to borrow a pair.

Ned, the surly barkeep of this tale, sprayed the insides of the shoes with an unlabeled can of aerosol. He only stopped to wipe out the inside of "clean" glasses, to fill one of said glasses with lukewarm ale, or to sneak a few pages of a book he'd been reading for one of his day classes: *Foundations of Astrophysics*. Hey, some of the simplest people dreamed the biggest.

He hadn't paid attention to the patrons bowling at lane three when they came in and continued paying them no attention, other than on the increasingly frequent occasions when the lady came up for more beers. Her companion, a bearded man dressed for a trip to Woodstock, kept dropping his ball in lane four. Luckily, Ned had a teenage son to deal with that kind of thing while he learned how the universe worked.

Ned didn't care much for hippies. Smoking the wacky tobacky, stinking up the place with their "all-natural" attitudes, thinking here and now when there was so much *there* and even more *later* to consider. This couple, if they were a couple, was taking Free Love to a whole other level. He couldn't be sure, but they looked familial, like a mother

105

and a son. Maybe he was wrong. Maybe they were simply on a trip together, attempting to repair years of strained communication.

Or they were freaks. Most outsiders were freaks. It was a simple fact of nature.

The lady loosed a wobbly spinner that curved to the left, teetered on the edge of the gutter for a second, and then willed its way to the center of the lane. Not enough, though. She ended with a seven-ten split.

"Ah-hah!" the bearded man cheered. "That's gonna hurt."

Or so it seemed.

She crossed her arms and smiled. The pins rattled, wobbled, and toppled. Once they cleared, she ambled to the benches and chugged her beer.

"You almost had me on that one, my boy. *Almost*. You're up." She regarded her empty mug. "And I'm out."

He waited for her to leave before rolling, that way there could be no funny business—no miraculous, last-second pin-downings. The ball went straight down the middle of the lane—hard, fast, and true. It struck the front pin, toppling the others.

"Booyah." He pumped his arm as he walked away. "That's how it's done."

The lady returned, holding four full mugs and shaking her head.

"Sure about that, son?"

Reluctant, he turned to see the front pin was erect, standing in the exact spot it had started. He rolled his eyes but didn't confront her. They'd argue. She'd win. He'd go home, self-esteem crushed once again—all the worse for having spoken out in the first place.

Instead, they shared an anonymous toast before taking a breather.

"Shouldn't we be drinking wine?" he asked.

"Always been a beer girl."

"Ah, well, I'm not sure there's a miracle for that. Why are we here, mom?"

For the first time in their millennia-long relationship, his mother looked sad. He noticed bags under her red eyes and lines across her forehead. Her hair was disheveled, her breathing raspy, and he couldn't help but notice she kept looking over her shoulder.

She took off her glasses, finished her drink, and said, "We've got a problem."

"I know. I'm working on it. Things are going pretty well. It's just not as simple as it usually is."

"What do you mean simple? The facts are clear to me. My shrine's been desecrated by the freakin' Adversary! Some of our most devout people have let the Devil into their souls and done a most foul and unholy act. Do you know how bad that looks, and the trouble something like this can cause? We're supposed to be protecting them, looking out for our followers. Ever heard of a shepherd driving his sheep straight into a wolf's mouth? Or turning the other cheek as it tears them apart?"

He hung his head. "No, ma'am."

"We taught these people to be kind, thankful, and courteous. Gave them fulfilling lives, small problems to keep their pitiless minds occupied. We handed them justice. Fairness. Mercy. The Golden Rule. Do unto others as they do unto you."

"Those last two are the same thing." His voice was mouse-like and broken.

"Shut up." She wiped moisture from her face. "They've fish to eat, wine to drink. Jobs. Wives. Kind neighbors. Hell, most of the kids in Mio aren't total screw-ups. They have all this because of *us*. Because of me. We opened the gates to the garden and let them in."

107

He wanted to stop her and remind her all they did was dictate what was right before they left humanity to their own devices. They'd had no guidance, no reassurance. Only each other.

"Do I ask for too much?"

"I'm not sure what you're asking for, Ma."

"One day." God held up a finger. "One. A little Me-damn respect from time to time. Pass around a collection plate on Sunday, shell out just a small fraction of their mortal earnings. What is money, anyway, if not a false idol? We have to spread the word, somehow, and real estate beyond the Golden Gate[1] is not exactly cheap. Don't kill each other, don't covet thy neighbor, don't crap with the door open, etcetera, etcetera."

Commotion from the opposite end of the bar caught her attention. A fat man with shoddy clothing had fallen off his bar stool. An older gentleman with a shaggy beard helped him to his knees.

Jesus was impressed by a beard as glorious as his.

The fat man was not.

After shoeing away his helper, the fat man began waving his arms and ranting. Finally, two ancient succubae glided to him from a corner booth, but the fat man couldn't see through their disguise. Just another normal day in Michigan.

"Poor sap."

"Boy, are you even listening to me?" the mother said, smacking him upside the head. To herself, "I should whip up a plague or two, remind them I'm still here."

---

[1] Not to be confused with the aforementioned gimmick down in Ohio. This is the real, bonified, have-I-atoned-for-enough-of-my-sins Golden Gate. It's maintained on a regular basis by chubby, winged creatures in diapers (hint, hint ODOT) that don't take kindly to bureaucracy.

"Yes'm. Sorry, ma'am. What do you want me to do?"

She picked a ball at random from the mechanical dispenser and lobbed it behind her head. It landed with a thud, chipping the ball and denting the lane. It collided with the pins and an invisible bolt of lightning splintered them. The lights flickered and the floor rumbled. A beer mug fell off someone's table.

"No, no...that won't do. I need to do something *big*. Something...21st Century big."

Ned, inspecting a fly at the bottom of an empty glass, pretended to not notice any of it. Sometimes ignorance was indeed bliss. And it was almost always cheaper than intervention.

She took a deep breath, counted backwards through her commandments. "Thou shalt not covet. Thou shalt not bear false witness. Thou shalt not steal. Thou shalt not commit adultery. And thou shalt not *kill*." She side-eyed Jesus, directing the last one at her son.

He cowered but held his ground. "Seriously, what do you want from me? I'm never good enough for you, admit it."

"Why can't you figure out who's doing this, god dammit?"

"God's name," her son pointed out. "Well, Mother, to be honest everyone in town is a bit, uh, suspect. Not that they're all guilty, but kind of dumb. There's this new guy in town. This Chase Cross, detective something or another. He's complicating my investigations."

"Well?"

"Good guy, really. Means well. But he's the dumbest of them all, you see? Getting in the way, making a mess of things, ruining evidence, and rubbing people the wrong way."

"So what?"

"He's the most suspect of them all."

Invisible lightning cracked again. God stood over her son, veins throbbing. A strong wind stirred outside and howled through the cracks of the bowling alley. She squinted over her glasses. "Do I look like I want excuses? I see everything."

"Then why don't you know what's happening, *Mother*?"

The whole place rumbled. Glasses fell off shelves and even Ned took notice. The ground beneath the building rocked and rumbled as if the earth itself would split like his tiger pants during Zumba class.

"That's it! You hippy-dippies need to leave before I call the sheriff."

"On what charges, sir?" God asked.

He scratched his head. "Well, I don't know. For being a nuisance, I suppose."

The barkeep was right. It was time to leave. Their argument was going in circles and Jesus was developing a killer headache like he hadn't had since leaving Bethany. He'd been hangry then, took it out in all the wrong ways.

Growing up, his mother had put a lot of pressure on him to be all omniscient and benevolent and forgiving and vengeful and yada-yada. It was a big shadow to stand in, that of God—lord and savior. Especially when all you wanted to do was chase girls, turn wine into lowered inhibitions, and make lots of friends. How did one find work-life balance given those parameters?

"Anyway," she said as they walked past the table with the fat man and the succubae. "I need you to double your efforts. God—I mean, Me—only knows who will die next. And something is shrouding my all-knowing eye. I can't...I can't see through this one. Can I count on you?"

"Sure."

"Sure?"

"Yes, Mother. You can count on me." Jesus closed the door and stepped into the night.

"Good." She kissed him on the cheek, leaving a smeared lipstick splotch. "Oh, one more thing. I think this case is bigger than humanity. They're capable of a lot of atrocious things, but it might not be their doing this time. There's a weird force at play. Whatever it is, it's affecting even me. I'm not...as in control as usual."

"Why do you say that?"

"The walls have grown thin. A lot more is getting through. More than ever. And earlier today I started spouting off new verses...like the old ones—the classics. But wrong. As if someone was satirizing my work."

If that was true, then the worst-case scenario was unfolding while they drank at the bar. Why were they wasting their time bowling? If they weren't already too late...

"My life is a bad fan-fiction right now."

"Right," Jesus said, not wasting any more time. "Sounds...uncomfortable."

She nodded, faked a smile, kissed him again, and stepped in front of an oncoming semi-truck. Instead of *splat*, a sound like golden bells and a chorus of tenor angels erupted and she was gone, returned home.

Watching the blank space that used to be his mother and the trees swaying on the side of the road, Jesus sighed. *The woods are lovely, dark and deep, but I have promises to keep. And miles to go before I sleep.* He'd heard it his fifth time through college, while studying English literature and poetry. It had resonated with him as elegant and catchy, but now hit way too close to home.

Language was funny. Language painted beautiful images across the mind, brought you to happy places beyond imagining. Language caused introspection, forced empathy. Language rang like music for the soul.

Language also reminded you how totally, completely, irrevocably screwed you were.

"Shit," Jesus said before blinking out of existence.

Chapter 11:

Lights Out

"Last one," Ned told Chase as he slid him a frothy beer. Foam sloshed over the top of the glass, adding to the crusty, sticky layers already fused to the bar.

"Tenders not supposed to, *hic*, whatchamacallit… Tenders not s'possed to be a judgy mcjudgebag, you son of a—"

"Weigh your next words wisely, stranger."

"Donya be bringin' my weight into this," Chase said, wagging his finger at a poster on the wall.

Ned rolled his eyes and turned his back to the drunk.

Chase had gotten lost. He'd been walking backwards his entire trip to Mio. If he flipped himself around, things might right themselves.

Earlier in the night, he began putting together fragments of this and pieces of that. A theory began to form in the dark recesses of his mind. There was something going on in Mio—something greater than any Sherlock Holmes plot, but he couldn't figure out what.

Yet.

He contemplated his theory over a beer. Out of the two bars in town, he chose the bowling alley. Any hard-working detective knew a bit of good-spirited fun kept the inquisitive palette clean. Besides, it was a popular place. The chances of him meeting a key witness or stumbling across something *weird* were slim to none across the street. Another fact of nature, everyone liked bowling. Even killers.

When he arrived, he did what he set out to do. He drank a beer.

Then another.

Then, a third.

After three, a number he didn't wish to disrespect—especially with the religious connotations of the whole shrine murder-mystery deal—he switched to vodka. Then whiskey. He didn't want to conform to the stereotypes of the modern detective but getting sloshed was so gosh darn wonderful. You could *forget*.

The problem was, as he forgot the pieces of his theory, it all drifted away. No matter how hard he tried to keep things straight, his mind went all swirly. The effort made him thirsty, which only led to more imbibing and more drifting.

Woe was the blight of the modern drunkard.

His ideas became fleeting thoughts. His head pounded with recollection. Why'd he come to the bar? Why'd he come to Mio, so far from home and a comfy bed?

Maybe the answer was in the bottom of the next—and according to Ned, the final—glass.

Grumpy and confused, Chase overpaid Ned with a handful of cash and prepared for a walk to clear his head. Chase stood and his barstool grabbed his leg. He knocked a bunch of glasses off the bar and fell face first, cushioned by his forehead.

A strong hand grabbed him by the scruff and helped him to his feet. Chase looked at his helper, at the ceiling, and at his shoes. Or, at least, where they had been last he checked.

Then, he yacked.

"D'you tie my shoes? I thank you, sir, to not…" He slurred and drifted off. "Took my shoes? You bastards."

The man wore suspenders and a fabulous auburn beard. For a second, Chase saw two men. No, three. Back to two. They snapped together, and he yacked on the man's ankles.

"You alright, kid?" The man tried to guide him to a booth.

"D'you take my shoes?"

"I think we need to get you home. Where do you stay?"

The man motioned to the exit and offered his shoulder as a crutch, but Chase stood his ground; or rather, he flopped on his back and became as immovable as possible. A toddler could have pulled him up or rolled him off, but the man remained patient with him.

"Who," he hiccupped again. "Who you?"

"Hezekiah." The man's beard rose and fell with his genuine smile. "Come on now, young man."

"No. I'm na Hezekiah. I'm Chase, Detect... Detective Cross. Never met this Hesi...guy. You have the wrong persons, friend. D'you take my shoes?" Chase scrunched his face to look angry and felt dizzy again, so he stopped.

"No, no. *My* name is Hezekiah. But that's not important. And I don't know where your shoes went. We can find them together. Then I'll get you home."

"I'm not supposed to talk to strangers. Momma says so."

The man gave up; there was no helping a man without shoes who wasn't willing to help himself.

But there were two others willing to try to help a drunkard down on his luck. Even though he could barely stand—and somebody had turned on the "spinny, swooshy thingy"—he recognized the twins approaching him.

"Mary Kate and Ashton? What'n'da are you two doin' here?"

Chase swayed, pointing an accusatory finger and beaming—cheeks flushed, eyes unfocused. He'd never met celebrities before, and these two looked much better than when he'd seen them on the cover of Esquire.

Amelia grabbed him, wrapping her fingers around his. Her tongue played at her lower lip.

Lily beckoned him to their corner booth. Naturally, he obliged.

Like a door frame, it jumped out of nowhere and smacked him across the head. These two women were not, in fact, Mary Kate and Ashton.

"You're from the jails," he managed.

"Bingo," they said in their singularly upsetting voice. Worms crawled through his veins.

Lily scooted closer to him, put her arm around his shoulders. "You're perceptive, Mr. Cross. Care for a beverage?"

"Nah, I'm toasty. A burger would be nice. Or an om—"

Before he could finish, a large plate of food appeared before him, complete with a greasy cheeseburger, western omelet, home fries, and two scoops of lemon ice cream—his favorite. He didn't ask how they'd known or what hole they'd pulled the food from. He realized he didn't care. He was absolutely ravenous.

Amelia and Lily congratulated each other with a wink. Sure, he'd get through his meal and back to business, but the Ambien in the ice cream should knock him out long enough for their boss's work to come to fruition. If not, the cyanide in the fries would do the trick.

They chatted freely while he gorged himself.

"He is so cunning, so brilliant. When he sees an opportunity—say the acting ruler of the underworld going on his honeymoon—he hops on. Hypothetically speaking."

"Of course." Amelia gagged as Chase shoved a fist of fries into his beef-filled mouth.

"If all goes according to plan, Management will have a new face."

"And we'll have cushy seats by his side."

"Can't get more perfect than this."

"Then why does *nothing* feel perfect?"

Eisa was a professional. Nobody had ever turned her down. Not one person one time. What had gone wrong? How had this "detective," a complete pervert, not *fully* fallen for her womanly charms? It didn't make any sense.

Amelia's skin tingled as the mother and son who'd been bowling walked by their table. His robes brushed against her knee, and it was all she could do not to hiss at the pain shooting through her body. Only one thing could have wrought so much chaos with such little effort, and she wasn't ready to accept it as a possibility.

"Did you?" she whispered to her sister, who recoiled in fright.

Lily quivered. Lily shook. Lily groaned and writhed in her seat.

Chase stopped gorging himself, a dribble of cheese hanging from his mouth. "She gonna be okay? Should we hold her mouth open or something?"

Lily leapt across the table, shrieking, and knocked Chase's plate across the bar. She was no longer the gorgeous blonde—rather, a sunken-cheeked, pallid creature with thin hair and hollow eye sockets. Onion stench wafted off her.

Chase hated onions. He'd take anchovies over onions. He'd take an enema over onions.

Ned glanced at the corner table, shook his head, and shrunk behind the bar. If they couldn't find him, maybe they'd leave.

In a voice like a volcano eruption, the creature screamed at Chase in a harsh, alien language. His blood boiled, the hairs on the nape of his neck stood straight up. Meanwhile, he silently lamented the loss of his lemon ice cream.

After an eternity, Amelia grabbed her sister and pulled her off the table. "Sorry about that. We, uh, must go. It's, uh, late and we have a busy night ahead of us. You know how it goes, right? Best you, er, forget we were ever here, yeah?"

And forget he did. He'd forgotten everything else tonight, so why not one more thing?

Like his prospect at enjoying some dessert, the women-demon things were gone. He, as always, was utterly, totally, completely alone.

Chase stumbled out the door—letting it hit him on the ass on the way out—and vomited his entire meal into the gutter. The streetlights and the kaleidoscope of stars above hit him like a rising sun. He tried to shield his eyes with his feet and fell into one of the numerous stone planters lining Main Street. Somehow, he pulled himself out and blinked away the blindness.

"Where's to now?" he said aloud. It was passed Mio's bedtime, but he was too drunk to consider sleep. Or consider anything, for that matter.

Down the street, a neon "closed" sign buzzed in the window of the local pizza shop, interrupting the quiet of the night. It also gave the neighborhood moths and mosquitos a slice of entertainment after a long day of flapping around annoying people. Chase remembered a giant pink elephant in front of the restaurant. It wasn't where he thought it should be, but he'd been wrong before.

He penguined his way north, towards the Our Lady of the Woods shrine. His legs moved without instruction, as if by divine intervention. If he was sober, he'd realize that was the way to his hotel, too. The cracks in the sidewalk were worse than Himalayan ravines. He might not have been prepared for such an epic journey, after all.

Half a block away from the bar, he stopped to have a long-winded and animated conversation with a buffalo painted on the side of the Chamber of Commerce. The social butterfly he was, he stopped again to talk to a discarded antique umbrella, seeing as it was the oddest shaped person he'd ever met.

"Oh ice...I-C. You're one of umbra Ellas, right? Makes sense. Thank you, sir. Keeping us dry one storm at a time. Good day." He shook the object's crank and stepped out into the middle of the road.

He zigzagged across the road, backtracking once or twice when his own shadow startled him.

The side street he took darkened as the streetlights faded, and the stars hid behind the trees. It grew longer and narrower every step he took. His mind wandered. In part to the day's events, but mostly to his mother. On nights like these, he always thought about his mother.

While most parents encouraged their children to pursue their dreams and be all they could be, Mrs. Evelyn Cross did not. Not by a long shot.

As a kid, Chase had been an avid reader. He wanted to travel to space one day. Mother reminded him he couldn't even find his way to the front porch. He wanted to sail to Europe or Asia to rescue some princess or fend off the evils of a powerful wizard. Mother insisted he couldn't even rescue a fish from drowning. How was he going to rescue anybody else?

Besides, those things were children's dreams; he needed to grow up and face reality. When he decided to be a detective and she laughed in his face, Chase Cross packed his backpack with all the money in her purse, a few changes of clothes, a four pack of pudding, and hopped in his station wagon. He never looked back, leaving Minnesota in his rearview mirror and trying his damnedest to tune out the scratching voice of his mother telling him he would fail.

"You were born a failure, you'll die a failure."

I'll prove her wrong. Nothing's stopping me now.

Especially not some half-pot sheriff's deputy in a tiny town like Mio. No matter how close they watched him or how many times they threw him in jail. No matter how many guns they had in their shed...

"Bloody hell. They've got those guns," he said to a crumpled fast-food wrapper on the sidewalk.

He had let thoughts of murder consume his mind and forgot about the arsenal in the shed—enough to equip a small army. He made a mental note to remember why he'd started drinking in the first place and another to remind himself to remember not to forget about the shed.

"S'lot to have to remember..." Chase belched and teetered.

He didn't have time to dwell on any of it. A branch cracked behind him. A hyena cackled from within the trees. His stomach twisted into knots, and the remnants of his late-night dinner made its way up his esophagus.

Shadows loomed towards him. Long, slender, menacing shadows. They flickered as they drew nearer.

He sped up.

They continued to draw nearer, dancing macabre and mocking him with their insidious patterns. Then, they dipped behind the trees, snapping out of view. A smell like burnt pine needles and sage invaded his senses.

When the shadows reappeared, they were closer yet, flicking in and out.

A grumble like the devil.

Ember eyes, bright as supernovas.

His eyes widened; his heartbeat quickened. Nowhere to hide; he couldn't escape the monsters in the night.

They were on him. Then, they were gone again, but the scent of burning lingered.

Chase needed to find his hotel and sleep off these delusions, but he had no idea which way to go. So, he kept on walking. *If I walk far enough in a single direction, I'm bound to end up where I started*, he thought. *Or somewhere else, at least. The sun will rise, and I'll sober up.*

That, or he'd die of cold and exhaustion. Either would mark progress.

"Hey, fat man," a voice in the dark said. "You lost?"

Was that voice real? Or was he hearing things again? He ignored it and kept going.

"What, are you deaf?"

Why was his mind playing tricks on him?

Chase stopped. A few paces off the sidewalk, in front of the local high school—home of the Thunderbolts, according to a large blue sign next to a much smaller football field—three teens approached. The embers of clove cigarettes lit, illuminating angry, slit eyes, before dying out and leaving sharp, pearly whites in the shadows. One teen walked right up to him, and the other two fanned out to flank him at either side, beyond his peripheral vision.

"Pine needles and sage," Chase whispered.

"Look at this idiot." The leader laughed. "What to do with you? What to do?"

"Why are you…what…it's late? You kids should be in bed. Mommy and Daddy must be worried sick."

He sobered a bit, mustering all his strength to fake courage. Chase had never enjoyed conflict—at least, not real conflict—but he wouldn't let three punk kids intimidate him.

You're a grown-ass man, dammit. Stick out your chest and show these twerps who's boss.

"Were you all following me back there, trying to be spooky? Did you…Did you really sneak around me and act like you were casually coming out of the parking lot? Real smooth, kids. And super lame. I wasn't scared. Didn't fool me for a second."

The leader flicked his clove close enough to Chase's face for him to feel the warmth of its lit end. His lackeys threw theirs down and stomped them with their pristine combat boots. One of them had spray painted a skull jacket.

The other wore a spiked, pink ankle bracelet. Chase smiled on the inside, picturing some rebellious princess picking out her accessories for the day. It made the kids much less menacing.

"What's it to you, fat man?"

"Lotta strange things happening in this town the past few days. Wouldn't want ya to get hurt. Or implicate you in certain…unpleasantries. I'm a detective, and I don't appreciate wanna-be thugs lurking around."

One lackey coughed. "Tony, man, he's a cop. Better leave him alone. Your dad told us to lay low."

"Shaddap, Chaz. I know what my dad said." The leader, Tony, scratched his head. "So, you're a cop, huh? All y'all are good for is getting drunk, waving your badges around, kissing the sheriff's ass, and letting this town go to hell."

"I don't know anything about that. Something else your dad said, I'm sure. Sounds like a wise man… Wise enough for a swift kick." Chase judo-chopped his arms, flicked his leg two inches off the ground. "But I'd kiss an ass like hers…" he added, under his breath.

"Don't talk about my dad like that."

Chase puffed out his chest but was overtaken by dizziness. He blinked the spins away and stepped closer to Tony.

"I'm not a cop, anyway. I could care less about the dribble that comes out of your dad's mouth."

"My dad's takin' over this town, so you better learn to respect him."

Before Chase could respond or defend himself, the teens jumped him. Skullpaint held his arms behind his back. Pinklet punched him repeatedly in the stomach. He tried to wriggle free, but they were too strong.

Tony stood back, lit another clove, and took a swig out of a small hip flask. Chase blubbered and whimpered with every blow, but his gut absorbed a lot of the damage—one benefit of carb loading. After several long minutes of torture, the leader blew a large cloud of smoke into his face and threw all his weight into one final, devastating punch. Chase's dark night became darker before fading to black.

Chapter 12:

The Shrine Alive

A deep gray, broken only by the fabulousness of the Hunter's moon, enshrouded the Our Lady of the Woods shrine. Gawkers and close family members of the Stillmans, unwilling to let go of their memory and acquaintances along for the ride had long since dispersed from the scene. They remembered their jobs, their kids, and all the other better, less depressing things they spent their time on.

Nightfall was an opportunity for nocturnal creatures to slink through the streets for food, without interruption or fear of being squashed.

Willy, the groundskeeper, tucked his red wheelbarrow in the shed among the rakes and shovels he'd grown to consider family. Once he finished his work, he too left the grounds to catch some Z's before dawn. It was always difficult to leave his sanctuary; the church, especially the shrine which he devoted so much of his time and efforts to, felt more like home than his trailer down the road. He was often compelled to sleep close by, to spend some quality time with God. To that effect, the parish had built him his own apartment near Father's. He kept his trailer, though. Even Willy had things he'd rather the church not find out about.

Christ the King, stiff from a hard day's work being a statue, yawned and rolled his neck. He'd have stretched his arms, too, but actions of that caliber required enough energy to move a mountain, and he was feeling extra lethargic tonight. He took two bureaucrat-slow steps off his pedestal and greeted the night with his customary mantra.

"Urgh. Another night closer to death." *If only that were true.* "Oh well, time to visit the others. They'll be expecting me, I suppose."

All around the grounds of Our Lady of the Woods, the statues were awakening and stretching out their own stony limbs. This was their nightly routine. Once the people left, they stepped down from their predestined places. It was their chance to *live*.

They quarried, strained, and grunted to their usual meeting place in front of the shrine. It was close to where they each had to return at the end of the night; and, even if some wouldn't admit it, they all felt a little less dry being within earshot of the babbling brook.

King, their leader (not by choice), forced his legs up each step, leaving bits of his frock in a crumbling trail behind him. He moved at a glacial pace. Though he didn't care for the others, he had to live with them. When you were a ton of marble, it was hard to get away to someplace better.

This effect would wear off within a half hour. They'd all be closer to human, still stiff but able to twist and shout if they wanted. King didn't want it; King didn't want much of anything. But it wouldn't last long.

The globe in his hand was heavier than usual, as if the weight of a hundred worlds rather than the one, swirled within its crystal walls.

"Ah, good morning, son. How did you sleep? Can I get you some tea?" Mary of Lourdes asked.

She reached out, an act that stretched his patience to tears, and straightened his robe. Her own pearlescent, white gown—spotless, as always—was pressed smooth and flawless. Even her blue belt, hugging her waistline parallel to the cobbles at her feet, was the perfect embodiment of neurotic obsessive compulsion. It was so chromatic-clean King had to the fight the urge to slap a fistful of dirt across her midriff.

He was cynical; he wasn't cruel.

Speaking of pearls, Mary of La Salette, eyes puffy from her nightly cry, greeted her son with a kiss on his cheek.

Her golden earrings and beaded necklace did little to distract from the sorrow she held deep within her eyes. So deep, it became her.

King never understood what she was *so* sad about. They all lived the same experiences, the same night-in, night-out cycle of meaningless dribble. Maybe she just loathed being trapped as much as he did. But, still, *he* wasn't depressed. Nobody would catch *him* blubbering about it. It went to show, no matter how much you thought you knew about the people close to you, you could never understand what went on in their messy heads. They themselves probably didn't understand.

"Bonsoir, mon beau Prince," she said between sobs.

"Huh?"

All these years and Sal hadn't bothered to learn English. To be fair, they hadn't bothered to learn Elvish, or whatever language she spoke. There were night classes for these things. Nerds who'd dedicated their lives to language—lingerie-ists, he believed they were called. But it wasn't worth the effort. Why bother? Nothing else made sense, anyway.

"King, my boy." Lady Fatima, the third and final of the three Marys, embraced her son. She was under the impression that people around her—especially her conniving sons—were up to no good. But, despite being a consummate conspiracy theorist, she was a diligent mother. She sniffed him out, rifled through his robe, and searched him for any signs of foul play. "What have you been up to? You look guilty."

"Ma, I look exactly the same I've looked every single night for the last sixty years."

"All the same, you've always been a rabble rouser. Even before we got here."

"Ma," King whined.

Christ, already with the accusations? I just woke up. And before I've even had a cup of coffee. Do I still like coffee? It's been so long...

While his mothers—Lourdes, Sal, and Fatima (each in her own way)—showered him with anxiety-inducing affection, he watched the rest of the shrine come alive. He always enjoyed this part. There was elegance in its congenital predictability.

Up the rocky slope of the shrine, high above the covenant of Marys, the patron of the hunt, Saint Hubertus, shivered off the dust of the day. He wore his signature red homburg, a tuft of white baby's breath fastened to it, and stood tall, one gloved hand rested on the hilt of his sabre. A barbed spear, his weapon of choice when hunting more formidable game, was slung over his shoulder.

Nearby, a small flock of sheep rustled themselves into animation, and the hunt was on.

Rather noisomely, Hubertus crouched low. He shuffled closer, stopping every few seconds—still as a statue—to throw the sheep off his scent so to speak. Satisfied, he continued his approach, pulling his spear around and springing at his prey.

"Not this time, old boy," King muttered. "Surprise, surprise."

The sheep eyed him, *baa*'d in sympathetic annoyance, and went about licking their fluffy fur. Closer to their Lord vertically speaking, they enjoyed the privileges and benefits of life much quicker than King and friends.

"Oh, I'll get you one day, you wascally wamb," Hubertus cursed, preparing for another strike.

The truth was he'd never catch a single sheep. It was a cat-and-mouse game, where the cat always lost. It was ordained. Being stone, believe it or not, made it difficult to sneak up on one's prey. For Hubertus, the hunt would never be the same.

It made King feel miserable about feeling miserable about his own circumstances. The cyclical nature of the perpetually downtrodden: to live, but take no joy in the one and a billion-billion opportunities that was life.

Shouts of condemnation erupted from an alcove behind the shrine, overpowering the superficial conversation between King and the Marys. Its occupant yelled something about forsaking the name, leading the flock astray, and "falling into the caltrop of the Devil, himself. Snared in a lifetime of sin and evil," and yaddy-dotty.

King grimaced. Every night on cue, after Hubertus's inevitable failure, good-ole Maximillian Kolbe came to life. He awoke from a PTSD-induced nightmare, where he'd stood before a firing squad in Auschwitz. He claimed he didn't regret what had happened; he'd forgiven those who'd done inexplicable harm to the people he loved. But that didn't stop him from awaking with a slur of damnation, which inevitably degraded into "commie" bashing. Calm in life but seriously pissed off in death. Could you blame him? He'd seen the darkest side of humanity in Poland and nothing since to believe they'd improved their demeanor in the least.

As his outburst ceased, a man wearing gray robes and sandals ambled around the corner. This evening's victim of verbal assault wasn't fazed one bit because he was *every* evening's victim of verbal assault.

He appeared stonier than the rest (if you catch my drift). He had a dazed expression on his face, a squinty smile, and he bobbed his head as he walked like he was listening to the Whalers in his mind. His name was Christ—the Risen Christ, to be exact—and he was King's middle brother, though they had never been close. Riz spent most of his younger years performing miracles, his later days attending Woodstocks and Burning Mans, and more recently doing nothing of note with the rest of them. Given a second go, he squandered his rise by attending festivals and extinguishing brain cells. King never understood his brother's life choices and would never forgive his indiscretions.

"Sup, dudes?"

"Cut the surfer-bro crap, Riz. There isn't an ocean anywhere near here!"

Lourdes pushed her eldest out of the way and kissed Riz on either cheek. "Old Maxy acting out again? Poor guy. We really outta' get around to see him more often. Sometimes all he needs is a friend."

"Amen," Sal sobbed. "Parfois, tout le monde a besoin d'un ami."

"I won't be peekin' in on him, I'll tell you what."

"Why's that, young man?"

Riz smiled, lips curving, duck-like. "Cuz he's a square. I don't need that kind of vibe in my life. I already endure Kingy here. Can't be havin' it with two Negative Noahs."

Sal wailed. Woe upon the man who didn't reach out to others.

But King agreed with his brother on this one.

"Fumant toujours vos medicaments, Vous etes si paesseux. Pourquoi ne pas vous etre comme vous etes le frere? Vous aves tellement de potential. Corps du Christ, et tout cela!" Sal lamented.

"Mother," King said, "no one knows what you're saying. Especially this guy." He poked Riz in the ribs. "I doubt he knows what anybody's saying half the time."

"S'true. More like three quarters."

"We don't have time to check on Maxy. We have to discuss the murders. The Stillmans were among our most devout worshippers in town. Don't they deserve our sympathy and attention?"

King, startled by his sudden outburst, covered his eyes. *Did I say that?* He opened a rabbit hole he wasn't prepared to follow.

"It's all secrets," Fatima said. "Secrets and lies. They abandoned the church for their own pleasures. They left to plot...to improvise their own means to the Promised Land."

"They were old, man. Moved on like low tide."

"You've never been to the ocean!"

"T'was such a messy desecration of our sanctuary. A shame, too. It was difficult for Willy to clean up, but he doesn't have my secret recipes."

"You see? Secrets and lies!"

"No, mostly just borax and washing sodas. Essential oils if you want a nice, fresh scent."

Spit-shine stones and toothbrush-scrubbed grout came to mind. Lourdes sighed, and a motherly smile stretched across her face. That was when she got The Urge. She'd be busy scrubbing away for at least an hour, giving the rest of them plenty of time to address the important issues.

"Ma needs to chill out, man. Gonna have one of them, whatjeecallits? Annie-risms." Riz pondered for a moment, allowed the syllables to roll off his tongue like a stream of thick saliva. Then, he let it drop. "Yeah, sounds right."

Riz trailed off at the end, watching the waterfall cascade into the babbling brook. If you looked close enough, you could see the drool at the edge of his lips.

King smacked his forehead. Hard.

Why me? Why does it always *fall on me to solve* everything?

He measured the weight of the Globus Cruciger in his hand. The orb gave him dominion over all the kingdoms, but he didn't even want dominion over the shrine. He'd trade it all for a normal statue's life. Or a Porsche.

Alas, it was he who tended the flock of humanity, he who tolerated the constant nagging of his mothers, the uselessness of his stoner brother. It was he, Christ the King, who put it all on his shoulders night after night. Even on the rare occasion when he strayed from the steps of the shrine to consult his youngest brother—the most optimistic, despite being nailed to the cross by bloody hands and feet— he found no solace in the interactions. No amount of positivity could lift the strain.

And now this. Murder of an unholy degree.

Who would desecrate such a holy place? Who would use the shrine to dispose of evidence? Such an act, breaking one of the most important of the Ten Commandments, would condemn a soul to an eternity in the boiling lakes of Hell. Unfathomable. Everyone died in the end, but never like this. *And after a lifetime of such devout service...*

To solve the mystery was a matter of figuring out who-done-it, but they had no resources and little—if any— outside help.

King remembered where he was. For a brief glint of a moment, he realized he wasn't alone. A fleeting glint of a moment was better than nothing.

"Well, mothers and brothers, any ideas on where we should start?"

"Someone is keeping it a secret from us," Fatima said.

"Doivent etre entrangers."

"Secrets and lies! Secrets and lies!"

"Chill, man. Not everyone is out to get ya. Sometimes you just gotta relax and live in the moment."

"Is that a stain? I think I see a stain!"

King raised a finger to interject, but it was already too late.

"Sacre Bleu!"[1]

"Schemes! Conspiracy! Murrrrrda."

"Donner sa langue au chat."[2]

King scratched his head, looked from face to face with his mouth gaped open, and harrumphed. When they got like this, it was best to just let them go. Someone would eventually stop talking, and the rest would follow suit.

Maybe.

Hopefully…

Probably not.

When they didn't, he hissed, holding up a hand for silence. He needed to think, to process the stimulus overload that had been his family's ravings. But they had made two good points.

First, Fatima's:

"Mother." He addressed her directly. "I think you're right. Coincidentally right, but if you throw enough darts, you're bound to hit the bull's-eye. Whoever committed this heinous act wants to keep it a secret. No one goes around murdering people and bragging about it; at least, no one that wants to stay out of prison. It seems to me this was likely a weak, last minute cover for an accident."

---

[1] Referring, of course, to a clandestine cult of mute, 20-somethings who spend their lives following Blue Man Group tours. Not to be confused with the Sacred Blue, a cult of women named Karen who revere all things blue cheese. Both groups, while different in every conceivable fashion, should be avoided at all costs.

[2] We're not entirely sure what Lasalle meant to convey here. There are two lines of reasoning. One, she meant to invoke a common English idiom. Two, she had some funky Chinese food in one of her past lives. Neither makes sense in this context, but people hardly ever make sense when you bring too many of them together in tight spaces without enough snacks.

A smirk crossed Fatima's face. It wasn't often anyone took her seriously. They "Hmm'd" and "I see'd" while nodding their heads and going over their plans for next week, but they never actually listened.

"Also," King continued, turning to the lovely and linguistically-challenged Sal. "I think I heard something in that Klingon nonsense you spew that sounded like stranger. Yes. I do believe our perpetrator has to be a stranger. No one in Mio would ever hurt the Stillmans. They were loved by one and all at St. Mary's, and *everyone* went to St. Mary's. The worst conflict this town has ever seen was a passive-aggressive note passed between neighbors written ten years ago...about a broken fence slat."

"Ah, Slatgate," Riz reminisced. "Mary Sue hated those geraniums..."

They all reminisced with him while Saint Hubertus took a tumble down the side of the shrine and Maxy began spouting another string of obscenities.

Were the killers inherently evil? Or had they acted in mad desperation? Or were the deaths accidental, like he suggested? Had the killers put it in God's hands afterwards, as a penance of sorts?

Either way, what they did with the Stillmans was sickening; there would be a reckoning.

"Anyone hear about any visitors or tourists coming through town?" King asked the crowd.

"Oo, I love meeting new people," The Crucified Christ hollered across the lawn. "You never know what wonderful stories you might hear."

"Even if they end up being killers?"

"No one is all bad. I'm sure they have a good explanation. I'm sure they're sorry for what they've done."

King ignored this. His youngest brother's glass-is-half-full-even-though-I'm-stuck-to-a-damn-cross-with-nails attitude wasn't helping the situation. If King needed a self-esteem boost, which he often did, he knew where to go. Until then, he tuned his brother out.

"My, uh, colleague Rico is in town?" Riz said. And by colleague he meant his pharmaceutical rep. "But he's a chill dude as long as you don't owe him any money or anything. I doubt he'd string up those poor folks for no reason. Think they were smokin—"

"No. I don't, Riz," King said. He threw a finger up. "Everyone freeze."

A single shadowy figure stumbled by across the street. It stopped across from them and stared in their direction. Nobody moved, not even the moon, until the shadow went about its business.

"That was a close one." King shook his head. "Anyway, you all have been so *helpful.* Thank you."

It was more apparent than ever: it was his responsibility to figure this one out. Mother was watching; he had a lot of pressure to do the correct thing. Such a desecration couldn't go unpunished, yet alone unsolved. No amount of Hail Mary's could absolve the perpetrator.

Two more shadowy figures appeared. One was tall, his bald head shimmering in the moonlight. The other was dainty, slipping between the dark places of the night.

King squinted. His vision, despite being well-adjusted to darkness, wasn't as it once was. He couldn't discern any distinct features. Just two people dragging two other people behind them…

"They're back," someone said.

"There's two of them."

"Let's get 'em."

As one, the Christs and the Marys beelined—if beelines were made of several tons of marble and moved slower than a boulder rolling uphill through honey—for the back of the shrine. They grunted and strained and (if they weren't made of stone) perspired at the temples. Riz giggled to himself at the collective effort.

By the time they got around, the sun was peeking from the east, and the perpetrators had gotten away, leaving the bodies in a flower bed of red and yellow petunias. King recognized them: the Carters. Loud, obnoxious, and rotund enough to crush the entire flower bed, but neither deserved that kind of death and discardment.

They were too late. All their efforts to catch the murderers red-handed had been for naught.

"Nothing ever goes well for me," he mumbled. "Okay, people, nothing else we can do tonight. Better get back to our places before it's too sunny."

Resigned, they all turned towards their respective homes for the day. They raced against morning's clock.

Maxy got in a dozen more profanities about commies and breaking the law as Riz past his chamber.

St. Hubertus, resigned for different reasons, straightened his cap and hung his spear over his shoulder once again. Another night without a lamb.

Lourdes wiped a last speck of dust from her chamber wall.

Lasalle dabbed at a single tear.

Fatima took a seat between a hundred burning candles.

King cherished the new day, cursing the night like every other night.

A pink stone elephant stampeded towards the other side of town, unsure if it would make it home by sunrise or not, but not giving two tusks if it did. Tonight had been the best night of its life.

Chapter 13:

In a Room with Death

A honeymoon was supposed to be filled with young love, exotic foods, and new experiences—the kind you remembered for a lifetime. Copious amounts of great sex, for example. Or, for those who had followed God's plan and waited for marriage, working out the kinks and hoping to have copious amounts of great sex in the future.

So far, Stan and Anaya hadn't pursued any such activities. Instead, Anya ruined it all. She'd managed to get motion sickness on their trip north, accidently killed a precious, wrinkled old couple at their motel—after the two had renewed their vows for their sixtieth anniversary—then topped off their trip with the Dale and Rhonda incident.

It was all going to heaven.

None of this was supposed to happen. They were on vacation, dammit. You were supposed to leave your job at the office when you're on vacation, not traipse around wearing it like a nametag.

The Stillmans only tried to help.

Anaya's husband, despite contrary belief, wasn't as strong as he claimed. She didn't love Stan for his brute strength. She loved him for his cunning and guile, the way he manipulated and persuaded people into doing his bidding.

He struggled to help his dizzy, sun-poisoned wife to their room. Truck stop Indian food with the top down all day hadn't been the best idea. He swayed to one side, knocking them both into the wall. His legs wobbled. Sweat beaded at his temples.

Mr. Stillman—bless his arthritic heart—heard the commotion and, upon seeing the struggle, hobbled over to help. She tried to say something, to warn the poor, unsuspecting Good Samaritan, but her words came out as dry heaves. Bracing himself on his walker, he wrapped his other arm around her for support. As soon as his hand touched her bare shoulder his heart popped, and he crumpled like a poorly baked soufflé. Mrs. Stillman, witness to the whole scene despite her glaucoma-glazed eyes, clutched her own broken heart and joined her husband. Not even Death could do them part.

The younger couple didn't know what else to do. The people of Mio were God-fearing people, so why not blame it on God? She *was* a good person to blame in times of doubt and tragedy.

It had been Stan's idea. He just couldn't leave his true nature behind. Before they embarked on their honeymoon, he'd read about a shrine in Northern Michigan, a small town somewhere deep in the woods and far away from larger settlements like Detroit and Ann Arbor; it sounded like the perfect retreat for two anthropomorphic lovebirds.

Mr. and Mrs. Stillman weighed a combined one hundred pounds, a load they handled with some difficulty as they shoved them into their rental. When they got to the shrine, they arranged them at its apex, in the light of the Lord. A sacrifice of lambs to silence the beast.

To Stan, it was as innocent a practical joke as tying someone's shoelaces together.

Despite their feather weight, draping them over the apex was a challenge. Getting them down was easier. All that so-called "detective" had to do was hit the shrine with his car. Funny how these things worked out sometimes.

Mr. Cross was a convenient distraction. A blessing in disguise to anyone else. This outsider fascinated the whole town, and infuriated them with his desecration, leaving the honeymooners free to go about their business. His claim to find out all the answers, though most likely a farce, might prove to be the end of his convenience.

Pun intended, he seemed Hell-bent on finding answers. Anaya assumed he'd snoop around a bit, dig up skeletons that belonged to the town's leaders, and blame some teenager or vagrant. Then he'd move on.

They had no such luck. Chase Cross wasn't like most people; Chase Cross didn't quit.

Stupid? Sure. Weren't they—humans—all? A drunk and a klutz? Absolutely.

But he was relentless.

Then there was the night of dancing and drinks. Anaya had let her hair down to enjoy her honeymoon. She loved meeting new, interesting people—people who weren't terrified of her, not living to avoid her. She liked gossiping about women she didn't even know, the rush of the breeze on her bare skin, and the glimmer of the moon on the surface of their lake. Even Stan seemed to enjoy himself, but he sometimes put on a front for her sake.

Then, she let her guard down. *I can never let my guard down.*

Dale and Rhonda didn't deserve to die. It wasn't their time. Dale's was coming soon enough, but she wasn't one to mess with schedules. Her only crime had been getting too close to someone, and it was a crime she would commit again.

They carted them to the shrine. It worked once, why not try it again? It absorbed people's problems; it was somewhere she might find a shred of mercy. Good lord, those people were heavy. Disposing of them took much longer, and she was sure they were almost caught.

And there *he* was. The moon was hiding behind passing clouds, shy on a ghoulish night, and Chase failed to catch them in the act. To be fair, it hadn't seemed like he was trying very hard, squinting and swaying from across the street like he was, only to give up moments later. Still, they hadn't had time to deal with Dale and Rhonda as elegantly as the Stillmans, partially due to yet another honeymoon disaster.

Her face swelled and her breath grew short. She didn't need to breathe, but perception was important. At first, she assumed it was the adrenaline and the wine. However, she was having an allergic reaction to her dinner. The Harbinger of Night allergic to shellfish? Who would have guessed? What an absolute nightmare.

Stan rushed her to the nearest clinic, which served as the town's urgent care center and veterinary hospital. Once admitted, she insisted her husband hook up her IV and administer her shots. The nurse was furious. She was nearing the final hours of a sixteen-hour shift and didn't like being told how to do her job, yet alone having to watch someone else do it for her. Stan pulled out a blank business card from his wallet. To her it read something like *Stanley T. Edgerton, M.D., P.H.D.* Outranked, undereducated, and short on patience; she backed off and let the good doctor do his thing.

Stabilized, Anaya told her husband to wait at the motel and get some rest. She wanted to be alone. She was used to solitude and needed a break from everything else—especially her new husband.

After Stan left, Chase Cross wheeled in on a wheelchair and the nurse helped him up onto the bed beside her. It bent under the pressure of his immense size, as it had been designed to hold 180 pounds of dog. He was drunk and beat to a pulp. Was this destiny?

A bit wobbly, he grinned and waved to her. As he did, he winced in pain, but the stupid ear to ear smile never left his face. "Howdy, new neighbor. I'm Chase Cross, detec…"

"'Detective,' yes. I know who you are. We need to talk, Mr. Cross."

The nurse asked if either of them needed anything.

Anaya needed a lot of things but shook her head. A mere mortal couldn't provide any of them.

Chase said no thank you and told her how lovely she was and how she was doing a fantastic job. She rushed off to respond to a dog-related incident involving a mess and a plastic bag, happy for any excuse to get away.

Chase shifted his mass on the hospital bed; or rather, he attempted to shift his mass. As he did, he ripped the cord of the IV out from the machine and the heart monitor went crazy. Before Anaya could start her conversation with the "detective," the nurse rushed in to respond to the sound of flat lining. Annoyed he wasn't dying and only a clumsy idiot, she reattached all the right cords and left them in a huff. On her way out, she cranked the morphine, hoping to knock him out for a few hours.

"How exciting." Chase giggled, enjoying the effects of the increased drip. "Now I know how death's edge feels. What a rush, huh?"

A guttural voice rumbled from somewhere deep inside Anaya. She had perfected the voice but hadn't expected to use it. "YOU KNOW NOTHING OF DEATH, OF THE FIRES OF OBLIVION. HOW DARE YOU? YOU'D COWER AT THE EDGE OF MY CHASM."

For once, the smile vanished from his face, replaced by sheer terror. He moved to call the nurse, but at the last second she stayed his hand. Silent tension filled the room, thick enough to cut with a spoon.

Anaya laughed in her normal, coquettish voice. It was soothing, and he forgot the last few seconds.

"Kidding. I'm afraid I'm not the best at making jokes. And these drugs have put me in quite the state. You understand, right?"

"I don't know what you're talking about, my lady. You've been nothing but charming this whole time."

He believed it, too. She was maternal, better than his own mother in a dozen ways. She was the woman he needed in his life. Loving and full of wisdom. Beautiful, of course, but not in an oedipal sense.

"Anyway," she said, "you're a determined young man, Mr. Cross. But trouble seems to follow in your wake. I can respect that, to an extent."

"Thank you?"

"I think it's time you left Mio. The police can handle it from here. I don't know her well, but Sheriff Grace seems like a capable woman."

Chase thought about this for a moment. She was capable. She was *exciting*. Her deputy might even become a decent police officer, with time and lots of training. He could leave and move to something bigger and better. Somewhere they needed him. It was the duty of a proper detective to fight for those who couldn't fight for themselves. With Sheriff Grace, Mio had that covered.

Then, starting to feel manipulated, Chase grew cross. If there was any one thing he liked the least in the world—besides onions—it was being used.

"I won't leave. I've made a promise to these good people that I intend to keep. But hey, do you think the nurse'd mind bringing me something to eat? Maybe a steak. Hell, I'd settle for a Jell-O," he said, remembering his swollen jaw.

Mr. Cross, I'm trying to help you. You could get hurt."

"Want anything when she comes?"

Anaya sat up in bed, facing him. The quick motion made her lightheaded, but she leaned in close and stared deep into his soul.

"Did you hear me, young man? I'm afraid if you don't leave, something horrible will happen to you."

Up to this point, she'd tried handling herself with a cordial demeanor. She had nothing against humans, per se. When there's a job, it's just that: a job. It was never anything personal. She didn't wish unnatural harm on anyone, but she longed to slap Chase Cross across the mouth. His mere existence annoyed her, and she imagined he had that effect on most people.

"'Detective,'" she began again, after taking a deep breath and counting to ten. "It will be best for your health and wellbeing if you forget you were ever here. Trust me."

"Wait a tootin' minute."

"What?"

He held up a finger and stared off into space. His wheels were turning and, even through the rust, she heard them squeak.

Does he recognize me? Did he see me across the street?

He smirked. "You're threatening me, ma'am. Did you have those boys beat me up, too? What did I do to you?"

"I don't know what you're talking about."

"You're telling me you had nothing to do with this?" He showcased his swollen face and the bruises tiger-striped down his side.

He was getting ready to undo his pants to show her the welt on his hip when she said, "Absolutely not, 'Detective.' I'm on my honeymoon. Why would I get a bunch of kids to beat up someone I hardly know? Just worried about your safety, is all."

"Oh, *now* you're worried? Where were you when your young punks were kickin' me in the beans?"

She clenched her fists, clinging to what little composure she had left. The earth rumbled, a meteor streaking across the sky in a far-off galaxy collided with the surface of a small planet, ending the reign of a vast, arborous civilization over a colony of talking poodle-like creatures. A large one-eyed raven landed on the windowsill of the hospital room. It cried out into the early dawn, staring at Chase with its one crimson eye. She hadn't meant to call it, but she was losing herself.

She was spontaneously omening.

Chase didn't notice any of this. Instead, he said, "Well, I've got a duty to help this town. I gave them my word I'd solve the case and solve the case I will. No matter who tries to stop me. You're concern is appreciated, but unnecessary."

"Your," she corrected. Even Death hated bad grammar.

"Whatever. Now, if you'll excuse me, I'm going to have a lie down."

The voice returned, guttural and shaking the machinery. "YOU WILL LEAVE. I DON'T NORMALLY ACCEPT WALK-INS, BUT I MAY HAVE TO PENCIL YOU IN FOR AN APPOINTMENT. I'M THE ONLY CERTAINTY IN LIFE, AND YOU WILL OBEY."

Eyes wide, Chase clicked the button to call the nurse.

She looked up from behind her station, down at her watch; she had twenty minutes before her shift ended, then she could go home. "I need a new job," she mumbled. "Or to move far, far away. To another planet, preferably." Then, without looking back at Chase, she continued to ignore him.

Chapter 14:

Jesus Laments

An old man—though you'd never be able to tell how old he really was given his sandy, blond hair and sun-kissed skin—approached a bed of flowers behind the shrine. Their pistils craned in his wake. The morning glories, fast asleep in the darkness of night, awoke and embraced his presence. They felt no anger at this sudden arousal from their slumber. If flowers *could* feel, they'd feel humbled, honored, and awash in the fulfilment of their greater purpose.

The man didn't walk, rather he floated inches above the moist lawn like a gentle wisp of wind, breathing life into every blade of grass, every worm, and every individual molecule. Mother Nature pulsed sapphire, fuchsia, and gold all around him. His aura was life and everything life entailed.

The still-warm bodies of Dale and Rhonda matted a patch of flowers. Such blatant waste sickened him. Throughout the history of humanity, he'd witnessed violence and deceit among levels of grand achievement and opportunity. People couldn't have one without the other. A savage bunch, humans. It was something he never understood. They inherited the Kingdom of God and, instead of unlocking their full potentiality—traversing the mysteries of time and space while working together to solve the world's problems—they killed each other, plundered their neighbors, and raped the weak and weary. Over what? Politics? Food? Ego? Religion? The latter of which, if you must know, was counter to Mother's intentions.

God never meant it to turn out this way. Sodom learned, but it was a lesson forgotten to time.

But this atrocity was not the work of humanity.

The stink of Death lingered. Her presence was stifling, and not in the metaphorical sense—the one written about by poets, cheated by no one, and embraced as an idol by the kid down the street with the nose piercing and neck tattoo. No, this was a physical presence. Death loomed nearby, hiding in the bushes or just beyond the horizon.

Oh Death, where is your sting? Why have you come?

At least he had the start of an answer. He understood why he'd had such a difficult time figuring this one out and why God had complained about everything feeling so clouded.

Someone else was involved in the killings, too. Not directly, but as an accomplice. He thought he knew who, too. The most unholy of matrimonies had taken place on Earth—eighteen-year-old couples, fresh out of high school, running off to elope. A man in his fifties driving his twenty-year-old bride to their wedding in his Ferrari. Mormons with ten wives—but none compared to the wedding that had taken place outside the realm of humanity.

Humans concocted farfetched theories about how the world ends. Nuclear destruction, pathological disease, or the sun burning out. In one case, the tidings were inscribed on the shell of an egg by an avian prophetess. "Christ will hatch," she wrote. While entertaining, these stories came nowhere close to the truth.

Even the righteous weren't safe. Not after this union.

Put on the full armor of God, so that you can stand firm against the schemes of the Devil.

Do not lead us into temptation but deliver us from evil.

Evil had already arrived, no delivery necessary.

The words of his Mother, written by his disciples, repeated in his mind though he doubted their power for the first time. No amount of armor—mithril, adamantium, Kevlar, or otherwise—could save humanity now.

Both the Adversary and Death lived, walked, and breathed. They'd conjugate, bringing The Void upon this world and beyond. It was a matter of time before the Four Horseman showed, a party Jesus didn't want to attend.

Willy, the Groundskeeper, unlocked the shed behind the shrine. Despite the early hour, he hummed a cheerful tune. The old man knelt, blessed the bodies lying in the flowers, and vanished. An aura of gold shimmered in his sudden absence and dissipated into the light of the rising sun.

His Mother, watching the whole time, finished a bottle of cheap whiskey. "Now, my son, you understand why I've been so damn grumpy."

***

Nearby, Bob watched, seeing everything for the first time:

The statues, all three Jesuses and Marys, Saint "Elmer Fudd" Hubertus, and even the little lamb running for its life.

The couple dragging the dead bodies, which his mind couldn't fathom. He'd been close to Death once, and he evaded the Devil his whole life. They were closely acquainted now, tethered to the streams of reality.

Chase Cross, drunk, getting beat to a pulp by a bunch of teenagers.

Quiet and hunched in the shadows, Bob witnessed more in one night than he had his entire life.

The old, robed man bore a sort of family resemblance. Maybe an uncle. Either way, through the man's aura of warmth, Bob saw the light.

Jesus. He was freaking Jesus. Was he here? On Earth? It couldn't be a coincidence.

It was crystal clear, smacking him upside his big head. *God needs my help; humanity needs my help. I am Bob, and my life begins here, in Mio.*

A voice sneaked into his mind. It said, *Light shall shine out of darkness, my son. See you soon, Bob.*

"But I can't do the things you ask."

You can, Bob, for you are my son, created in my image, and will carry on my vision for all of humanity.

Oh, bugger, thought Bob. "That's a lot of pressure."

Chapter 15:

Something from Nothing

The sun rose and a nothing kind of day happened. Funny how it worked out this way, more often than not. At least, for the individual. Days had certain obligations, certain pressures. People relied on days to tick off their calendars, to track their weeks, and to waste their years. Days were the building blocks of how they planned their lives. Day after day, week after week, year after year, until each lived their last. Then, the days kept on keepin' on.

This wasn't a particularly interesting day in Mio, Michigan. It deserved a participation medal for trying, but beyond that—meh.

Elsewhere, a baby was born in the backseat of a pearlescent Camaro with others conceived in even less convenient locations.

Far away, in the highest chamber of an ivory tower, a physicist awoke from a troubled dream to realize she'd discovered the secrets to unlocking faster-than-light travel. Before she could record her equations for posterity, a grad student knocked on her office door intent on coercing her for the higher grade he so justly deserved. He'd never understand how far his entitlement set back scientific progress for, like a fading dream, the numbers faded from her mind forever.

It was just *that* kind of day.

Oddly, no one died. This was happening more frequently. Even the biggest dimwits[1] were noticing.

Mostly, Mio used this day to recover. Everyone needed to take an occasional mental health day. Despite the

---

[1] If you ask Darwin, these are the ones that should be paying the most attention to Death anyway.

deep wounds of losing two of its most beloved couples in the same number of nights, time would heal all. Or wash it away entirely.

***

Chase Cross took this opportunity to rest. He struggled to compartmentalize the fact a bunch of kids kicked his ass, but he took solace in the pampered life of a patient in Mio. It was in the pudding, really. He'd never had all-you-can-eat pudding. The rump of his dark-skinned nurse helped, too, and every shift change brought the prospect of uncharted waters for him to dive into, harass, and ogle. It was all the salvation he could handle.

Jade was her name, the one with the rump. She'd come in to check on him at the beginning of her shift. Her silver dollar, emerald eyes caught his, and his pants tightened. When she leaned over to check his IV, and the V-neck of her scrubs came open, he'd lost it. He never had *it* to begin with, but it was gone, nonetheless.

Her high school sweetheart recently cheated on her, so she moved back in with her parents, taking on extra shifts to pay for 8 years of student debt. Her self-esteem was at an all-time low. Despite the fat man's creepiness, his catcalling and pathetic attempts at flirting made Jade feel sexy for the first time in months. She strutted out of his room with a hop in her step and moths in her stomach. Not butterflies, because butterflies assumed euphoria and bliss. This fluttering came from self-loathing.

It was just *that* kind of day.

***

Not far away, Stan and Anaya enjoyed a leisurely float down the Au Sable River. The gentle rocking of the waters calmed her stomach. Anaya recovered from the sickness of the day before, but she'd never recover from what happened during these long nights in Mio. Four billion years and Death still wasn't used to the nitty-gritty of her job. Nothing in her

149

experience prepared her for accidents at the workplace. Though they happened to everyone, when they happened to her, worlds burned.

The river was theirs and theirs alone. Earlier in the week, a pipe broke after decades of corrosion. The lead designing engineer was a week out from retirement. The project came across his desk—one last hoorah, so to speak—and he put as little effort as possible into constructing a sewage line for the campgrounds upriver. It consisted of a massive, Olympic pool-sized tank and one pipeline to taper off the sewage levels in the tank. He didn't even bother to inspect it.

The fish's misfortune gave Stan and Anaya the peace and solitude they sought. Neither could smell, anyway.

It was just *that* kind of day.

***

Bob continued to wander about, wondering who he was. *Soon, my Son, Soon*, he heard repeatedly but failed to make sense of what the words meant.

As he wandered, he noticed the true wonders of Mio, Michigan. He enjoyed the various quilt blocks hidden in wooded neighborhoods, plastered above the doors of small-town general stores, and displayed on the broadside of barns with paint peeling in every direction. His favorite block depicted a moose, stopped at the bank of a stream for a morning drink. The sun peered over the tops of evergreens, much like the sun did today. Despite not knowing who he was, he knew someone with a true gift had made the quilt and appreciated every individual stitch.

***

Hunched over her desk, under the light of a single bulb, Sheriff Grace poured over a stack of paperwork related to the deaths of the Stillmans and of Dale and Rhonda. She also poured another couple fingers of whiskey and drank without tasting. She knew they were related. The deaths, that is. Why else would four bodies, on two separate nights, of two couples both old and young, show up at the shrine? No amount of whiskey in the world could convince her it was a coincidence. It also couldn't help her make any sense of the facts.

Deputy Lawson sat behind her, nodding off. He'd ran her copies, poured her coffee, and made phone calls for her all night. Eventually, she'd forgotten he was there.

"What the hell is happening in my town?" she asked the sunrise, continuing to ignore Deputy Lawson.

He was okay with being ignored. It meant he wasn't getting yelled at.

She needed to find answers, quick. Mio was the sort of place where people enjoyed their peace and privacy. It was the place where old men went fly fishing every day of the week, young couples spent their time gazing out across the big sky at a trillion glinting stars, and teenagers revved their four wheelers as they wound through the forest. Consequently, it was also the kind of place where people unraveled when their privacy was disturbed. Newcomers (often tourists) struggled with too much excitement— especially the murdery kind—and the Unknown riled the people. Sheriff Grace couldn't afford her town going all riley on her. Her men were far from equipped to deal with a full-scale rabble without a lot of messy, unnecessary bloodshed.

She slammed her fists on her desk. "Where are the damn others? Deputy?"

"Yes, ma'am?" Deputy Lawson said, quick to her side like a puppy waiting for a biscuit.

She ignored the red streak across his forehead from where he'd fallen asleep on his desk. "Where's the mayor?"

"Not sure, ma'am. Seems to be M.I.A."

"And what about Dietrich? I swear that sumbitch has been beggin' me to give him extra responsibility around here. It's not like shovin' his sausage hands into these folks' pockets and takin' their hard-earned pennies ain't causin' enough harm."

"Yes, ma'am. Him, too."

Peachy. Just peachy. Sheriff Grace always found herself at the top of the totem pole. People begged her to solve their problems for them, as if they didn't have minds of their own. To be fair, most didn't. The sheep needed someone to look to for guidance. Christ—that's why they introduced Christ to begin with.

Her mind drifted. To her chagrin, it drifted all the way off the end of the world, landing in a bottomless chasm of misery. The chasm was filled with prismatic projections of Chase Cross's face—that stupid, infectious smile of his.

"He could pull this off." She bit her lip and tugged at the collar of her shirt.

"Excuse me?"

"Er, uh," she stammered. "Nothing, Deputy. Don't be stupid. We don't have time for stupid."

Was she having feelings? She had no time for those, especially for someone like the "detective." But maybe he wasn't so bad. Maybe...

It was just *that* kind of day.

Chapter 16:

Premium Rabble

On the outskirts of Mio, deep underground in the basement of an abandoned, hot pink grocery store, rabble kicked into full swing. A group of angry men—and possibly a woman (no one was sure)—did what groups of angry men did best. They argued, talking over each other, all saying the same thing in different ways while refusing to hear a word of it from the others.

They were split into two groups, each huddled and facing towards the center of the expansive, musty room. Group was a loose term. It was every man for himself, but someone had drawn lines in chalk. Whoever brought the chalk had angry children at home who would just have to deal with it for now.

Between the parted groups, idle time passed.

One man stood in the middle, arms folded, chewing on a toothpick. A week's stubble and a lifetime of disappointment covered his face. He was a man of fewer words and more action than the rest of the town combined. The problem was he enacted them underground, beneath the all-seeing eye of the powers that be. Usually they were harmless. Manipulative, profitable, deviant and self-serving, but harmless.

When he could no longer stomach the droning on of the others, he unfolded his arm, flicked his toothpick onto the concrete floor, and stood on a crate.

"Shut up. Everyone." The reverberation of his voice froze the crowd in place, most with their mouths still hanging open. "Good. I appreciate your enthusiasm. Really, I do. But enough's enough. I assume you all know why we're here."

There were nods and fist bumps. Agreement murmured from wall to wall. Despite their differences, both sides knew something had to be done, and none of them could do anything alone.

"The mayor and the sheriff have let our town go to hell. I, for one, can't sit idle and watch it burn. Mio is a good place with decent folk. Folk who go to church on Sundays, clear their sidewalks when it snows, and pay their taxes when it's convenient. Not folk who deserve to live their days in fear."

He hopped down from the crate and walked to crowd, stopping from time to time to shake hands or talk one-on-one with someone. He knew how to include people, even if he wanted nothing to do with them.

"Do you all want to go through your days thinkin' you're next?"

"No!"

"Do you want to put your lives in the trust of a woman?"

"No!"

"Yeah," Shirley said, twirling her mustache. "I'm okay with it."

He ignored them. "Wouldn't y'all like to stand up and take our town back?"

"Yes!"

"Are we gonna let these outsiders dictate to us how to solve our problems?"

"No!"

"Are we gonna start being our own men again?"

"Yes!"

"Are we going to dress up like Madonna and sing show tunes?"

"Yes," Jake Clive, well-digger, said.

The rest of the rabble answered with crickets. Someone in the back sniggered.

"Got ya, Jake," Tony Dietrich said, booping the young man's nose. "Anybody got any ideas on how we make this town great again? Kurt, how 'bout you? What you got for me?"

A younger man, dressed in a baggy, navy blue suit, beamed. He was the only non-native Mionite in attendance. No one listened to him, but he never said much anyway. Unless it was about Med Supps or Universal Life policies. Kurt could talk the birds silent about those. Insurance was in his blood.

"Well, uh," he began. "We need to act, that's for sure. I protect families from untimely deaths—at an affordable rate, of course—but I can't protect people from their *own* untimely deaths. My product serves those left to mourn, not those who've moved on to the afterlife. I provide insurance, but I can't provide assurance. Not like you can, sir."

Tony Dietrich rubbed his stubble. He relished the affirmation but moved on without acknowledging it. He appreciated a good brown-noser but would never admit it out loud. You couldn't go around giving them too much credit; it went to their heads. There was finite space for ego in the world, and there was already too much hot air in the room.

Someone cleared their throat. It was one of *them*. Usually, *they* were the opposition. Real estate agents got under Tony's skin and drove him into fits of rage. The poor folks of Michigan had limited resources. To him, it seemed a waste for them to spend all their hard-earned money on houses. What good did a house ever do for anyone?

The throat clearer was Marcus Anderson, owner of Big Bear Realty, and big bear was the understatement of the century.

"We are keeping people safe, sir. You know better than anyone. I think I speak for everyone when I say having solid roofs over their heads is the best thing for the people. We need to keep doing what we're doing, and I think Mio will be fine. Nothing a favorable, low-interest, explodin' arms mortgage[1] can't solve."

"You haven't written a quality mortgage for anyone in this town for ten years!" Shirley pointed out. Her Adam's apple vibrated as she enunciated *ten years*.

"And *your* premiums are through the roof. My daughter came to your office the other day, healthy as a whistle, and you underwrote her as 'high-risk.' The audacity of—"

"She smokes a pack a day, and I see her cutting in and out of traffic on her motorcycle like she's late for brunch with Death. You're lucky I wrote her up at all. What about the Joneses? Sweet couple, expecting a little one any day now. You refused them a loan for what? On the grounds of bad credit? What in the hell is credit, anyway? This isn't some hoity-toity college town where you can just not take advantage of people."

"Hey, we all gotta make our money. You know that same as anyone else, Franny, but I couldn't in good conscious—"

"Don't call me that!"

"I saw you in that chatroom, Frank. Don't think you can hide your dirty little secrets from us."

"How dare you!"

The men in the room returned to doing what they did best: yelling at the top of their lungs. Soon, there was going to be a full-blown riot, a battle royale.

Tony Dietrich, returning to his usual silence, made his way out of the crowd and to his crate in the center of the

---

[1] Mio has always had a problem with bootleg fireworks. In certain circles, losing a limb is a rite of passage. In others, it's just good, plain fun.

room. He'd let them duke it out for a while. If they talked long enough, someone was bound to offer something resembling useful he could claim as his own. Both groups offered the best solutions to the problems of modern, everyday living, but neither had a damn clue how to help themselves.

The insurance people thought a new Whole Life policy—discounted for a limited time only—for every man, woman, and child was the answer. What better way to lighten the stress of death than by protecting family finances? Funeral expenses were on the rise. It cost more and more to put you in the dirt. The only reasonable course of action in such uncertain times was preparation. If they couldn't put a stop to the murders, they might as well ease the financial burdens of any future occurrences.

The real estate people disagreed. Shelter. It was all about shelter. A firm roof over your head—offered by an agency loyal to the area, with affordable interest rates—provided the best defense against the unknown. A locked door promised people safety. Two locked doors were better than one. So, they urged the necessity of getting everyone a second home. The third best safety measure was safety in numbers. More people, behind more locked doors, each provided by local agents. The trifecta of death-defying real estate investment. Buy, buy, buy!

Around the time the argument devolved from yelling into beating their chests and throwing poop at each other, Tony Dietrich spoke again. His voice carried through the cavernous basement. Everyone shut up to listen.

"I appreciate your ideas, people. All of them have provided me with, uh, insight in this matter. However, I have a much better idea, involving all of you. It might also involve some unsavory things. I need to know if you all will follow me. Do I have your full support to do what needs to be done? Do you trust me?"

Without hesitation, the room said, "Aye." And, the ayes had it.

The wheels were in motion, and Tony Dietrich had his army.

Chapter 17:

Jesus, Meet Jesus

King shook off his daytime stiffness. Stiffness became a seventh sense for a statue, but that didn't mean he couldn't dream of fluidity.

Speaking of dreams, he'd had one while the humans were out. That might have seemed unnatural because, the fact of the matter was, statues didn't dream. Subconscious thoughts weren't built out of chicken wire and stone. They couldn't be plastered together, bit by bit; they were amorphous, built out of desire and fear.

He peered into the depths of his Globus Cruciger, seeking an explanation. It never revealed much to him, and he didn't have high expectations this time so he wasn't disappointed. All he saw was the swirling of clouds over a deep, blue ocean and the ghostly reflection of his own hollow eyes.

The colors before him contrasted the colors of his dream. He had dreamed in red and black, fire and death. Of flames that licked the sky, covering the surface of the earth, incinerating everything in their path. A slow burn, starting from the very grounds where he stood—the true heart of Mio, Michigan—and spreading like wildfire. It engulfed trees, creatures, houses, and skyscrapers—as if each were a match to a book no one would ever read again. When everything was scorched and the oceans were evaporated to dust, the fire moved away from the atmosphere, eating the stars and turning the whole universe to ash.

When all matter, on all planets, across all space was incinerated, the flames raged on. First the heavens, then time itself burned, leaving nothing else for the flames to consume.

He started it, standing beside a small fire pit in the yard near the shrine, robes blowing behind him in a ceaseless wind. There were others around him. He never saw their gray faces but knew the essence of their souls. It was a cold night. As he blew on the embers to stoke the flames, the shadows of those around him disappeared one by one. The pit could no longer contain the flames. With a flash of light, he too was gone, leaving no one to douse the inferno.

The masonry of the shrine melted away, as did the faces of his brothers and his mothers. Even the rain couldn't save him. History flashed before his eyes. He stood high above the Temple of Jerusalem on a storm cloud. Then he was at the Acropolis, peering down from a nearby hillside. As soon as he arrived, fire dispersed across the land to leave Greece in ashes. Bits of singed papyrus floated in a gentle breeze, spilling out of the fiery mouth of the Library of Alexandria.

Fast forward to the marvelous cities of modern days. A woman on a bench off of Pudding Street, enjoying a hot cup of tea and a scone from a nearby bakery. It was not where she usually stopped, but no one would bother her here. London was a loud and nasty place, and she feared the worst—brigands, thieves, and rapists, oh my. She never expected to be taken in a great conflagration, however.

Stockholm. Copenhagen. Moscow. New York. Detroit. In his dream, King lived them all as if they were one massive burn, crossing all boundaries. Their smoke rose in the sky, twisting into the horrible visage of Death, whose laughter started earthquakes and erupted volcanoes. It was a cackle that spilt Earth wide, spilling its layers into the black void of nothingness.

He never personally visited these places, but he recognized each of them as if he'd been born there. They represented human ingenuity and perseverance at its finest. People built great civilizations only to have them torn down in their prime. Instead of giving up and moving on, they built again, starting each time from scratch. They built them stronger until their walls were impenetrable and their inner workings so complex that their leaders no longer understood how they worked.

The cycle never ended. People died. Buildings burned. Families mourned. The next day, still covered in tears and soot, they grabbed hard hats and shovels. It would be disrespectful to the dead to quit. It might have been easier to curl into a ball in the corner, but it took real courage to start over again. King respected this trait of humanity more than any other.

But, in his dream, it all ended. There was no one left to scrape together the pieces. Rainforests, deserts, plains, and even mountains were wiped off the face of Earth. Forgotten. All that remained was an insidious laughter riding in on a pale horse to claim the realm of the living and the heavens alike.

She had a face: the face of oblivion.

King woke from this dream in a sour mood. Not known for his sunny disposition in good days, this boded poorly for the others.

"Good morning, son," Lourdes said as he scooted his way towards them. "You look awful. Chin up. Straighten your robes. Did you wash your hands yet?"

"Urgh."

"Le Seigneur vient," Sal explained. "Prepare toi."

"Urgh?"

"She says the Lord is coming. He's got a lot of explaining to do, doesn't he? Something's not right here, and I'm sick of all these secrets. I will not have our home desecrated further," Fatima said.

"Urgh," King said.

Nothing about the day before prepared him to deal with his mothers. He loved them, sure, but couldn't deal with their little "quirks." Not tonight. One was already off to clean cobwebs, while the other, *still* refusing to learn

161

English, blabbered on in French. They had apps for that sort of thing! And Fatima, the worst of them all, looked over her shoulder at every crunch of leaf or gust of wind. What could possibly happen? They were trapped, useless.

He wished he was far away. The farthest he'd ever gotten was around the church. It took all night and exhausted his limited energy. When the sun rose, he froze in place a few inches from the sidewalk. Mio people were not capable of comprehending moving statuary, but somehow, he arose the next night in his normal spot, dusted and polished.

Since he couldn't run and hide, King did the next best thing: he retreated into the shallow recesses of his own mind, wondering if he should tell the group about the dream he had the day before. Would they understand what a dream was? Would they care? Could he do justice with a description? The primal parts of his soul understood the significance of such an event. His learned nature, however, reminded him how little he cared. They wouldn't understand either.

Once again, this burden was his alone. He was born into the responsibility of being king. If you bothered to ask, he'd tell you it's not all it's cracked up to be. People relied on him for both wisdom and solace. Around every corner laid someone waiting to dump their problems on him. If he couldn't solve them, they'd run him through a gauntlet of mental-martyrdom and outward shame. Sure, they'd bend the knee when the situation called for it; but, when there were tough decisions to make and he made the wrong ones, they'd drive a knife into his back.

Instead of humoring their incessant needs, King turned his back and hung his head low. As he slid away from the group he said, "Please, not today. You're on your own."

Dumbfounded, the group watched him go without trying to stop him. Best to leave him alone when he got like this. He'd come around; King always came around.

The night droned on, though King wished it wouldn't. That's the funny thing about the dance between the moon and the sun. No matter what people wanted—no matter how dark times seemed—one rose and the other set. No matter what, this little light of thine would shine.

He developed a migraine (if a statue could have headaches). He pawed at his stony temples, paced back and forth in the depths of his Mother's candle-lit temple. The flickering flames of a thousand prayers gave the impression that the features of his face were rocking under the gentle lull of crimson waves—an apt description, for he felt lost at sea with no boat, waiting to drown or be eaten by sharks.

He'd never been down here before. Sal's sanctuary was constructed on the backside of the shrine, in between two meticulously kempt flower beds. It hadn't been worth the effort before. Scooting was serious work only to return before sunrise. Not to mention the cracked pavement and shredded lawn. Willy wouldn't be happy in the morning when he discovered where King had dragged through his flowers.

King didn't care. If only for a few minutes, he needed to escape the others. Was that too much to ask?

His dream was something greater than them, greater than himself. Nothing else mattered anymore.

End Times were coming. They would be hot, and they would be dark. The only question left was when. How much time did he have left?

He sat on a bench, facing the altar. The clamor of his joints cracking and popping echoed throughout the chamber shook the entire shrine. It wasn't as loud as the wooden bench snapping straight in half as he relaxed onto it and slammed onto the polished floor. A small earthquake rocked the entirety of Northern Michigan. King laid there, unable to find strength to stand.

"*My child*," came a voice through suppressed laughter. "*I have come.*"

Then, the weirdest thing happened. King stood, as fluid as any human gymnast, and found himself running out of the alcove towards the front of the shrine. He ran out of fear. He ran out of joy. He ran because, for the first time, he could run. The wind blowing on his face and through his hair breathed new life into him. It was a sensation he'd never felt before. If he knew the words to describe it, he'd describe it as showering in microscopic diamonds or floating through the void of space on ecstasy, tiny pins and needles of pleasure prodding his every pore.

The grounds of the shrine, things he'd watched in slow motion his entire life, whizzed by him. Streaks of blended color appeared and disappeared behind him until he got to the steps and tripped. As he fell forward, he spread out his arms to fly. Instead, he crashed into the side of the shrine and shrieked with laughter. He couldn't fathom feeling anything but entirely and utterly exultant.

Sure, he'd experienced loosening stiffness before. The body broke free of the clutches of inactivity after a while, color returned to the face, and blood to the veins. But this was something different. This was *humanity*.

Riz helped King to his feet. "I want whatever you're smoking, brother."

King hugged his brother for the first time, and all three mothers for the thousandth. They were taken aback, staring at him and wondering who this new King was. It was amazing how big a difference ten minutes of meditation could make.

"He's here," King said. "Our Lord has come. After all these years, all this misery, he's here."

164

"Mon cher enfant, etes-vaus fou? Avez-vous besein de fixer?"[1]

"You better not be lying, son. You know how much I hate liars…"

An ecstatic squeal, like a teenage girl in a shopping mall, pierced the night. It was Cruc, shimmying on his cross. He danced as well as someone nailed down could dance, throwing finger guns at an approaching figure across the lawn. If he danced much harder, the cross might wiggle out of the ground; that'd give Cruc something to be giddy about.

It was less of a figure approaching and more of a sphere of intense light breaking the darkness around it. As it floated closer, the grass grew taller and greener. Flowers, once closed for the evening, opened their buds towards the sphere. The shrine's creatures pranced in and out of the light, chasing each other, and stopping to lick the man's sandaled feet. Night's cold grew suddenly warmer than summer's noon.

The trinity of Marys and the triumvirate of Jesuses watched the man with restless elation, knowing full well who he was but unable to comprehend the magnitude of his sudden appearance. The light that enveloped him was the light of the sun itself—the light of a thousand suns. Everyone shielded their eyes, but no one dared look away.

King felt a foreign wetness on his cheek, which he recognized as tears. Though his mother, Lasalle, wailed and moaned, she'd never shed a single real tear.

When the orb bearing Jesus—the true Jesus— reached the steps of the shrine, King half-expected to evaporate and return to dust. *We all came from dust and return to dust*, but no one exploded or anything. Not this time.

---

[1] Here, Lasalle is reaching out to see if…ah, you know what? Screw it. She's asking for a croissant with a side of jelly and a Fuzzy Navel.

Instead, the orb brought flesh and blood to their faces. Rosy cheeks, wet, veiny eyes. Flowing blond and brown hair falling over their shoulders.

Lourdes rubbed her fingers through Riz's hair, speechless. Dandruff flaked off in every direction, but it didn't bother her in the least. She grasped her son's face.

He removed her hand. "Ma, you're embarrassing me."

By that time, they were all kneeling. No one remembered doing so but they each took turns kissing the ground at Jesus's feet.

"Rise, my children. No need for that. You are all a part of me, and me of you. Please, stand so I can look upon your faces."

They rose as one. Lasalle. Lourdes. Fatima. Riz with his glassy eyes. King, staff and Globus Cruciger in hand. Even Cruc was standing there, nail holes healed, beaming.

"Now, tell me about these desecrations. What evil hath infected my holy place?"

As he said this, his orb flickered and went out. They were once again shrouded in darkness. Blood no longer flowed in their veins as it was replaced by chicken wire and stone. Returned to their normal states, the bickering returned with a vengeance.

Fatima started them off, saying the same things she always said while jiggling her many bracelets in everyone's faces. "All these damnable lies. Pardon my English, my Lord and Savior. This is a good and clean town. The people are pure. Pious. But powerful hands steer good people astray. Whose hand is guiding them?"

"It's that Saunders kid. Fretful dirty boy. I've never seen him with clean hands or laundered Sunday dress. But, then again, he probably never tends to his own room," Lourdes added, matter-of-factly. Her eye twitched the more she thought about piles of trash and dirty clothes. It spiraled out of control from there. She could no longer resist scurrying off to clean a smudge on the shrine.

"He was always an honest boy, though. There's something about a dirty child who knows how dirty he is. That boy's convictions are stronger than the Devil himself."

Silence for a moment. King never met this kid, but the innocence of a child was a difficult thing to corrupt absolutely. They were talking about a murderer, not a vandal or truant. Kids didn't turn violent overnight. It took years of abuse and neglect, a life filled with violence. Or a one-in-a-million chromosomal dysfunction. This decidedly did not describe the Saunders boy.

"Nous avons vu deux personnes, l'autre soir."

"No one cares, woman," Fatima said, sticking up her nose.

"Peace, Mothers. No need for such hateful language," Riz chimed in, looking up from whatever it was he'd been doing. Whatever it was, his marble eyes looked even glossier than before, and a faint cloud of vapors escaped into the atmosphere.

"I like your thinking, brother," Cruc said, excited to be a part of the inner circle for once. His smile cut the top part of his head off, making him look like a cartoon character from the Funny Pages.

"You leave my thinking out of it. She's got feelings, you know."

"Well, tell her I say, 'Pardon me, miss.' No offense meant." Cruc winked at his brother. They both giggled, but their childishness was cut off by Lourdes' return.

"There we go, all clean."

"Good God, woman," Fatima said. "His name not in vain." *With this again? Her name.* Her *name.* "You ever just relax for once?"

Lourdes hung her head. She had a problem but couldn't help it. Something deep inside of her rang a bell, tugged at a leash. She had to obey. Besides, if she didn't tidy from time to time, the shrine would be unlivable. It wasn't her fault they all took her for granted.

"Pensev-vous qu'il etait quelqu'un qu'ils connaissaient?"[2] Lasalle asked after several uncomfortable moments.

"I'm thinking, no."

"That can't be what happened. Can it?"

"Anyone see the new hedge row? Willy's outdone himself this year. Impeccable work. Always reliable, that Willy."

"Quoi?"

King's headache thrummed back into action. He hadn't yet spoken a word and the rest of the group was getting nowhere fast. This happened with them. There was nothing left to talk about after spending so many years with the same people. So, they repeated themselves. Constantly. Over and over and over again.

"They're right about one thing," he said. "We saw them, Father. I knew they'd show themselves. I just never expected..."

"Please, I'm not your Father," the real Jesus said. "If anything, I'm merely your, uh, cousin? Brother-in-law? Er...half-brother? Not sure. Mom never explained that part."

"Brothers in arms?" Cruc offered.

"Brothers in *peace*?" Riz amended. "We have arms, but I will not go to war with you, bro. Or any bro, for that matter."

"We're not damn soldiers, and Woodstock isn't for a few months still."

"Brothers with arms? That could be okay."

---

[2] This one might also be about a croissant.

"Fellow carpenters?" The real Jesus asked.

"But we're made of stone, my man."

"Yeah. And you're just stoned. What of it, *my man?*" Cruc drew out the last word, like it was riding a gnarly wave off the coast of California. "What about me and King, here?"

"King and I," Lourdes corrected, licking her finger and rubbing a streak of dirt off her son's forehead.

"Enough!" Jesus's divine cool was back and hotter than Hell.

Reality itself pulsed and shifted around the ripples of his anger. Somewhere, not too far away, a kid taking a bath screamed as his wooden boat cracked down the center and took a dive to the bottom of the tub. The boat, with its wide hull and a dozen plastic dinosaurs shoved into it, was the only toy he had left. No one heard him cry. If they had, they'd remind him God worked in mysterious ways. If the arc must sink, let it sink. There was no way to understand her master plan.

Everyone stood, shaking in a metaphysical sense, and no one dared say anything else. They had forgotten themselves and forgotten who was among them. The pang of embarrassment stung them all, but none more than King. He'd awoken on the wrong side of the lawn and life had rolled downhill from there, gathering clumps of grass and pieces of discarded garbage on the way in an Ugly Katamari.

"Now, Mothers. Er, Cousins? Not sure where we landed on that…" Jesus looked for confirmation. No one offered any. "First disciples of this holiest of holy places— yes, that sounds good. A mouthful, but accurate. Anyway, you've failed me. In turn, I have failed Mother. This shrine, a sacrament to everything we stand for, has been turned into a mockery of our beliefs. It has become the Devil's playground, and no one's bothered to disinfect it afterward."

Lourdes perked, reaching for her hanky. Jesus waved her off, nodding his appreciation of her enthusiasm before continuing.

"Since it's obvious you have no idea what's going on, I will fill you in. Armed with the truth, you will be offered a chance at redemption."

***

The Devil and Death first met at the 3000-somethingth Annual Heaven and Hell Convention, which took place early in the year somewhere outside of Atlanta, Georgia. The planning committee decided on a Gangsters and Flappers theme.

It was the type of gathering where people set all their differences aside, if only for a couple nights. Angels and demons sat together, picking each other's brains, swapping war stories, and debating the philosophies of life...er, eternal life.

Why do humans walk the earth, while demons and angels are exiled to the farthest reaches of the universe? Who was responsible for atrocities like Hitler and bell-bottom jeans? How hot are the hot tubs in Hell? I mean, really, they can't possibly be that hot. Most importantly, is angel's food cake superior to devil's food cake?

They spoke on history and fine art, the best practices of both divinity and depravity—complete with live, interactive demos. A 14th century demonstration by Aerico got out of hand. Showing his colleagues the best way to spread the common cold to their enemies, Aerico sneezed in the middle of an incantation and wiped out over one hundred million people over the span of seven years. Tim, the valet/security officer, was forced to remove the demon from the premise and died two years later from the worst case of skin cancer ever reported.

But that sort of thing didn't happen anymore. Or at least not as often. There were contingencies in place for that kind of thing. Besides, most of the uppers and lessers learned over the years that human life was precious. Without it, their own lives wouldn't be half as entertaining.

Life was good once a year. Even those holding the balance between good and evil needed to let down their hair on occasion. It was hard to balance the two sides; but, as it turned out, the balance was even harder to disrupt.

So, the demons arrived at the south gate and the angels flew in from the north. Father Time made a rare appearance. Even Mother Earth, draped in garments woven of vines and tree roots—refusing to conform to the mainstream dress theme—stopped by for the affair. Why let the lessers have all the fun? In fact, the two surprised the crowd with impromptu musical performances.[3]

Death showed her face, too, bringing with her the other horsemen of the apocalypse: War, Famine, and Pestilence. Though they kept busy with their humanitarian work, they never missed an opportunity to get together and knock a few back. Ole Pesty was delighted when word of Aerico's mishap reached his ear and, to this day, claims it as his own accomplishment. He was teaching the lesser demons well.

The Heaven and Hell Convention was a two-day affair, starting February 28th and lasting until midnight on the 29th. The first day tended towards the low-key. Caterers provided hors d'oeuvres, ranging anywhere from tapas to Brazilian barbeque to half-frozen cocktail weenies. Only the serious drinkers arrived early enough to partake; the other attendees arrived around midnight. Humans kept both demons and angels too busy during the day for them to

---

[3] Father Time is the lead singer of the band Pendulum, a post-rock staple. Mother Earth plays the drums for the Screaming Gaias, an all-girl punk band that does Earth, Wind, and Fire covers. Both shows were smash hits even though the Fire Marshal was only called twice.

party; hence, why they hid this particular day from them. Every four years, everyone got a few extra hours to rage.

The coordinators hired The Devil as the keynote speaker...again. He prepared his usual speech, changing a few of the jokes he'd used for centuries. Some of the raunchier ones always got a blare of raucous laughter from young Gabriel, especially after a few Meso mules. Midway through, the Devil made eye contact with Death, really seeing her for the first time. It was love at first sight, as if every other sight over millennia never happened.

A lot of harmless flirting followed. Blood-red Cabernet walked hand in hand with the two lovebirds. They danced the tango, laughed at each other's stupid jokes, and bullied Gabriel—who was losing his dinner in a soup pot. After being sick, Gabriel continued his talk with Aamon, who was looking more wolfish than usual. Death sneaked behind Gabriel and stole his staff, giggling as she ran off with it. The Devil held the door for her and they both left the banquet hall.

In their minds, they were just two immortal beings enjoying themselves. They assumed no one else thought anything of it. Rumors abounded, and they were the talk of the convention, but that didn't stop them. You couldn't deny love, especially between the Prince of Darkness and the Angel of Mercy. No one imagined they'd elope, taking their honeymoon in Michigan, to bring humanity to the brink of destruction.

There were no instructions in the manual for that sort of contingency.

***

"So that's how it all started and how it will all end." Jesus stopped to take a deep breath. The world breathed with him. A mighty wind shook the trees and rattled the shingles around the shrine as he exhaled.

"That's all fine and dandy," King said, "but has nothing to do with Mio. Or the murders."

"Right on, brother. Right on."

The real Jesus patted Riz on the shoulder. "Right on, indeed. This happens to be the place in Michigan where the Devil and Death have come. Flew a plane from Atlanta to Detroit, stopped to make some new friends. They had to reveal themselves with more flair than usual to keep their strength up. Us divine entities need to 'feed' on what makes us whole to remain in our corporeal forms—Death on souls, the Devil on sin, myself on belief. The Devil intended to return home, but the blushing bride insisted on seeing more of the countryside. She'd never had an opportunity to get to know her clientele and how they live. Now they're shacked up in a motel up the street, preparing to consummate their unholy union."

"Alright, Devs. Gettin' it done," Riz said, holding up his hand for a high five he wasn't going to receive.

"Not alright. Not even close." These were solemn words. The Son of God pulled Riz's hand down. "This union will bring the End Times. I was blind and didn't see it coming. I need your help to stop it. Or, at least, to slow the bleeding."

There was a collective and ineffable gasp, followed by soft, en francais sobbing. Lourdes stopped cleaning. Fatima forgot all about conspirators and liars. For once, Cruc looked gloomy and Riz came down from his high.

"Pfft. Of course, you do," King said. "Why wouldn't you? What's it got to do with us? We're confined to the bars of night and restricted to the church. These hallowed grounds don't allow us much opportunity to help."

The rest might have been quick to abandon themselves, but King held his ground. Created in the image of God—or, rather, constructed to be the image of her son—he'd be damned if he abandoned his woe-is-me attitude. It was who he was. Period. Pessimism was his brick and mortar. It was home.

But then, something interesting happened.

They always had an inkling that someone took care of the grounds, they had a name—Willy—but failed to recall the laborer's face. It was one of those things that happened—as common as breath. They dragged their massive stone bodies across the lawn, digging divots in the grass and leaving ruts wherever they went. The destruction they wrought sort of put itself back together during the day as they rested. Everyone knew that.

From inside a shed across the way, a shy, aging man with a salt-and-pepper beard stepped out. He watched his feet move as he approached the group, pulling a wheelbarrow behind him by one handle. The man stopped beside Jesus.

"This is Willy, the groundskeeper," Jesus said.

"Hello there. Nice to meet y'all."

The group stared, mouths agape. A human had spoken to them. This too was definitely not in the manual.

Reading their minds, Willy said, "Don't think nothin' of all the work you leave me. S'kept me young all these years. Idle hands, ya know? Feels good doing God's work every day."

Their jaws dropped further. King attempted to blink away the illusion; but, when he stopped, Willy was still there.

Riz patted his robes, looking for another doobie, but gave up.

Lourdes twitched like a tweeker. Willy was the dirtiest man she ever met. The last time he took a shower was during the reign of the Roman Empire. Julius Caesar would have ordered this man quartered for his lack of hygiene alone.

The rest of the group dug into their figurative pockets, shuffling around and wondering what the others were thinking. Until now, no human had witnessed their nightcaps. They were always so careful to keep their secret meetings, well, secret.

But Willy had known from day one. Imagine your world being turned upside down. Now imagine you were turned upside down like a bully turns out his victim's wallet to shake out loose change. Now imagine you were the loose change and built out of a half-ton of stone. When you hit the ground, you crumbled to pieces. The joke was on you because those pieces formed themselves back together the next night. Every night, without fail.

Willy, sensing their confusion, set the wheelbarrow down and removed his straw hat out of respect. "I worked it out as a wee lad, you see. Liked to explore the shrine. Oh, I've known for years. I saw y'all wondering around by the light of the full moon in the 60s. Just reckoned y'all nice folks 'preciated your privacy. Wanted to leave ya to your own dee-vices. Sorry I wasn't more upfront. Was nice, having something all to myself."

Willy was not a learned man. But he was pious and hardworking. No one could deny his politeness or his devotion to the Lord. Something about his bucolic tone put their minds at ease. Everyone but King.

"How's he fit into all this?"

"Well," Jesus began, "Willy's your eyes when you cannot see. Your ears when you are deaf. Your lantern to guide you when it's light out, so to speak."

"Lanterns are—"

King waved off Fatima. "Hush, Mother. It's a metaphor."

So, it looked like they were enlisting a human's help. No one was at ease, but the cat was out of the bag. Though, it might have been too soon to bring the cliché back into use. Ever since the Farmer Kelly incident, people in Mio had a sore spot about putting cats in bags. Then again, maybe the time was nigh.

Regardless, the statues were finally connected to the daytime world. The burden fell on King to guide Willy. He wasn't looking forward to the extra responsibility and hoped something cataclysmic might save him the effort.

"There's someone else," Jesus said to King, as if he knew what he was thinking. For extra assurance, he continued, "Yes, I *do* know what you're thinking. What can one man do to save Earth? In the end, probably not much. But I want you to meet my son, Bob."

This man, Bob, caused a commotion for two reasons:

First, he appeared out of nowhere. One second there was only Willy by Jesus's side. Then the body of a simple and indistinguishable man filled the empty space. Some of the more astute members of the group remembered seeing something there, but even they couldn't picture what exactly it had been.

Second, the syntax of "son" felt odd. Jesus put a special inflection on the word as it rolled off his tongue. Weren't all men sons of Jesus? Among the group, family lines were drawn crooked and muddled, but this one was especially off-putting.

No conclusions were drawn on either front. At least not until Jesus explained who Bob was. He *had* been there the whole time. People only saw what they wanted. Or only what they were comfortable seeing. This also applied to the statues, as it were. The theatrics of the Lord's approach overshadowed Bob's arrival.

Also, Bob was indeed blood related. That was a *long* story.

"What happens in Atlanta stays in Atlanta, amirite?" Jesus winked. "I'll tell you about it after the world ends. Which will be sooner rather than later if we don't act fast."

After pleasantries, the trinity of Jesuses and triumvirate of Marys accepted Bob and Willy as their own. It would be nice to have flesh and blood around.

Even King came around and hugged Bob. "Welcome to the family, Mr. Robert."

"It's just Bob."

"Just Bob?" Riz laughed. "That's a weird name, isn't it?"

So, with the first glimpse of light on the horizon, the statues returned to their places. Bob and Willy slinked off with Jesus. King returned to slumber, worried the problems of the days to come were certain to outweigh the opportunities. The path would be hard and, in the end, they'd all be disappointed by their attempt to assuage the red tides of apocalypse. Disappointment and failure fueled the world. Why should it be any different now?

Chapter 18:

Serena

With that vile woman gone—the one who had seemed so sweet, but who, like all the rest, turned out to be a manipulative harpy—and the steady flow of morphine creeping through his veins, Chase began to enjoy himself again. The hospital bed wasn't comfortable, but he *was* getting plenty to eat.

Press a button, food. Press the same button, fluffy pillow. These concepts should catch on elsewhere; he made a mental note to pitch it after this was all over. Some practical examples included twist cap, get drunk. Unzip pants, get laid. Lay down, burn fat.

A part of him, deep down and hidden under multiple layers of flab, knew he needed to get out of bed. He could suck it up. His injuries weren't unsurmountable. It was high past time to work instead of getting high to pass the time. At this rate, he'd find Mr. and Mrs. Stillmans' killer by the time hell froze over (unlikely given lava, hot springs filled with widow's tears, and other infernal devices).

Somewhere, somehow, someone needed his help. Another victim could meet their maker any minute. Mio needed a hero to provide the answers they deserved, to bring them retribution.

The police weren't doing much. Sheriff Grace was a dedicated woman but naive to the possibility of corruption in her town. Deputy Lawson was, well, about as much help as putting shaving cream on your toothbrush early in the morning when you're running late for work and fighting halitosis from a night of rum and fish tacos.

They needed an outside perspective. Someone to objectify them, at least the sheriff. He pictured her curves, the nape of her neck.

"That's not right." He licked chocolate pudding off the corner of his lip. "Objectify them? Sheriff Grace? No, no. That's all wrong. I like objectifying things, mostly women, but not the sheriff. We need to be objective. Yes, we need someone to be *objective*. And to get more pudding. More pudding would be great. Nurse?"

She had heard him talking to himself and was already in the room, hands on her hips and tapping her foot. Chase winked and put his hand on her back as she fluffed his pillow. She slapped it away. Without a word, she left him, but stopped in the doorway to pick something up. She stood slowly, glancing at the fat man with *eyes*. Hey, everyone needed attention from time to time, even if it came from a loser like Chase Cross.

Despite his animalistic desires, Chase considered himself a complex creature. Take, for example, what happened next.

With the nurse gone, and his pudding cup empty, he started to feel empty himself. Maybe it was the bitter quiet of the hospital, or the heightening pain nagging at his ribs, but Chase started crying.[1] His eyes became miniature monsoons, blurring the room around him.

He wasn't crying because of his many mommy issues or the loneliness looking over his shoulder every day. He wasn't crying because of the hunger pangs in his stomach. No, he was crying because he missed his friend, Bob. It was Just Bob, and he couldn't turn off the waterworks.

Bob disappeared at the shrine. Chase thought it would be fun, kind of like a Sherlock Holmes story, to investigate the Stillmans' murder with a sidekick—a foil of sorts. Two pairs of eyes, even one untrained in the fine arts of detection, were always better than one. Besides, not being

---

[1] Despite popular opinion, men are allowed to cry, too. Especially when doped and out of dessert.

alone for once brought Chase an ineffable clarity in life. The man, despite his simplicity, had an undeniable quality. One couldn't help but like Bob. Anyone capable of sleeping so soundly (and snoring louder than a Metallica concert) on a metal prison bunk, had to be trustworthy. If not trustworthy, at least easy to please. Easy to please was good. It meant maybe Bob wouldn't leave him in the end.

As a man of action, or so he considered himself, Chase Cross needed someone of intellect. Bob fit the bill. He might not wonder much, but he wandered enough.

"I wonder if Bobo is doing okay," he said to nobody at all. "And where he got off to."

Chase didn't make quick friends. In fact, Chase didn't make *any* friends. He either met people he liked, who "mysteriously" disappeared, or people he couldn't tolerate, who ended up following him around anyway.

His mind, woven like a rusty chainmail shirt, wandered to the complexities trapped therein. It protected him, but at a cost. First, his mother, and then to school, where he first discovered his love for the female form. His first crush had been the school nurse. A kind, blue-eyed bombshell who tended to his emotional scars every time he got bullied. Thinking about bullies, his mind took him back to his mother. Thoughts of his mother made him want more pudding. And more morphine.

Before he had time to summon the nurse, a wave of excitement washed over his wing of the hospital, drowning each room with confusion. The hospital staff—docile, from what he could tell—erupted with energy as waves broke on the beaches of their boredom.

It was all running after gurneys, running with gurneys, grabbing stethoscopes and hooking up electronic machinery, slipping on blue latex gloves, and clopping down the hall in high heels. Chase wasn't sure if the shoes were appropriate hospital attire, but he admitted the legs leading down to them were acceptable.

His favorite nurse appeared at the door, unlocked the wheels of his bed, and pushed him against the far wall without saying a word. She checked his vitals, squeezed his IV bag, and held his wrist, counting under her breath.

She glanced over her shoulder before sprinting out. "You seem alright, but it's going to get real cozy in here real fast. Can I trust you to behave yourself?" He nodded.

Chase watched a handful of doctors roll in new patients, then zip by the door to his room to meet others at the front entrance of the hospital. Inaudible dialogue was taking place between staff members, like a dozen quarterbacks calling out plays to the line. Heads nodded and orders were carried out. Despite the number of injured patients, they handled the inundation like the professional veterinarians they were.

Six people. No, a dozen.

They came in in droves.

After a while, he lost track. The chaos's dizzying speed made Chase sick to his stomach. It was like triage in the Cambodian rainforest, and there didn't seem to be an end to the wounded. At one point, a man much larger than Chase wheeled in two patients in two separate gurneys with only one massive hand.

The cries of pain were unbearable. The saddest part? No joke could make light of the situation. No one bringing him pudding came in close second.

But they did bring him three new friends.

First, two police officers were wheeled into his room, both unconscious. One he'd never seen before, but—despite severe burns across the entire left side of his face that wrapped around his neck to the rest of his body—he recognized the other.

Chase thought back to the day they freed him and Bob. He'd noticed the small shed between the police station and the courthouse. When the door opened, a broad-chested officer sat at a card table playing poker with a skinny redhead. Further in the shed, a rack of automatic rifles stuck out like hay in a needle stack. The burned officer was the man in the shed; his caterpillar mustache gave him away.

The third person, a woman in her late twenties with matted, sooty blonde hair came to rest right next to him. She wore a tight blue dress and thick-framed glasses. Compared to the police officers, she was unscathed by whatever calamity had brought them to the hospital. Gauze stuck out from her shoulder, covering minor burns, and she smiled at Chase when he winked at her. As the nurse hooked up an IV, the woman squirmed to stay out of the way, knocking over a tray of utensils and a plethora of doctor-type instruments.

"Pardon me," she said, her voice shrill like dissonant harp strings plucked all at once. "I'm just so clumsy."

The nurse struggled with the tools, holding the woman down. She looked exhausted. "Please, ma'am. Relax. You've been through a lot today."

Chase fell in lust. He was Mount Ararat and she was the Arc. Somehow, in the expanse of miles of desert, high in the peaks of insanity, she'd found him. But did she carry an olive branch in her teeth or something sharp?

Silence fell over the hospital. They had apparently wheeled in his roommates last. The officers slept, their chests rising and falling to the sound of EKG. The woman stared at him.

"So, what happened?" Chase asked.

Her voluminous eyelashes fluttered like angel's wings as she spoke. Her words, reserved and coy, sent shivers down his spine.

"I'm Serena. What's your name, handsome?"

He told her. The detective within him wanted to move past the formalities of small talk to get down to business. Chase, the man, desired more informal things. Those would have to wait.

Serena had other plans.

"Chase, eh? And what is it you're chasing?"

"Well, a few things." She dangled the lure in front of his face, and he had no choice but to take a bite. "Presently, I want more pudding."

"What else are you after, Chases Pudding?"

"I'm a detective. I'm after answers. Can you tell me what's happening? Where did you come from?"

"I was born in a small tow—"

"Be serious now. It's important."

Taken aback, she straightened her posture as best she could in the clumsy hospital bed.

"Fine, then. If that's how it's going to be…I'll skip all the stuff about me, the 'un-serious' stuff." She side-eyed him. "There was a fire at the courthouse. Started at the police station. Nasty ordeal. They hadn't fanned the flames by the time they took me away."

Chase didn't have the heart to correct her idiom. In fact, he didn't even notice. She was too damn adorable. Instead, he barraged her with a line of questioning, ranging from semi-coherent to completely, outlandishly off-track.

She held up a dainty left hand, clad in a gold watch and not a single ring, to stop him before he hurt himself.

"Why don't I just tell you what I know?"

And so, she did. She'd overheard a lot of things. In the heat of the moment, secrecy and emergency protocol flew out the window. What he couldn't glean from her recounting, he pieced together with careful deduction. Everything else he filled in with his mind's eye—the third eye of the great detective.

Since most of what he took from her recollection was wrong, here is what actually happened.

***

The fire started during the uncomfortable time of the morning when the moon hadn't tucked itself in and the sun had yet to finish its first cup of coffee. Mio, awash in haphazard strokes of pale gold, felt no different at this time of day than any others. The drunks and the third shifters, both equally dangerous given the right circumstances, stumbled home after finishing their last bites of hash at the local greasy spoon. Those few successful and driven people—a ratio phenomenon not particular to Mio—were up and ready to greet the challenges of the day. If Mio had a mall, this was around the time a hundred old people would be rounding their seventeenth lap.

No one had anticipated the fire. How could they? Nothing like it had ever happened before, a resting status that was becoming so common they might as well have changed their slogan to, "Mio, Michigan: where things that never happen always happen."

Officer Miles, nearing the end of his late shift of watching over the police station—and, by default, the people of Mio—toddled around the station. He was a simple, ginger-headed young man in his early twenties. His shift had been quiet, besides dispatching a team to thwart a group of punk kids vandalizing the bridge again. One of them had been Tony's boy, though, and they were let off with yet another warning. There was also Crazy Ira, who liked to harangue the general store employees about demons and sexually deviant nuns, but Miles ignored that call. Ira usually went away when you ignored him.

It was all in a day's work. In fact, Officer Miles had even snuck in a nap or two.

He'd been engrossed in an infomercial for a brand-new home innovation sweeping the nation: the BrushSnatch (patent pending). From what he gathered from the soundless, black-and-white television, it was the hottest tool on the market since the VacMower (no explanation necessary). It served as both a common household sweeper and a bug catcher, for those rueful housewives unable to stomach murder in the sanctity of their little, tidy homes. He found himself overwhelmed with the call to action, especially when bold letters flashed across the bottom of the screen urging him to "call now to take advantage of a limited buy-one-get-seven-free deal."

No one would notice if he stashed a few of the extras around the station. He was convinced they would come in handy one day, so he dialed and read off his credit card number with the satisfaction that only comes with the smart purchase.

He patted his own back. "Good job, Officer."

As a reward for his excellent service, he kicked back to catch a few more Z's. If the world needed him, he'd hear the call and answer it.

A few minutes later, he awoke famished and drenched in sweat. The usual station smell—manufactured tropical breeze and body odor—was gone, replaced with the comforting smell of a campfire under the stars. He wasn't sure where the smell was coming from, but he wanted a rack of ribs or a roasted marshmallow between two stale graham crackers—no chocolate. Chocolate made him hyper.

Someone ought to open a twenty-four-hour barbeque joint around here, he thought as he stretched his legs. Since he was already up, Officer Miles figured a drink and a snack were in order. He'd earned it.

Part of his job was to patrol the station every hour. The station was empty, but police work was thorough and routine attention to detail. They taught him that in the academy. It was one of the few pieces of advice that stuck. The rest he learned along the way.

As a part of his patrol, he checked the nice visitor's bathroom at the far end of the hall—the one with faux-marble sinks and plush, three-ply toilet paper. While he was there, he relieved himself. Then, he found himself in the kitchen. Why not grab a snack? He peered into the cupboards. No intruders or vandals, but he helped himself to a day-old donut. And another. Although they weren't baby-backs, they were cinnamony-delicious. He checked; the side door was locked.

He jiggled the hot doorknob, glanced perfunctorily outside without really looking at anything, and nodded his head, satisfied by a job well done. He wiped cinnamon sugar off his face and wondered why there was so much flickering brightness coming from the porch. Next, he wondered why the doorknob had been so hot to the touch. Now that he thought about it, it seemed a bit abnormal.

Neither of these peculiarities connected in the vast emptiness of Officer Miles' mind. Even with the thickening, black smoke and the flames licking the outside wall of the police station, he hesitated to draw conclusions.

An explosion rocked the station

"Uh, hello? Please, go away."

It didn't.

The fire spread through the wood. What at first was a warm, Bahama day grew into a lava bath in the bowels of Phoenix, Arizona. He backed away from the door, aware to some degree of danger (about 1,500 of them, in this case) but still couldn't comprehend the volatility of his situation.

Fumbling around the kitchen, using the counters to navigate, he found the cupboard by the fridge. He needed another donut. How was he supposed to respond to the situation on an empty stomach?

The crackle of his radio, barely audible over the crackle of the flames, reminded him who he was and that, as a police officer, he had certain obligations. But none of his training taught him what to do if the criminal was eight feet of white-hot fire and his was the life that needed protection. This stuff wasn't even covered in the "special edition" training videos, the ones his classmates had given him his first year on the job.

Officer Miles unclipped his radio and held down the talk button, organizing his thoughts as he did. Sheriff Grace hated when he did this but, given the circumstances, he needed to get it right.

"Uh, guys? Anyone? I mean, if you're awake yet and all. Yeah…there's a, uh, something happening here."

Tsst. "Miles what are you on about?"

"Fire, sir. Or, I mean, ma'am. Sorry. In the station. It's moving fast. Making itself at home, if you ask me."

Tsst. "What?! The station is on fire?"

Miles recounted the facts. Thick smoke obscured most of his view. Despite this, he was pretty sure he knew how to answer the question. First, he needed to stop coughing and catch his breath.

"Yes, ma'am," he managed. "Seems to be."

Tsst. "Dammit, Miles. Are you still in there? Get out. Call the fire department. I'm on my way to you."

And that's what he did. Well, after knocking over two end tables, flipping feet-up over the couch, and somehow spilling coffee on his uniform. His parents never allowed him to drink caffeine. Claimed it turned him, a "special boy," into a raging calamity. He never quite knew what they had meant. Maybe they were worried about him ruining his only pair of work clothes. *Other than that,* he thought, bouncing off walls on his way through the building, *I don't see a problem.*

By the time he made it outside, the fire had engulfed the three-story police station. He was crispy around the edges but alive. A fire truck was screaming down Main Street towards the scene. The chief was already there, getting things ready for his crew.

To Miles' horror, he remembered the first-shifters. Two of them were sleeping upstairs. Jared, with his caterpillar mustache, and Todd. Both outstanding officers. Miles told the chief about them and crossed his fingers. They'd be alright; God watched over Mio and her people.

Other people in town, especially the Main Street business owners, were operating a bucket chain of sorts, drawing the water from a mystery well. Miles ran over to help. No one was there to open the fire hydrant yet. The five-gallon buckets didn't do much good, but they had to try something. If the flames spread to the courthouse, everything that kept the town afloat was at risk: ledgers, tax documents, court cases, deeds, permits and the paged of every single law ever enacted in Mio.

They needed a miracle, and they needed it fast.

They got their miracle around the time the flames spread to the courthouse. A small one and too late, but a miracle, nonetheless.

A gray cloud sauntered across the sky, directly above the building, and opened the floodgates. People gazed around, refusing to admit what they were seeing: it was only raining on the courthouse.

Sheriff Grace pulled up around this time with Deputy Lawson riding shotgun. As she got out of the car, the last of the fire not snuffed out by the rain retreated into its cloud with a whimper. She pretended not to notice.

"Miles," she yelled. "What the hell did you do?"

Stooped near the rubble of the police station, Miles finished coughing up the last of his lungs. He shuffled to her, head held in shame. He felt bad about the mess he made inside the station. The knocked over tables. The coffee stain on the carpet no one would ever get out no matter how hard they scrubbed. Hope remained: the sheriff didn't know yet, and he was going to do his best to keep it that way. He was sure the fire would cover up most of his damage.

If not, he could always fall back on the BrushSnatches.

"Sorry, ma'am."

"What were you thinking in there?"

Good question, he thought. No wonder the sheriff was in charge. Excellent questions like those led to excellent police work.

"Well," he said after a long silence, "I was thinking about a glass of ice water and a cold shower."

Good answer, he thought.

Miles took pride in two things:

First, he'd gotten through the tenth grade with only three D's and no failing marks.

Second, and this was the important one, he set a record during the county police physical examination—he liked that word, examination. You needed real smarts to use words like examination. Heck, for fun he had ran the course a second time and finished before the deputy but held no anti-moss-eats towards the man.

Now, he had this. It had been uncomfortable in the station. The temperature reminded him of a hot summer day. When he thought about summer, he thought about air conditioning and sweaty glasses filled to the brim with ice water. He straightened up, brimming with rediscovered confidence.

Now, he had *logic*.

"Miles," Sheriff Grace said, holding back the desire to punch him in the throat, "are you messing with me? Or just completely brainless?"

"Ma'am?"

"Go help them clean up, Officer. I think I saw some poor man coming out of the courthouse coughing up a storm."

He followed orders, bounding with every step and congratulating himself on a night of policing work done right. No matter what else happened, he'd always have that.

Even with two officers wounded—both a more than crispy around the edges—one building burnt to dust, and another chewed by a hungry inferno, it could have been worse. Miraculously, no one died. Too many people were dying in Mio, and only Mio.

***

Serena, she explained to the detective, had been in the courthouse, preparing for a civil lawsuit against one of Mio's many real estate firms. They'd been urging tourists from Ohio and Indiana to travel north, enticed by the investment opportunity of a lifetime—think timeshare, erase the sharing, erase the actual property, and that's close to what they were doing. She was sick of these greedy stiffs taking advantage of worn-out, naive city folk.

Alone on a wooden pew, paper sprawled beside her, she was reviewing her notes. They were careful in their dealings, but a few mismatched signatures and a fake routing number provided the evidence she needed to put a few crooked men behind bars.

Then, she caught her first whiff of smoke. Odd, she was the only one up at that ungodly hour. Serena didn't look away from her work. "No smoking, please." She absent-mindedly pointed at the printout on the wall above her head. "Take it outside."

She coughed as the air was sucked out of the room. Growing up, her parents smoked, and Serena hated everything about the filthy habit. Fed up, she slammed her binder on the pew and stood to confront the culprit. There was no one around.

A faint crackle came from behind her, followed by the sound tape makes when it's peeled off a rough surface. She took off her sweater, dabbed at the sweat beading around her temples, and started fanning herself with a memorandum. A circular portion of the cedar wall seemed to darken, the blackness spreading in all directions. Because of the smell of burning wood, she sniffed her armpits to make sure she put deodorant on before she came in.

She shrugged. "Not me."

A noise from behind the clerk's counter startled her. When she turned again, she was facing a young man wearing all black who she thought she recognized—perhaps one of the high school mouth-breathers from down the street.

He stepped out from behind the counter with a pile of documents jammed into the wing of his arm and a gas can in his hand. He smiled at her with one corner of his chapped mouth and pulled a pack of cigarettes out his pocket. His sneer remained as he lit one, never breaking eye contact with the lawyer. In a single, drawn breath, the cigarette was ashes.

"Might have to reschedule your appointment, ma'am." He flicked the butt behind the counter and exited the building through the front doors.

She wasn't sure what to think about the encounter, but she didn't have time to dwell. The wall behind her peeled apart with flames. It was like a cardboard coffee cup, left to sit in the sun all day—liquid seeping through the thin bottom layer until it was picked up, spilling the contents everywhere; but, in this case, the hot coffee was a full-blown inferno exploding into the room.

While she recalled the latter portion of the story, she held Chase's hand. Neither of them realized it was happening; he was too absorbed in the details, and she was too frightened by their recollection.

"I heard someone say it started in the parking lot of the police station." She raised an eyebrow at her companion. "But I didn't realize pavement was conducive to fire like that."

"It's not."

"What then?" she asked, letting go of his hand.

"Arson."

"How do you know?"

"Well, you said he had a gas can. Duh."

"What are you going to do, Detective?"

Normally, after a look like the one she'd just given him, he'd be head-over-boots in love. However, all he felt was relief that he wasn't—wasn't holding her hand anymore, wasn't thinking about all the things he wanted to do to her.

Instead, he was thinking about Sheriff Grace. The whole time Serena told her story, he had awaited the arrival of the badge-wearing, dark-skinned superhero. In his imagination, the sheriff rode in on her white horse to save the day. She scooped him up and dropped him on the saddle behind her just in the nick of time.

When Serena first mentioned the sheriff's name, he knew everything would be okay. But Sheriff Grace needed his help, and she needed it fast.

"Serena," he said, "I've got to go. There's work to do."

"Can't you stay with me a bit longer?"

He peeled himself from her arms and shook his head. It was a tempting offer, but he was sick and tired of losing to his temptations. She might not be a succubus, but if she wasn't going to help him solve the case, she wasn't worth the effort.

"Good-bye, Serena."

"Until we meet again?"

He shook his head. There wasn't going to be a next time, not if he could help it.

Chapter 19:

Rabble Rally

A not-so-starved-anymore-but-still-mangy coyote, rather triumphant after spending much of the night stalking a plump hare and undoing his belt after a meal, stretched out alongside the highway. He was content to lay on the damp asphalt and lick blood off his snout. The coyote watched a hovering mosquito before it buried itself in his fur. This should have been the last thing he saw.

His last thought should have been how illogical the sensation of prey moving in his stomach was. The coyote dismissed this as a delusion.

"Uh, Sheriff?" Deputy Lawson scrunched as low as possible in the passenger seat. He pointed out the window at the critter, but it was already too late. *Thump, thump.* "Never mind. It's nothing."

Sheriff Grace white-knuckled the wheel of the cruiser. She wasn't slowing down, not even if angels descended from Heaven. The people of Mio elected her to do a job, and she had only one vice: an obsessive need to serve and protect. Every man, woman, child, feral cat, and rodent relied on her to keep them safe. Her billy club was ready.

Deputy Lawson, sitting shotgun and keeping a close eye on *her* shotgun, held on tight. He grasped for a handhold on the door of the car, scratching and pawing at the dashboard. His superior liked to drive fast; crime didn't wait. This, however, bordered on psychotic. She was driving *away* from Mio, at about the speed of sound, utilizing both lanes and the shoulder—even the grass around particularly sharp bends.

He opened his mouth to say something—raised a finger and cleared his throat—but something about her ember eyes and the lava veins shut him up. He resigned himself to sheer terror. There were fates worse than death.

Damn anyone who questioned the sheriff's dedication. Deputy Lawson, despite his current trepidations, had nothing but respect for the woman. Right out of juvenile detention, passing his cadet exams by the hair on his chest, she took him under his wing when no one else would. Despite his past mistakes, she pulled him into her far-reaching web of protection and taught him everything he needed to know.

He took no pleasure in seeing the sheriff like this. Her infallibility replaced by anxious compulsion hurt him to the core. In the moment, Sheriff Grace was throwing a temper-tantrum like a teenager whose mother just took her cellphone and changed the Wi-Fi password.

Finally, he said it. "I think you ran something over back there, ma'am."

"Deputy…" She took a deep breath and relaxed her grip on the wheel. She tried to convince herself not to throw him out of the car. To be fair, it wasn't his fault he was this way. Nurture only went so far. People were born into their life, not the other way around. She glanced at him and said, "Don't you think I know that?"

"It's just…I think it was a coyote."

"So?"

"So what, ma'am?"

"So, what's your point, Deputy?"

"No point, ma'am." He glanced back at the shrinking carcass on the road and shivered.

One minute the coyote had been chasing rabbits and howling at the moon. The next, he was slinking off to find a safe place to rest through the day—maybe on the way a bird flew by, low and intent on stirring up some early morning play. Maybe the titillating scent of a vixen wafted by. Either way, what harm could come from stopping to smell the flowers? Then, Sheriff Grace came along to smear his entrails across the underbelly of her black and white. Before the coyote could react, before the moon was yet out of sight, everything went dark again. Forever.

Still, Deputy Lawson swore he saw it move off the road, still slinking but only because three fourths of its body was as flat as a pancake.

Impossible…Right?

He shivered again.

Sheriff Grace didn't have time to worry about such trivialities. She left that to Deputy Lawson. That was why she hired a deputy to begin with. Worrying was one of his talents. Everyone had to excel at something.

Ahead, a clearing in the depths of the forest rolled into view. As she applied the brakes, she willed her heartbeat to match the faint rhythm of the road underneath her tires. She reached deep within herself to find calm. Even deeper, she found the will to bring herself back to the moment long enough to realize they'd passed the park.

By the time they circled back and found the entrance, her rage returned hotter than before. No one started fires in her town. No one killed their neighbors, defiled the wholesomeness of their neighborhoods. It was still a mystery who had done it, but one thing was certain: By the finger twitching over the trigger of her revolver, Sheriff Grace would find out who and make them pay.

Sheriff needed to compose herself. People relied on her reliability, and Deputy Lawson looked up to her. She'd called this meeting and needed to articulate her feelings in a productive manner before pulling the trigger, literally and metaphorically. And she frowned upon the possibility of having a heart attack. An untimely death would hamper her ability to rally the rabble and put an end to the chaos. That was not something she'd let happen.

Rifle River came into view. Like Loud Creek, it was aptly named. On any given day, upward of a dozen rifles— Winchesters, Remingtons, Weatherby Mark V's, and even knock-off Walmart brand models—washed onto the bank. Some got tangled in the weeds, others jammed upright in the wet sandy bottom; but somehow, someway, they always found their way to damn near the same place. Some of the most scientific minds[1] in Mio examined this phenomenon. In the end, no one could quite figure it out. Instead, they wrapped the "hot zone" (or so it became known as) with yellow caution tape, paid a revolving door of teenagers minimum wage to stand guard all day, and chalked it up as one of the unexplainable mysteries of the universe—like chunky peanut butter or dark matter.

One day, one of those hoity-toity southern types, all learned and dressed in fresh-pressed flannel, arrived on what he called "safari." As an Ohioan, this scholarly fellow needn't look any further than the close northern realms of the unchained Michigan wilderness for excitement. Not Scotland, or Nepal, or the Moon—the latter, of which, many Michiganders would have preferred he visit. "Conducting research," he also called it: his version of documenting a primitive group of native peoples in their own natural habitat. "Anthropology," or so he claimed. Pretension was a better word, but Mionites believed that was the moment before a fishing line went taut. So, we'd call it snooping.

Anyhow, this professor of the Deep South, this tweed, ivorybilly, came across Rifle River on his last day in town. Martha, the teen on guard that day, told him about the mystery and why she was there—with sleep glazing her eyes. He offered her coffee. She reminded him she was only

---

[1] See also: the Michigan DNC and a young man named Pete with a lazy eye.

thirteen. He wondered why a thirteen-year-old was working and if he should report it, but time was short. With the power of careful research, painstaking triangulation, and a whole lot of luck, Dr. Know-It-All[2] deciphered the riddle.

A mile upriver, the local NRA chapter–everyone and their grandmothers and their grandmother's grandmothers—had their private campgrounds. Here they came to drink and shoot guns and celebrate the American Dream. They were decent, upstanding, 2nd Amendment revering citizens of the greatest country on the face of God's green earth. Every now and again, a chapter member wobbled to the bank to relieve him/herself. A bob and a frigid dip later, they'd find themselves face first in the water, watching their gun float away in the current. He suspected the reason behind the sudden change in the river's speed in this area was due to a congenital desire to get as far away from those people as fast as possible.

But that was mere speculation. He never put his latest theory to the test; he also wanted to get as far away from those people as fast as possible.

It was in this way Rifle River became the only river in recorded history to literally bear arms to its visitors. Also, there was always the bears along the bank to contend with. Thank God they hadn't figured out how to bear arms with their own bear arms. We would be telling a whole different story...

Not particularly worried about the possibility of militant bears running around in her forests, Sheriff Grace parked. She grabbed the shotgun from the backseat and gave Deputy Lawson a desperate look. *It's time to go. The troops are*

---

2 PHD, not medically licensed in the State of Michigan or anywhere else. This disclaimer is brought to you by medical malpractice and poor decisions.

ready. She planned for them to be there early, waiting. The show couldn't start without the host.

"Get 'em all riled up," she told the deputy. Make them squirm in their boots, that way they were already boiling over with anger and ready to make somebody pay by the time she arrived. "Deputy?"

"Yes, ma'am?"

"Sunglasses." She held out her hand and, after a few beats, added, "Please."

He hesitated, bent forward to look out the window at the sky. Not a sliver of sun peeking through, just fast-moving gray clouds. Still, she'd said please. "But ma'am, its—"

She slammed the door, glaring at him. With the shotgun resting on her shoulder, she had to admit he was right, but today was too important to admit to a mistake or show weakness. *Stick to your guns, lest someone sticks them to you instead.*

"Deputy, what do I pay you for?"

"No disrespect, ma'am, but I think the people pay me. For police work. Or something."

"Or something is right." She ignored his sass, this time. "Now, give me my damn sunglasses. They're waiting."

"Wasn't that the whole poi—"

She snatched them from him and growled.

Deputy Lawson watched himself in the mirror-fronted lenses of her aviators. He looked like a scared child, ready to cry after his mommy yelled at him and sent him to bed with no dinner. It wasn't a good look on him, but he'd accepted it a long time ago.

When her pearly whites disappeared behind those lenses, so did the remainder of Deputy Lawson's confidence. She revealed her wants and desires by the way light glinted off her eyes. Or by how she hung her shoulders. Or by the twitch of her nose. When she wore her shades, though, she was a total enigma, giving the impression of a loose cannon. Given his position, the deputy would inevitably get caught in the crossfire.

Across the park, the troops awaited. They weren't really troops rather a hodge-podge of concerned citizens angry as all get out with what was going on in their town. Not as angry as Sheriff Grace but simmering like boiling macaroni noodles in a far too small pot. They hung around a cluster of picnic tables, avoiding eye contact with each other. Common interest had brought them together—they wanted to do something about the murders—but they despised each another.

They were like a pride of lions, this bunch. Solitary creatures, giving themselves enough space to mate and sunbathe without interference from the rest of the pride. They bit at each other's ankles, bared their yellow fangs, and lifted legs to mark their territory.

Agatha, proprietor of Agatha's Eats, a popular diner on Main Street, even resembled a lion. Not a lioness, either. She stretched, catlike, and scratched at her mane as the two police officers approached. Through the years, the townspeople of Mio developed an odd affinity for Agatha. She always did well in school, at least when she wasn't cursing someone's eternal soul or singing folk songs. English, history, and cooking were her strongest subjects, but fairy lore had always been her *favorite*.

So what if fairy circles and dribbled candles made her seem witch-like? She made it work, even among all the uber-religious zealots in town.

Despite these distinctions, no one considered the possibility that Agatha might've actually been a witch. Come on, she had the name and everything. She expected the accusations to come any day, but that day never came. Each morning she opened her restaurant, hung a crucifix on the wall, and fired up the grill. Her cowl of mystery, strengthened by true belief, was a powerful tool—a tool she'd use until her dying days.

Sheriff Grace came to a stop and said, "Gentlemen," but a tiny throat cleared in the crowd. "Yes, yes Katt. I was getting there. Gentlemen and ladies. Better?"

"Ahem, times are changing Sheriff. Ladies should be *first.*"

Katt, who owned a small baby store in town—not the kind that sells babies, but the kind that sells things to put on babies—was busy finishing her makeup. A recent addition to the Mio family, relocated from the distant south (Kentucky), she'd been appalled by the fact the only place to buy diapers also sold liquor in brown, glass jugs.

Sheriff Grace ignored her. Katt was good at being a distraction, especially to wound-up, bull-headed men. Well, any men really. Men were easy. But Sheriff Grace was hard.

"Do you all know why I called you here today?"

"Better be good. Too dang hot out 'ere," Jacko, of Jacko's Ice Cream and Cigars (hard to specialize in one thing in such a small town), said as he moved forward in the crowd.

Jacko's sweat pooled through his musty white t-shirt. Spiders of hair stuck out from the wrinkled V-neck. His comb-over stuck to his red forehead, dripping marbles of sweat onto the rest of his face. The smell emanating from him was almost too hard to describe, but rotten potatoes and fossilized feces came close.

"Ahem." Katt cleared her throat. "If only you'd take care of yourself, Jacko. Life's too precious not to treat yourself."

"My dear, you know nothing of 'treating yourself.' A cheap tube of lip gloss and dark eye shadow doesn't make you a lifestyle expert. Not by any means," Charlotte, the town beautician—and beautiful, to boot—said. "Expertise makes you an expert. And just having the knack. It's a gift from God, in my case."

Charlotte stuck out like a pool of blood in a white, padded room. As did the meticulously applied rouge on her pale cheeks. The depths of her sapphire eyes had drowned many a seasoned swimmer over the years. If it weren't her eyes, people got caught in the crimson vines coiled neatly atop her head. Words like blue and red were too of-this-world to describe Charlotte with any justice. She had to be described like the precious gem she was.

"Real profane," Phillip said. He considered himself a masterclass astrologist and ran a small gift shop on the outskirts of town that sold incense, cosmic calendars, and knock-off tarot cards. The internet was his best friend. When questioned about the alignment of the stars or the possibilities of the future, he retreated into his "safe space" to breathe in the enlightening qualities of solitude. The beeps and moans of a dial-up connection could be heard anytime he disappeared behind the curtain. "Your constant wisdom is a blessing to us all."

"Profound," Gus, owner of Gus's Yum-Yum, said. "It's profound, Phillip. Surprised your stars didn't tell you that."

That shut Phillip up for the rest of the book. They never invited him to these kinds of things, but he came anyway to give his two cents. The moment others acknowledged him usually marked his time to butt out. Call him what you will, Phillip knew where he stood in Mio: about as close to the border as possible, while still close enough to keep an eye on things.

Gus, on the other hand, was loved and cherished by all. Other than Agatha's Eats, the Mio Pizza Shoppe, and the McDonald's adjacent to the Dam, he ran the only edible specialty restaurant in town. He even hosted a buffet on Sundays and every other Wednesday. His Chinese food was the best north of the Au Sable River, which put him in direct competition with exactly zero other establishments. Men like Jacko and Tony Dietrich—men of significant mass and stature—frequented his restaurant. They kept the fryers on and the grease a-bubblin', so to speak.

People came to Gus for two things: trans-fat and fortune-cookie advice. In his younger days, he'd lost his wife to heart disease and his small fortune betting on black in the underground of Chicago's Chinatown. So, he was alone in this world. He'd made a few deals with the Devil, ended up in Mio, and appreciated the closeness the people provided. He had no problem giving them the answers they thought they needed. He didn't understand why anyone would come to *him* for advice; but, somehow, it felt like redemption. His proverbs became legend. Proverbs such as:

Confucius says, go to bed with itchy bum, wake up with stinky finger.

We are born alone and die alone. Dress accordingly.

The end is near, and it's all your fault.

Today will be at least a minor improvement on yesterday, but a step down from tomorrow.

Real, sage advice. Things people didn't realize they needed to hear. Wisdom for workers of the modern day. His idioms didn't replace God, but they were sometimes a desperately needed supplement.

The last person at the tables was Richard Schloss. He owned a seedy bar in town. One of those places with a flickering neon Harley Davidson in the window and about a foot of sticky beer spilled on the floors, walls, and even the ceiling. He also chain-smoked hand rolled cigarettes and had a vocabulary consisting entirely of grunts. He'd probably killed a man before (though all the evidence proved circumstantial in a court of law), so murder in small-town Mio was his opportunity to flex his potential.

These were the most powerful people in Mio. The real movers and shakers, though some shook more than the others when they moved. It might've been Sheriff Grace's town, but she pretended to consult them before making big decisions. Whether or not she listened depended on if they agreed with her.

"Where's Mayor Gunderson?" Sheriff Grace asked. Everyone shrugged. "Tony Senior?"

"They don't seem to be here, ma'am," Deputy Lawson said.

"Leave it to a *man* to point out the obvious," Charlotte whispered, glaring at the deputy. "Figure that one out without the Sheriff holding your hand? I'm impressed."

"What's that 'sposed to mean?" Agatha said. She got in the beautician's face and cracked her knuckles as if ready for a fight.

"Well, Katt was right about one thing. She doesn't even realize it, but the world is changing. It's not a man's world anymore. We're starting to see how much better us girls are."

"Oh, sweetie," Agatha said, putting her hand on Charlotte's shoulder. She squeezed a bit too hard for the gesture to be reassuring. "Bless your heart."

Monkeys beat drums around the inside of the sheriff's head. She took her sunglasses off and rubbed her eyes. These meetings were never straightforward. The fact she thought this one would be different, considering the situation, surprised her. She was the butt of some joke and the only person not laughing.

"After hundreds of years of life, you should appreciate the modern woman's plight. We have to stick together," Charlotte said.

"What ya know about feminism, child?"

"I know men are dogs. Give them a bone to chew on and a hydrant to—"

"Serious? You spend ya days dollin' up these sculpted women for men to ogle and parade around. With ya litta brushes and tiny paints. I even saw sparkles in your shop once. Who wants to sparkle when they can shine instead?"

"And *you* spend your days in the kitchen, slaving over hot stoves to cook for those same men. Seems hypocritical to me."

"Hippo nothin'. Least they payin' me for it, while you're takin' the money off these hard-workin' ladies. Damn shame. I built my empire with mine own sweat and blood, sweetie. There's dinnity in that if you ask me. But you? Psh."

The monkeys in the sheriff's head invited their cousins and their cousin's cousins to build tree houses with rubber mallets while they drummed. It was time to get down to business. Every important beginning started with an even more important end. She wanted this to end and for these women to stop yapping.

Before she could, Gus fanned the flames. "I've always thought that woman who seek to be equal to man lacks ambition. Ouch!" This was, in fact, word for word off of one of his most confusing fortunes. Adding "in bed" made it a bit more fun but no clearer.

"What? Feminism hurts now, Gus? Too bad. You're just going to have to deal with it," Charlotte said.

"No. Bee stung me. Dig too deep for the honey and you're bound to get pricked on the finger."

Everyone nodded. Bee stings stung; no one argued the contrary. Once again, sage advice from one of the town's most trusted advisor.

The sheriff's monkeys were building with sledgehammers now and blaring EDM.

"Enough," Sheriff Grace said, slamming her fists on the table in front of her. "I didn't call you here for you to waste my entire afternoon. You'll have to discuss gender inequality another time, far away from me. For now, understand I'm a woman, I'm the sheriff, and I run this town. I think we're doing just fine, *Charlotte*."

"Well said, ma'am," Deputy Lawson said. "Brought down the glass ceiling, you did."

Agatha scoffed. "Careful where you step, lass. Them shards can be sharp."

Sheriff Grace ignored the old woman and walked around the troops in a semicircle. She inspected them, staring dead in their faces and locking eye-contact with each one until she snapped to the next. They stood straighter, zipping their lips and their legs. The deputy followed at her heels, almost tripping over her when she stopped suddenly to address them.

"The Devil's in Mio. He's in her people. In her waters. Sleeping in her beds. Death is in the air, the stink of it is rank. I just can't find the source. We're all scared and pissed off. People are dying, and we can't figure out why. People don't kill without repercussions. Not in my town. Mr. and Mrs. Stillman had lived here all their lives. Longer than any of the rest of us put together, besides maybe Agatha. Looks like you've been here for at least three lifetimes, no offense, Ag."

"None taken, lass. T'ain't too far off, anyhow."

"They practically built the church. They placed the last stones. Mr. Stillman led the UAW and was active with the legion. His wife volunteered at the library on the weekends, started the summer reading program for your children. Dished out soup to the poor in Gaylord over the holidays. They were loyal and charitable. Neither of them ever as much as jaywalked. How were they rewarded?"

"Murder, ma'am."

"Murder is right, Deputy. Thank you, as always, for your insights. It's called a rhetorical question. Now shaddup, would ya?"

He tucked tail and retreated behind big Richard Schloss for safety from the blades of her words.

"Anyway, they were a wonderful couple. Loyal for over fifty years. Never straying from the righteous path of God. Now, they're dead. Murdered, as our helpful deputy pointed out. Along with Dale and Rhonda. Sure, I picked up Dale a few times. The man couldn't handle his whiskey like the rest of us, but they were decent enough folk. At church Sunday mornings. Hard workers. Taken well before their time and no one has a damn clue what happened or who dunnit."

"Ahem, what about Mr. Cross?" Katt said, barely audible.

"Speak up, woman. What about him?" Jealousy boiled within the sheriff.

Katt stepped forward, shuffling her feet in the dirt. When she realized everyone was glaring at her, she attempted to make herself look big by puffing out her chest and pulling back her shoulders. Compared to Sheriff Grace, she was a grain of sand. Baby retail she understood. Powerful women, not so much.

"The detective, Sheriff. Surely, he's figured out something by now. Bad driver, but he seems nice. Why isn't he here? Couldn't an outside perspective help?"

Sheriff Grace laughed. It echoed off the surface of Rifle River then back at the troops, louder than a gunshot. It was a guttural and maniacal kind of laughter, inspired in part by the absurdity of everything and by her exhaustion. If it wasn't for a picnic table to hold on to, her laughter would have brought her to her knees.

Deputy Lawson laughed, too. It was forced and uncomfortable.

One by one, the others joined in with obligatory titters. No one understood what was happening.

"You're hysterical, lass."

"Should have seen her on the drive here," the deputy muttered, retreating behind Richard Schloss again. He couldn't make himself small enough, even behind the muscular hulk of the bartender.

Sheriff Grace composed herself. She wiped tears from her cheeks and ignored the stitch in her side. God knew how much she needed that. Without wasting another second, she said, "I'm not hysterical. I'm pissed off to hell and back. I don't know about y'all, but I won't stand for it anymore. Burning down the station—my home—was the last damn straw. This town is sick. Does anyone know the best cure? Anyone?"

Gus stepped forward. "The greatest medicine is the emptiness of everything."

"Excuse me?"

"You're excused, Sheriff," Gus said.

She stared at the man for a long time, making two decisions: whether the little man was worthy of a response and whether Gus had brought Kung Fu with him from the big city. She sized him up, considering if a swift punch to the throat would be enough. Her fingers drummed her billy club. In the end, a fight with Gus would be counterproductive, compounding the violence problem sweeping through Mio. Besides, he fried up one helluva delicious Crab Rangoon.

"The only emptiness this week has been filled with, *Gus*, is answers. These are acts of war. We need to retaliate and fight fire with hotter fire. We can raise a white flag, roll over on our backs, and hope Chase Cross possesses a fiber of competence. Or we can fight back. What do you all say?"

"Ahem, Mio is a peaceful place."

"No one can buy ice cream if they're dead or strung up in a hospital bed. Broken bones and bleedin' and stuff. I've got a family to feed," Jacko said.

"You live alone," Charlotte pointed out.

"I've got a *me* to feed, either way. And my cats."

"Y'all can go on being peaceful, for all I care, while whoever is terrorizing us laughs at your cold corpses," Sheriff Grace said. There was a collective gasp, as if she'd gone too far, followed by a murmur of agreement. *I finally have their attention.* "Makes no difference to me. You're just an ice cream man. And you, Katt, sell baby clothes. I'm lactose intolerant and menopausal, so no extra skin off my back if someone else dies while you're busy doing nothing."

She waited for a response, but none came.

The deputy crawled out from behind Richard Schloss and puffed out his chest. His boss was right, and he knew it.

Katt had even forgotten about the detective. It was best she kept him out of her mind, for her sake.

The sheriff continued. "Ask the Stillmans. Ask Dale. Ask Rhonda. Is Mio still a peaceful place? Are they going to tell you who killed them while *they* were busy being peaceful? What do you think they'd say—"

"Ahem, I was just thinking—"

"We don't have time for your thinking, Katt. We might not have time to act before someone else gets hurt. They burned down my station, God dammit. I'm going to war, people."

***

She could no longer wait. They were getting rowdy. The borders between their realm and hers were broken. Something had to be done, but what?

I'll write a strongly worded letter, *she thought. That'd really show 'em. That'd tell them she knew what they were doing down there and, hopefully, they'd sort of knock it off on their own. If not, she'd have to dress for a personal appearance. That sounded like* work. *She hated* work.

Besides, the letter would be to her, wouldn't it? How productive could that be?[3]

***

There was a lot of grumbling among the group, but no one dared defy the sheriff anymore. They weren't brave enough. Her fingers were still drumming on her billy club, and they all saw her revolver teetering nearby. Despite their reservations, something had to give (and we're not talking about giving thanks).

She motioned to the deputy, a subtle nod he understood. Without a moment's hesitation, he ran off towards the squad car.

Everyone waited until he returned, shuffling their feet and looking everywhere besides at each other. Sheriff Grace paced, digging the beginnings of a trench in the damp, sandy soil beneath her feet. She fidgeted with her sunglasses, putting them on, taking them off again, and biting the ends. All the arguing and moaning was bringing her plan's momentum to a grinding halt. Meanwhile, a killer and potential arsonist walked free. A man—or, a woman, according to the oh-so-forward thinking of Charlotte and Katt—could be busy plotting their next insidious move in some damp basement.

Deputy Lawson hustled to the picnic tables with a black duffle bag slung over his shoulder, the clamor of metal against metal emphasizing each stride. He dropped the bag in the dirt, sending up a cloud of dust. Katt cleared her throat and forced a cough. Grinning at the sheriff, he unzipped the bag to reveal its contents. They all gasped, except Richard Schloss who grunted his satisfaction.

"Everyone grab a gun," the sheriff said.

---

[3] More productive than 99.9% of government offices. Less red tape, no waiting on hold for hours on end, and no stone-faced receptionist with weak knees and IBS.

One by one, they approached the bag and reached in. There was no pushing, no shoving, and no hesitation. Only solemnity.

When Charlotte's turn came, she said, "You can't be serious. I'm a lady. Ladies don't participate in such barbarism. Can you imagine? I have my 'dinnity' to think of." She glanced behind her at Agatha as she said this. One look from Sheriff Grace, though, and she shut up, grabbing the last rifle from the duffle bag before stepping to the side. She held it out in front of her with dainty, uncertain fingers. "Not bad. Not bad at all."

This left the most eager of the bunch, Agatha, weaponless. She was the only person there, besides the two police officers and Richard Schloss, who even knew how to handle a firearm. She hung her head as she peered into the empty bag.

"We seem to be one short, ma'am."

"Did you clear out the shed?" The deputy shrugged. "Well, we'll go back into town and grab the rest. We need to find Gunderson and Dietrich, anyways."

But Agatha had something else in mind. She walked towards Rifle River with a hop in her step. She concentrated on every minute ripple, every bend of the bank in front of her. A fish bobbed its head out every few seconds, curious as to what the hairy, old woman was planning. She paid them no mind, waiting instead for the perfect moment. She crouched and continued to scan the surface of the river. When she spotted her prize, she leaped headfirst into the water and disappeared. By the time the deputy got there to pull her out, Agatha had sprung out of the water with a scoped Winchester between her teeth.

"S'all right, everyone. Got me one here. Bit soggy but it'll do just fine. Do that rotten sumbitch killer much worse, I 'spect."

"What a woman," Gus said.

The troops clapped for her triumph, bowing to the sheer excellence of her discovery. Even the sheriff applauded the old woman's tenacity. They were all armed and fired up, besides Charlotte. Her gun lay dormant on a picnic table as she reapplied crimson lipstick—her own form of war paint.

"Okay," Sheriff Grace said once everyone calmed down. "This is the plan."

She told them the plan that wasn't quite a plan, but they listened intently. Everyone accepted their role in the production to come. There would be a lot of winging it, and it—whatever that entailed—might not work. But they had to do something. Mio deserved as much.

Chapter 20:

That's a Convoy, Huh?

A convoy of rusty trucks, green Astrovans, a Toyota Prius, and what looked like an old woman on a broom—which, of course, wasn't possible—whirred by. Repugnant Rachel had been walking a long, long time and, since Detroit, the road had put her through a lot of hardship. The fact that she was walking and breathing at all was an inexplicable miracle. Or, in her case, a tragic curse.

She'd fallen from the rafters in a train station, bled herself dry with broken glass, been hit by at least three vehicles, suffered a vicious attack by a small bear in her sleep, and was stung by a swarm of bees. All of them. The whole swarm. She'd be pulling stingers out for the rest of her life, which might last forever after all the deaths she'd already lived through over the past few days.

Rachel was no closer to her final destination. No wonder her mind was playing tricks on her.

But, wasn't that a cackle? That had to have been a cackle...

She shrugged, took a deep breath, and kept on her way.

Chapter 21:

Desperate Sisters

Back in the place beyond place, Naomi addressed her sisters. She should apologize to them for reprimanding their failures, but apology was akin to weakness. She'd apologize when she was dead.

"Due to circumstances beyond our control, we can no longer fulfill our duties," she said. Somewhere an adult pretending to be a kid giggled. "Matters will have to work themselves out."

Amelia and Lily pouted. They were self-aware, understanding their ultimate shortcomings. When sexuality failed to do anything other than slow the inevitable, poison had been a promising alternative. Poison was, according to the ignorant, the woman's weapon. It was sloppy, low-brow, and below the twin's standards, but it would have gotten the job done. It would have stopped Chase Cross from continuing down a path that led to complications for their master. Everything was sorted, then *she* had appeared.

Eisa, who still hadn't recovered from her prior reaming, and who was much less self-aware and unwilling to admit defeat, groaned. "*He's* been on Earth for quite a while now. That's gotta count for something, right?"

"Ah, wise and true. Wise and true. His grip on Hell is weakening—fact. But it's still under his domain. Confidence, sisters. Confidence and time. Though, I worry it won't be enough. I may have to meddle."

They embraced each other.

Though Naomi possessed enough confidence for them all, she couldn't help but fear the consequences of failure coming full circle. Not fulfilling their obligations to their master would mean a swift, permanent end to her unholy immortality. That was something she wasn't willing to accept.

Her talents were more elegant than her sisters', much subtler.

She grabbed a dusty mason jar out of thin air. It was labeled "Stan"—a cute nickname, to be sure—and red vapors swirled around inside of it. She twisted the outer ring and popped the lid off. She inhaled through her nose, bringing tendrils of vapor towards her, and exhaled them to the bottom of the jar. They spread out like winter across an empty field.

"Are you sure?" Eisa asked.

Lily and Amelia gathered around her, eyes wider than black holes.

"It's the only thing left." But she knew how inherently dangerous meddling was.

Naomi plucked tweezers out of the aether with her free hand, stuck them into her ear, and plucked a microscopic chunk of her Broca's area. She flinched but pulled it out without as much as a tear. She held the gray matter over the open jar, a wicked smile drawn across her face. Then, she dropped it in.

"Men are prone to slips of the tongue. This should send our buddy 'Stan' right out of his mind."

A *mwahaha* session ensued, followed by lots of scandalous dancing around the cauldron, some serious shrieking, and copious amounts of mead consumption. For all intents and purposes, their work was finished; it was time for the sisters to celebrate.

Chapter 22:

Detective Cross Drops the Quotation Marks

Chase Cross stepped out of the hospital and into the light. The difference between the artificial fluorescents inside and the full glory of the afternoon sun stunned him long enough for the door to hit his ass on the way out. Again. He blinked away the blinding whiteness from the edges of his vision. After the door shut, leaving the chaos behind him, he forgot all thoughts of Serena, leaving room for only Sheriff Grace. Stretching out the stiffness in his legs reminded him of the pain of his bruised rib cage, but he had no time to dawdle.

The nurse had pointed him in the right direction: out the front door, down the hill, and far, far away from her. The subterfuge of her unsolicited help was lost on him. He appreciated the kind gesture, and that was enough. Besides the killer and the kids, the town of Mio was treating him rather well. Sure, Sheriff Grace liked to give him a hard time, but hazing was expected from a colleague.

Everyone was ecstatic to see him go. As soon as the "detective" disappeared, they jumped with joy, patted each other's backs, and embraced. The only person sad to see him go was the lawyer, Serena, who watched him walk away until she lost him around the bend.

He took it slow. The effects of the pain medication lingered, and the afternoon heat was stifling. Huffing and puffing with each step, he trudged on towards the heart of town and recapped the last few days.

It started Sunday morning. Mass had let out and the people of Mio stood aghast outside of the church. Someone murdered the town's oldest couple and draped them over the top of the Our Lady of the Woods shrine.

Unaware of the whole ordeal, something had called to Chase, telling him he was needed. Who was he to interfere with divine intervention?

The drive had been long, his eyes grew droopy, his blood sugar low, so he pulled up as close to the crime scene as possible. It seemed like a good idea at the time. Weariness got the best of him, he hit the gas instead of the brakes, and got a little too close.

Nobody seemed to sympathize with *his* struggle. They were too busy worrying about their precious shrine.

He didn't *have* to come. He didn't *have* to answer the summons to help. He didn't *have* to care, but he did. Caring for others was part of who he was, especially when "others" were curvaceous women like the sheriff.

A voice had whispered to him. He ignored it at first until it spoke louder. He drowned it out again by turning up the radio. God stepped in, short circuited his entire entertainment deck, and made damn sure he was listening. She told him to go north. To some town called Silo or Mile or Milo... She'd seemed distracted, and the crackling static of the radio made it difficult to focus.

Mio, it turned out—*my-oh*—a small town that was changing his life.

His escape from his mother had him trapped in a bedbug-infested motel with an emptying wallet. He'd drive north, if only to break the monotony of existence.

One minute he was miserable, living with his mother in an apartment in Minneapolis. The next minute, alone and wasting away, trapped in the bottom of a bottle of whiskey in some flea-ridden nightmare of a town on the border of Illinois and Indiana. Then, he found himself locked in a broom closet converted into a jail cell, arguing with the sheriff of Mio.

Life was sometimes weird in its unpredictability; that made the whole ordeal worthwhile.

Sheriff Grace wasn't everybody's cup of tea, but she loved her town and would do anything to protect it. At first, that included locking him up. It was understandable. He'd made her look weak in front of the entire town, driving up like he did, undermining her authority. But she let him go, along with his new friend Bob. The simple act of swallowing her pride and releasing him proved her dedication to Mio (and gave him a glimmer of hope).

Oh well. There wasn't any point dwelling on any of it anymore. There was still too much work to do.

Chase came to a bend in the road at the bottom of the hill. The entire two blocks of the town unrolled as he rounded it. A group of children hung out under the bridge across the Au Sable River, skipping stones and smoking wacky tobacky, as his grandmother used to call it. Closer to the dam, their fathers cast out line after line. They never caught anything; they simply took pleasure in the act. They found comfort in having no expectations. Besides, their kids and wives didn't take them seriously so why should the fish?

A group of tourists from one of those places nearby—like Toledo—prepared to launch from the far side of the river. They each sat in the mouths of large tubes, holding hands, and drinking beers, unaware of the plight of the local fishermen. One of them, a tan, muscular man in his early twenties, wore a backwards baseball cap. On the brim of it rested a pair of sunglasses. As they kicked off the bank, he used his hand to shield his eyes from the sun instead. There were fist bumps and high fives all around, accompanied by an unnecessary number of "sup, bros" before they disappeared down the river.

When both groups were out of sight, Chase retreated inward to figure out his game plan. He didn't like games, probably because no one ever played them with him, but he wasn't playing anymore.

The Stillmans. Dale and Rhonda, who Serena had mentioned in passing. The fire. Something stunk in the town of Mio, and it wasn't the 80,000 gallons of sewage draining into the river.

He had been sidetracked too often. First, by the short stay in jail. Then, by Tony Junior and his punk friends. Finally, by an endless supply of pudding and the company of a beautiful stranger. From what he'd seen so far, Mio was not the kind of town where people mysteriously croaked or police stations spontaneously caught fire. In fact, Mio wasn't the kind of town where much happened at all.

Before he hit the road, Serena broke down the who's who of Mio.

There was Sheriff Grace. He knew her well enough already and planned to find her as soon as possible. She could help answer some questions, both those related to the case and others off-record.

And Mayor Gunderson, too. Serena warned that he would be hard to get in touch with. If he wasn't at nearby Garland Golf Resort, playing through the back nine, he might be floating down the river with a visiting sorority or soaking in his private Jacuzzi. When anyone attempted to question him on what the town paid him to do, he urged them to take it up with his secretary. Months of asking around would lead to the inevitable conclusion that he didn't have a secretary. By that time, Mayor Gunderson would be on a plane, first-class, heading to Hawaii for his semi-annual vacation or skiing the slopes of the Upper Peninsula.

Chase weighed the pros and cons of trying to contact the mayor. The scales teetered in his mind until they broke. A meeting with the mayor wasn't worth the effort. Besides, what kind of man interrupted another man while he was vacationing?

Now on Main Street, his stomach started gurgling. He realized he hadn't eaten for at least an hour or two. It had been even longer since he'd had a drink. Coincidentally, he was standing outside the bowling alley. He could pop in, scarf a burger, polish a fifth, and be back on the case before nightfall. Life was too short to rush, anyway.

Further down the road, Mio's only fire truck idled as the crew finished cleaning. They carried load after load of burnt wood and melted glass to a dumpster nearby. The station was ash, and the courthouse looked like something scaly with wings took a fiery bite out of it.

Seeing the damage, Chase Cross made a big decision—one of those life changing, character-defining decisions out of the stories he read. A hero had a choice: the right path or the left. To the right, an eternal cycle of disappointment and mediocrity. To the left, fulfillment of some deeply engrained desire—a dragon to fight, hoarded treasure to discover. This type of decision changed the course of the world. It was his great epiphany; his moment of divine clarity.

He made this choice with ease.

I'll wait until four o'clock to start drinking. Now just isn't the right time. A half hour would give him at least enough time to investigate the fire.

So, he moved on. Half a block later he came to Charlotte's Beauty Salon, a place Serena told him to go for answers.

"Real clever, Charlotte." He rolled his eyes.

These places usually tried too hard with names like Cutting Edge or Dying for Color or, his personal favorite, Curl Up and Dye (the only time the act of dying wasn't permanent). He appreciated the simplicity of Charlotte's Beauty Salon, even if it was phoning it in a bit. There was name recognition, and no one could mistake the shop's purpose.

Charlotte was a strong, feminine voice for the town of Mio. Little girls idolized her for her good looks and her success. Their mothers and aunts paid away their life savings for a few hours of artificial beauty, all expecting to take away some part of the woman with them. Anybody with that much power had sway over the masses. Also, he remembered from the movies, salons were the place to go for the juiciest gossip.

A life-sized poster of a redheaded JC Penny's goddess, peeling away at the edges, stared down at him. After saluting the ginger, he walked in. A young blonde woman greeted him at the counter. She wore a white button-down, of which she unbuttoned the top two buttons when she saw him looking in the shop. Her jean shorts were barely long enough to be a blindfold.

"Can I help you?" She looked him up and down. "Ew…I mean, er…no, thanks."

"What's your name, young lady?"

"Uh, Geneva."

"Well, Uh Geneva…lots of weird names around here, huh? Anyhow, I'd like to strike an accord with you, if you don't mind."

She twirled her hair, mouth slightly open. "Gross. I drive a Corolla. Better gas mileage. You need a haircut or what?"

He filled her in on the situation and offered to pay the price of a haircut if she would get Charlotte for him. Ensuring her it was of the utmost importance and urgency, he told her it was a small price to pay for the security of the town. He couldn't help her if she didn't help him. Besides, what type of detective would he be if he didn't buy the people's information from them? Certainly not the kind he wanted to be. Not even close.

After his long-winded explanation, Geneva took his money and said, "Sure talk a lot, don't ya? Charlotte's out. Won't be back until later."

"Any idea where she is or when she'll be back?"

Geneva held the twenty out in front of her, admiring Jackson's flowing locks and chiseled jaw. She'd almost never seen a twenty-dollar bill before and was already planning what to do with it. Chase tried to snatch it, but she pulled it away too fast.

"Thanks for the cash. Gonna tip me or what?"

"Dammit, woman. Of course, I'm not going to tip you. I demand you return my—" Before he finished, she turned and walked away from him, disappearing into the back room.

He left.

As soon as the door closed behind him, she reappeared; he stood there transfixed, appraising her through the window. The depth of her eyes, the curve of her thighs… She was almost too much to handle. She winked. He bit his lip, thinking about the prospects of a do over with such a beautiful woman.

Suddenly, where Geneva had been standing, playing with her hair, Sheriff Grace was leaning against the counter polishing her revolver. She pulled her sunglasses to the tip of her nose and there was menace in her eyes. He heard her voice saying, "You better just go, 'Detective.' There's work to do. Besides, you can do better than this hussy."

"Right. Of course."

Inside, Geneva raised an eyebrow and mouthed *what* at him, annoyed he was sticking around for so long. She made a move towards the front door, but Chase Cross was gone. That's when she surprised herself, finding herself fawning over the man—despite his fatness and general want-to-slap-repeatedly demeanor. With an opportunity missed, she returned to the other side of the counter and called her ex-boyfriend.

Chase's friend from the hospital had given him a few other names, too.

Some creepy ice cream man, who sounded more like a pumpkin than a person.

A feline who opened a baby retail store; impressive, considering the usual brainwaves of cats focused on eating, swatting mice, and knocking things off counters. Besides, who'd let a cat run a cash register? Everyone knew they couldn't be trusted with money.

There was another named Big Dick Schloss. He didn't want to go there for obvious reasons and one not so obvious: the man owned a bar, and it wasn't four o'clock yet.

He realized most of the places were behind him. His hunger moved his feet, and he passed without as much as a glance. Even though he was holding off on adult beverages, he told himself a man's gotta eat to keep his mind sharp. As fate would have it, the Mio Pizza Shoppe happened to be next door to the salon.

On his initial drive into Mio, Pinky the Elephant—a name he'd given the statue because, let's face it, it was such an obvious moniker—stood out among the other eccentricities of the town. It donned 1970s-carhops-and-poodle-skirts pink and stood tall for tourists and residents alike. Chase admired Pinky; the elephant knew its purpose and executed its duties with unwavering devotion.

Today, the most noticeable eccentricity in Mio was the missing statue. An elephant-sized depression in the grass was all that remained of Mio's vigilant watchman. Circular tracks led away from the spot, heading towards the street before disappearing. Bits and pieces of chipped paint littered the ground in an oval where Pinky once stood, as if he'd shaken himself off after a dip in the watering hole before scurrying down the road.

"Peculiar," Chase said aloud, before shrugging it off and entering the restaurant. A chime announced his presence to the best pizza chef in town.

"Welcome," the pizza chef said. "What can I get ya? Can I suggest the pizza?"

"Where's Pinky?" Chase asked.

"Pinky?" The man looked confused. "Right here, bub."

"The elephant? Big statue, used to be out front? I think I'd notice if it was still there."

"Ah, you mean Leroy."

He opened a steel trap on the side of the oven behind him. He grabbed an enormous pizza peel from a hook on the wall and used it to remove an even more enormous pizza. Chase's mouth watered as he followed the rivulets of pepperoni grease from one disk to the next. Veins of mozzarella and cheddar pulsed and settled.

Stay resolute to your cause, Chase reminded himself.

"What you know about Leroy?" the pizza chef asked.

"Nothing much. Where'd he go, by the way?"

The pizza chef grunted. "Can I get ya something? Slice of me specialty? Somethin' ter drink?"

Chase was hungry, but his need for information outweighed his hunger. He'd press the chef for more information and then celebrate his work with a slice or ten. "What's your name, guy?"

"Pinky. I told ya already."

"Pinky? But—"

"Did I stutter? Look, I'm a busy man. Sure you are, too. Those damn kids came around here the other night, stole Leroy right from under me paddle," Pinky said, as he cut the fresh pie into twelve symmetric slices. He scooped up the largest and flopped it down onto a plate for Chase. "Hot peppers? Parm-a-Sean?"

"Who's Sean?" Chase shook his head, though. Apparently, he was eating whether he wanted to or not. He dug in without waiting for his meal to cool. "So, what makes you think…oh good lord, that's delicious."

"I know it." Pinky beamed.

"Anyhow, what makes you think it was 'those damn kids?' What kind of kids do you people produce in this town? Strong enough to take that thing away…"

Pinky slammed his fists on the counter. The impact almost knocked the pizza clear off the plate, but Chase snatched it out of midair. He'd hate to waste such a sublime piece of pie.

Pinky's neck veins twitched. "Leroy is not a 'thing.' He's a member of the family, and you best not forget it. And it was just them damn kids. Doesn't matter which ones, does it? Isn't it always them damn kids?"

Chase half-heard Pinky. He was busy picking strings of melted cheese out of his beard and shoving them into his mouth. When he was done, most of the cheese was woven into his thick beard hairs, but it was the effort that counted.

In his mind's eye, hazy as it was as he focused on each bite, Chase envisioned the crime scene. He pictured a group of teenagers, led by Tony Junior, roping Pinky and dragging it onto a giant wagon or a series of skateboards strung together. In this mind's eye, the effort took them hours. The chances of nobody having caught them was slight to zilch and—as crazy as it seemed—there were elephant-like tracks leading away. Nothing seemed broken, either. Kids tended to break stuff. It was the modus operandi of even the most docile of teenagers.

"How big are the kids in town? Is it easy for them to get their hands on steroids?" Chase asked, holding his plate out for another slice.

"The hell kinda questions are those? We're a good Christian town, not some pagan, giant-raising, needle-stickin' town. How dare you come in here, eat my food, and insult our children. Only Jay-sus can judge them kids. I oughta—"

"Slow down, big guy. I didn't mean any offense. I'm a detective, you see."

But Pinky didn't see. He grabbed the peel from the wall again and scrambled towards the dining area of the restaurant.

Some people felt they have a right to judge and chastise their neighbors, but as soon as an outsider did the same, they lost it and acted like you were a complete monster. Like a bully marking his territory, giving poor little Nelson swirlies and wedgies daily. If someone else took a turn, they got their nose bloodied. About as reasonable as hot soup on a summer day.

Chase fumbled in his pockets for some money, threw it on the counter, and ran out of the restaurant. He was out of breath by the time he got to the door.

The missing statue perplexed him, but he had bigger fish to fry. Also, the prospect of getting paddled by a man bigger than him, an impressive feat in itself—though clearly not uncommon in Mio—was not high on his bucket list. He had to focus on one mystery at a time.

Speaking of mysteries, he found himself at the site of the former Mio Police Station, now Mio Rubble Pile. Officers, firefighters, and common citizens stood around the grounds, exhausted and covered in soot. It seemed to Chase they were too busy cracking jokes and drinking coffee to be worn out; but, then again, he was worn out from running ten feet.

Maybe Leroy was right. He shouldn't judge the people of Mio too harshly.

He surveyed the scene. Chase Cross was no expert, but one thing was obvious. There had been a fire. And recently. Scorch marks and wisps of smoke wafting from the blackened pile of debris gave it away. Where he'd once spent the night, there was only desolation. But none of this told him anything new.

He noticed his car parking among a row of police cars, boot and all. Other than the boot, and the depression from where he hit the shrine, it seemed unscathed. It must have gotten towed during the night, and Sheriff Grace must have taken it upon herself to rescue it from the chop shop— out of love, of course. There was no other possible explanation.

Sheriff Grace and Deputy Lawson were nowhere to be found. Not that he necessarily wanted to find them. They had locked him in a cell, called him fat, and embarrassed him in front of his new clients, but they would be familiar faces. Someone to give him a rundown of the damages and how the fire really got started.

Instead, he approached the nearest relief worker, a police officer whose badge showed yet another weird Mio name. "Excuse me, Officer... Wɪʃəs?"

"Oh," the man said, moving aside. "Pardon me. It's Officer Miles, by the way."

Chase brought his palm to his face. "Your tag's upside down then. Anyway, I have a question for you. I need your help." The officer tilted his head. "You *are* a cop, right?"

Officer Miles's face trembled like his head might pop from too many neurological processes. Sweat beaded on his forehead and around his neck. His face relaxed and he feigned composure for the sake of duty.

"I am, indeed, sir." Chase made the *ding* of an oven timer to celebrate. "Thank you for the question. Now, if you'll excuse *me*, I still have a lot of cleaning up to do."

Chase growled. Miles stepped back. No one had ever growled at him before. Well, at least not a fat, hirsute—he learned that word from a book he read once—man wearing a hospital bracelet. He wondered if Mio had a mental hospital and if they made a habit of letting their patients out for unsupervised strolls.

He was a child the last time he'd been growled at. The incident stuck out as a life-defining moment. He'd named the raccoon Ned, and Ned always seemed to have toothpaste caked around his mouth. Miles wondered who was brushing its teeth, thought that very nice of them indeed, and decided to take more time to care for others. Hence, joining the force.

When he went to help the big fellow clean up, Ned bit him on the hand between his thumb and his pointer finger. He tried again, and Ned bit him on the wrist. Then on the cheek when he leaned forward to calm the creature. Always resolute, Miles thought about giving it one more go, realized he was feeling faint, and passed out instead. Waking up alone and scared in a hospital bed was a lesson he wouldn't soon forget.

"Sir, I have grounds to believe you might have—" He paused and choked back a tear for poor old Ned, who they had to euthanize. "You might have Rabbis. If you'll just come with—"

"Impossible. I'm an atheist."

"Right. What I mean to say is… you might have Rebiss."

Chase brought his palm to his face, harder this time. "Just call me Cathy Lee, then."

"Sir, this hospitality is just a sympthumb of your disease. If you'd just come with me, I'll get you the help you need. The veterinarian clinic is just around the—"

"Good God, man. Are you having a stroke? I need to know what happened here. Jesus Christ." *How can I help you, Child?* Chase looked around and then at Miles. The voice didn't sound like the officer's, but no one else was around. "Didn't I just tell you how you can help? Cripes. I need to know what's going on. I'm a detective."

Officer Miles shrugged. He couldn't figure out why this man insisted on repeating himself. Maybe delirium from his infection. Sometimes a police officer had to make the tough decision and detain a citizen for his or her own good.

As he reached for his handcuffs, he said, "This is for your own good, sir."

When Miles reached for Chase to cuff him, he was unpleasantly surprised by how fast the man could move. Chase undercut his wrists, knocking the cuffs to the ground, and spun him around a hundred and eighty degrees. It all happened in one fluid, blurry motion. Miles was locked in a half-nelson. Despite his athletic prowess, he was trapped.

Out of breath, Chase said, "Station wagon...Fire...answers." He imitated driving a car and the rise of flames with his free hand as he spoke. It was clear he had to talk slowly and deliberately in order to get through to Miles.

"Oh, why didn't you say so?" the officer said. Chase loosened his grip, releasing the man. "The sheriff found the vehicle last night parked in front of—or rather, on—a fire hydrant. Seemed happy about it, too. Said, 'I'll deal with that bastard once and for all.' Kind of harsh, but hey, I'm happy whenever the sheriff's happy. She doesn't yell at me as much."

"And the fire?"

"Definitely arson. Just can't figure out how it started. We've been investigating all morning."

Blown away Officer Miles's sudden articulation, Chase bowed and turned to walk away. He stopped and turned back. As a child, he liked getting rewards for good behavior. A chocolate bar here. An extra soda with dinner there. Little treats, to tell him he was doing the right thing. Even a simple gold star did the trick.

He turned back to Officer Miles. "Remind me to buy you a beer when this is over."

"Ooooo, Sheriff Grace doesn't let me try beers. I'll definitely hold you to that."

"Smart move, Sheriff," Chase mumbled.

"What was that?"

"I said, 'Thank you, Officer.' See ya later."

Chase tipped an imaginary hat to Officer Miles and left the man alone to revel in the pride of police work done well.

It really had been a good day. After the fire and losing the donuts, Miles' confidence had been at an all-time low—which was still much higher than most people's—but this small victory helped bring back his normal, high-spirited demeanor. Sometimes small victories were important; they got people through the day.

After inspecting his car, which including tugging on the boot with all his strength and kicking it, plus taking careful inventory of all the empty bottles and cheeseburger wrappers through a filthy window, Chase crossed the parking lot to investigate the former Mio Police Station, now Mio Rubble Pile.

He circled it once. He circled it twice. With all the effort, he winded himself and became quite sweaty. If Sheriff Grace showed up, he'd use the excuse that the rubble pile was still emanating a great deal of heat. Sure, he sweat as much as a normal person, but the extreme amount pouring from his face was due to the intense temperature. She'd have to buy that excuse, and hopefully she wouldn't think he was some sort of disgusting slob.

Why was he concerned about the sheriff? Why was she on his mind? *She's only a woman...* A tall, dark, and handsome woman. A curvaceous and powerful woman, with a sweet-scented air of authority about her. A woman with eyes like supernovas. But a woman, nonetheless.

His thoughts were clouding his ability to do his job. The worst part was he knew his feelings about Sheriff Grace weren't simply intimidation or admiration for a colleague. His heart fluttered when he thought about her, and this realization made his stomach churn.

Exhausted from walking and afraid he might be sick, he knelt sometime during his third circle around the building's ashes. He looked out across the lawn towards the courthouse. The shed he noticed Sunday morning stuck out. Its doors were wide-open and its contents all but empty. Who had the guns, and the dangers they represented, depended on who else knew about the cache.

But who were they fighting? No one knew who burned the station down or who murdered those innocent people. Chase was worried Sheriff Grace might extract vengeance on the wrong person, and there was nothing he could do to stop her. No information he could provide to persuade her otherwise.

That's when he saw it, camouflaged against the blackened pile of drywall and splinters, half-buried under a section of a melted microwave, staring him dead in his stupid face. Anger boiled inside him. Here was a million and one chance for anyone but a detective. And not just any detective, Detective Chase Cross. It was a straw of hay in a needle stack.

There—on the ground, clear as day—was the black, wetted butt of a clove cigarette. The same kind he'd seen up close and personal a couple nights before.

"Viola," he said with a flourish.

"Don't you mean voila?" Deputy Miles asked.

"Oh, sure, you get *that* one right…"

Chapter 23:

A Beginning and an End

The Devil stared Death in the face. Death stared back. An eternity of happiness passed between them—sucking much of the world's happiness dry along with it—before they released it back unto the universe.

She kissed him on the cheek. His skin tingled where her lips had been, but the sensation brought him pleasure instead of pain. It made him feel *alive* for the first time since he'd thrown down his sword and cast aside his angel's wings. The fall from heaven, through the center of the universe, and straight onto the throne of Hell had been exhilarating, no denying. There was nothing like free falling through a million stars and stirring them into a frenzy as you shed your former self, feather-by-feather. All the while, the weight of eons of guilt peeled right off, freeing your soul from its last fears of God.

But this was better. Stan needed this.

Of course, God wanted to stop it, to stem the apocalypse and all that nonsense, but it would take more than omnipotence and an all-seeing eye to stop him from getting laid. It was *finally* happening, and it was going to be epic.

The Devil sat up, poured himself another glass of wine, and drank without wasting time to taste the sweet nectar. He was nervous, almost shaking. *Satan doesn't get nervous. Nerves are for puny humans. Satan gets it done*, he thought and poured himself more wine. "You're the man," he whispered.

"What's wrong, dear?" Anaya—Death—asked, pressing her warm body against his. She rubbed her fingers through the curly-q's on his chest as it expanded and contracted. She made her way down to the fire of his loins. She stopped below his waist. "Oh, I see."

How embarrassing. After all the setbacks and distractions, he hoped at least *this* part would go on without a hitch. He was the Prince of Darkness. Princes were suave, debonair, ferocious in bed, irresistible to women. Not impotent, God dammit.

Oddly, the image of God helped a bit. He pictured the night he met Death at the Heaven and Hell Convention. The two caught eyes, but he hadn't been seeking hers. Behind her, mingling with Zeus, God glowed in her low-cut dress of silver and gold. He'd meant to attract *her* attention. He *longed* for it.

He'd never tell that part to his wife. Death didn't operate under personal vendetta, but he didn't want to test her morals. Besides, she was almost as beautiful, and everything worked itself out in the end. When you were meant to ride a unicorn but found yourself riding a pale horse instead, it wasn't wise to complain. You could, after all, be riding an ass.

When she felt his hardness, Death squealed. "Well, hello there," she said, tightening her grip and clenching her jaw.

***

Somewhere far away, otherworldly and worlds apart, God felt a strange sensation start in her toes, snaking to her fingertips. God took coffee with her chaos and tea with her serenity. She was currently enjoying an afternoon tea.[1] Too soon, her serenity would be gone.

She had a tersely worded letter to compose. She couldn't put it off any longer.

---

[1] It's always afternoon in Heaven, somewhere between the rush of morning obligations and the disappointment of nighttime shortcomings.

God found herself compelled into reciting words she hadn't spoken in centuries. They bellowed from her mouth, hot like a breath held in for far too long. She said them to no one in particular but to everyone at the same time. Somehow, they didn't sound right to her. They were skewed, hijacked. They were a bad fanfiction of a book ghostwritten in the 6th Century: her book.

"I stretch out mine hand upon thine waters of Mio and beyond, upon thine streams, upon thine rivers, and upon thine lakes, that thine nourishment may become booze instead, leaving you drunk and lazy." Startled, she sat back in her throne and scratched her head. "No, that doesn't seem right."

But it had been said. And it *was*.

***

On Earth, taking a day's rest from a hard moment's work, Willy the Groundskeeper propped his red wheelbarrow against the shed. He clapped the dirt from his hands as he walked to a bench facing the shrine. His water bottle sat beside him, filled this morning from his own faucet. He drank to quench his thirst, but before swallowing it all down, he spat most of it on the grass. The vodka within warmed his belly and stung his nostrils.

"Odd," he said, sniffing the contents. It was without a doubt vodka—and not the cheap stuff. He was twenty years sober, blaming his alcoholism for losing his family and for finding God. He shrugged and started drinking. "Guess I won't be helpful to these folks, after all."

A few blocks away, somewhere on Main Street, the sound of sirens wailed for the second time in twelve hours. Tires screeched and someone yelled. The ruckus was drowned out by twisting metal and blaring horns.

People staggered about the streets like zombies, not hungering for brains, rather hungering for some late afternoon Taco Bell delight.

Anaya, standing with her husband, loosened her belt buckle. She pulled her shirt over her head as they both hit the floor with a clatter. Laying against the wall on the crusty carpet, drunk, they roared with laughter and kissed.

Stan struggled to his feet, using the bed to steady himself. He offered a hand to his wife and she took it. As he pulled her up, she looked him in the eyes and said, "How do you want me, Mr. Edgerton?"

"Exactly how you are," he said, embracing Death. "And that's *Doctor* Edgerton to you, young lady."

***

"Siri?"

"Yes, God?"

"Make a note for me."

"Yes, God."

"Then I will smite all thy borders with frogs, and salamanders, and newts. Possibly even some nasty, warty toads." God shivered. She sipped her tea while pacing on the wisp of a cloud charioting her across the sky. The words she spoke fascinated her. *Why not?* "Toads? Yes, now that's starting to sound better, isn't it?"

"I wouldn't know, God. Seems to be a question you need to ask yourself," Siri said.

God nodded. The words weren't right, but they were just.

***

Far below, Henry Fitzpatrick and Patrick McHenry, two "good-ole-boys" born and raised in Mio—who reigned as president and vice president of the local NRA chapter, respectively—sipped Bud Light out of tall bottles wrapped in paper bags. To occupy their minds, they fished from the shadows of the Mio Dam while they drank. The day's catch had been piddly, at best, but they were determined. Besides, the dwindling Styrofoam cooler of beer reminded them of a job well done and a day well lived.

Henry stumbled towards the edge of the river to relieve himself. He slipped on a slippery patch of the bank and tumbled into the water. Patrick mocked him relentlessly until something miraculous shut him up. Henry swallowed a mouthful of river water without hesitation.

"I'll be damned. It's booze?"

"You're daft, old man. No wonder they want to put you in that home."

"No, I mean it. See for yourself," Henry said, using his hands to cup more into his mouth. His friend did the same. From that moment forth, they wouldn't be leaving their fishing spot for quite some time.

"Whaddya suppose is happening?"

"Must be something in the water," Henry Fitzpatrick suggested.

Patrick McHenry grunted in response, returning to dry land with his mouth full to cast out another wobbly line.

They both stood with their feet spread wide, as to not fall in until they were ready for more drink. This wasn't common practice, but it was a wise man, they knew, who adjusted his techniques to his circumstances.

After a while, they hiccupped and gasped. The surface of the water rippled. The ripples turned into bubbles, the bubbles into waves, rocking the surface of the river and spilling boozy, foamy liquid onto the shoreline. They were drunk, but they couldn't be this drunk. One built a tolerance over the years, and Henry Fitzpatrick and Patrick McHenry had at least a hundred years of heavy alcoholism between the two of them. The thought of their love affair with alcohol reminded them of Willy, their old drinking buddy.

"Wonder how the poor old bastard is doing," Henry said.

"Willy? Probably better than us, currently."

Patrick's speculation was spot on. As he too went to relieve himself in the river, the waves on the surface ceased. He didn't dare move. The two men watched in silence, jaws wide, as something incredible happened. This was no miracle. This was a Devil-sent omen.

Hundreds, if not thousands of frogs sprung out of the mouth of the river onto the bank. Green frogs and mink frogs; western chorus frogs, singing the songs of their people; Red, white, and blue frogs; and wood frogs.

Squadrons of salamanders slithered out onto the grass. Shiny black ones with tiny lips opening and closing as they sounded out the letter "o;" fat-headed ones spined with yellow spots; and dirty, slivering mudpuppies, river dogs incapable of playing fetch or learning how to stay. They left slimy trails behind them as they took to land en masse.

Last, out lumbered the toads—wart first—croaking like Great Old Ones. There was a skink or two in the mix, but the men were too drunk and overwhelmed to keep track. Neither of them were herpetologists, although Henry's crotch burned whenever he forgot to refill his prescription.

The amphibians washed on land, flopping over each other, some getting trampled in the process, but most hopped and slithered their way towards Henry Fitzpatrick and Patrick McHenry.

The two humans, outnumbered and hopeless, covered their ears and curled into balls on the grass. The amphibians swarmed them, all slimy and bumpy and determined. Hundreds piled on, suffocating the men.

Or, they would have suffocated, but Death wouldn't find them today. She was busy, if you know what I mean.

The creatures didn't stop there. One by one they left the two would-be lifeless bodies and overtook the town of Mio. They slipped over the boardwalk, up the hill, and onto the bridge. As they spilled into the street, unsuspecting drivers swerved to avoid the flood.

Henry Fitzpatrick and Patrick McHenry remained in the fetal position, holding hands, until all the chaos had passed.

"Are we alive?" Henry asked, embracing his friend.

"I donnu."

"We shouldn't be. Should we?"

"Nope."

"But we are?"

"Uh huh."

"Hm."

"Yup."

They scrambled to their feet, hyper-aware of how close they had been to each other. Clearing their throats, they checked to be sure no one had witnessed their display of affection. Once satisfied, they nodded at each other and parted ways forever, a tradition abandoned in the face of machismo and lack of sexual confidence.

***

Death twirled her naked body, allowing her husband to take in every inch. He admired curves that led to crevices and followed the crevices to even more curves. She eyed him seductively and winked before returning to her dance of love. Once her song reached its crescendo, she turned once more, much slower and with a deliberation, to a Devil who would denounce his wicked ways for one more taste.

Lying in bed on his back, he swelled with anticipation. He beckoned to her with an outstretched finger, licking his lower lip. *No more setbacks. No more distractions. Time to do the damned thing.*

Death agreed, but Death was patient.

***

"Stretch out mine rod and smite the dust of the land, that it might rise and turn thy crops into…rice? Yes, rice. Thy people throughout the land of Mio and beyond will become so sick of the stuff it hurts."

"I've found three locations near you that sell rice," Siri interjected.

After she spoke this new verse and listened to Siri butcher her words, God threw her device over the edge of the clouds. Part of her own cloud swirled in four columns. The columns merged, creating a tiny vortex as she feigned a lazy stirring motion with her fingers. She quickened the pace and a tornado of condensation expanded until it took the shape of a writing desk. A golden bird flew overhead. She reached up, pulled a feather from its wings, and sat down.

"Now, that's more like it. Old-school, oh yeah."

Inspiration struck her again, harder.

"I need to be writing this stuff down," she said, scribbling an outline of what she had already spewed. "Never know when the muse might leave. Besides, memory's not what it used to be."

***

God was too far away to hear it, but the *meep, meep, meep* of a delivery truck warned anyone nearby that it was ready to be received. Agatha stood to the side with her arms crossed. Delivery day was always such a hassle, especially amid a local uprising *and* with a brand-new driver.

Always prepared, Agatha propped her rifle against the wall. She was already running low on bullets, though. Over the years, she labored to earn her restaurant the reputation of being the cleanest restaurant in town. Only the occasional splotch of black mold in the bathroom and mild-to-severe grease buildup in the kitchen disqualified her from running the cleanest restaurant in Michigan.

While she was scrubbing the grill, a bunch of frogs and things attempted a coup of her personal space. They came in through the propped back door and open windows. The larger ones, mostly the toads, tossed themselves bodily at the glass front door until it shattered inward.

They made themselves at home, hopping on tables to get a better angle at customers and causing a general panicked ruckus. The clientele—all drunk—ran around in circles, flailing their arms and screaming shrill screams. They tripped over one another, squishing some of the unluckier amphibians into the tiled floor. She shooed them out—the people, that is—so she could deal with the invaders.

When the broom was no longer effective at keeping the animals at bay, she pulled her rifle out from under the counter. A 'yee-haw' and 'hoop-holler' later, she let 'em rip (so to speak). It had been a while since she'd fired a gun, yet she was quite the crack shot, sans practice.

The battle raged, and the amphibians were winning. The creatures persisted, flooding in as the new ones replaced the dead.[1] They decided the slaughter wasn't worth the reward. Eventually, they headed off down the street, leaving a gutsy mess all over Agatha's Eats.

So, when she greeted the delivery driver, she was already agitated. When Todd, fresh off his first actual delivery, unlatched the trailer and swung open the door, she was less than pleased.

"S...sss...sorry ma'am (hic). My Paul-geez." Todd stared at the contents of the truck. He checked his clipboard, scratched his head, and hoped it wasn't him who had made the mistake. "Thas not (hic) right. Thas...uh...rice? Ma'am, why'd you (hic) order all this rice?"

"What do you think? This ain't Gus's Yum-Yum. I demand you take this away and bring me what I ordered. Discounted, of course. Completely comped if you know

---

[1] It's important to keep in mind that the rules of Death do not apply in cases of spontaneous omening. This is partially because of the laws governing matter. You cannot have new, real-life matter where there was none to begin with. Fiction also plays a role in this uncommon phenomenon.

what's good for you." Agatha was at her most professional when dealing with incompetence. Holding people accountable gave her a sense of fulfillment. "Have you been drinkin', boy?"

Todd focused with glazed eyes. He rocked, then fell forward onto his hands and knees. He laughed but didn't know why. Instead of trying to get up, he vomited on her shoes. It took every fiber of her patience not to kick him square in the jaw.

"Think I...lay down first?" He passed out on the pavement.

***

Death straddled her husband, kissing his neck and nibbling his earlobe. He cupped her breasts and kissed her all over, losing himself to the pulse of her body. He paused to take in every aspect, every pore on her skin. The part of him still thinking about missed opportunities was long gone. He drug his fingernails down her spine, resting his hand on the small of her back. Their muscles contracted together in perfect harmony.

"Take me now. Take me like it's our last day on Earth."

It is, the Devil thought, but he didn't linger on the idea. After the deed was done, they would have to return to their stations. There was work to do. For now, he enjoyed the moment. He opened his arms to embrace Death.

***

"Behold," God continued, her quill working furiously. "I will bring Ford Focuses into thy realm, and they shall cover the face of Earth in time, and thine cherished trucks and SUVs and sports cars shall forever more be fuel efficient, family-friendly, and painfully practical sedans."

And so, as these things go, it was.

***

240

Tony Dietrich Senior opened the door to his three-car garage, flicked the light on, and nearly had a panic attack. Sitting in the middle, where his black Hummer and candy-red Ferrari once sat, was a brand-spanking new Ford Focus, fully loaded—CD player and everything. There was nothing special about this car besides the fact it wasn't the car it should have been.

Walking around to the rear of the car, he ran his fingers across the silver finish. "What are you supposed to be? And what did you do with my 'Rari?" It made him feel "cool" when he called it that.

He hit the garage door opener and waited as a sliver of sunlight grew into a bright afternoon day. Across the street, a blue Ford Focus swerved to avoid a stop sign, jumped the curb, and hit a no-parking sign instead.

"Oh, so close," Tony Senior said, sticking his tongue out at the driver.

Detroit-made Ford Focuses, either parked on the side of the road or speeding by in multiple lanes, stretched out as far as his eyes could see. The people of Mio had more variety in their choice of transportation...didn't they? Oh well. They were always simple people and he loved them for it. It was easier to take advantage of simpletons. It was a fact reflected in his swelling bank account and, until now at least, his reflection in the mirror of his sports car.

He didn't have time to think. *His* people were awaiting his arrival. There was much to do before his plan came to fruition. Having to fulfil his destiny in a cheap, mass-produced car was a mere inconvenience. Nothing would stop Tony Dietrich Senior from pulling off the greatest caper in the history of Mio: The overthrow of Sheriff Grace's regime.

"But first I gotta check out my stolen guns," he said, scooching into the driver's seat of his new Ford Focus. He

241

ran his fingers over the steering wheel. "Oh, this is actually kinda nice."

***

Death rode her husband like she rode her pale horse, his hands grasping her thighs, leaving imprints on her skin. She felt him inside of her; the ecstasy was overwhelming even for her. The room pulsed as he pulsed. It shook as the two lovers rocked harder and harder. She leaned forward to kiss the Devil.

"I love you," she said. He was the only man to win Death's affection. The only one to receive the kiss of death unscathed. "Ride with me, my love."

***

God wrote feverishly at her desk. After the last verse, she'd swapped out tea for whiskey. It seemed appropriate as words flooded onto the scroll.

"I will unzip swarms of flies of thee, and of thy servants, and thy people, so no man, woman, or child can ever again keep their pants around their waists. That'll really teach 'em, huh? But do they need to learn?"

She thought about this for a nanosecond and decided it didn't matter. Humans were always doing something they needed to learn a lesson for. It was her solemn duty to teach them that lesson, for Heaven's sake.

Besides, she remembered something was amiss down there. She'd visited with her son. Whatever it was, it was serious. She couldn't concentrate. Not with her brain revolving at light speed. Not with the smoke hissing out from the point of her quill as she tried to keep up.

***

Set in his ways, as stubborn as a bear, Pinky was never one to learn many lessons. Despite the events of the day, a few customers still waited in his lobby for their pizzas. Who was he to deny them cheesy bliss?

242

As he stuck the peel in the oven, his grease-soaked pants slid down to his ankles. Being a consummate professional, he ignored it until the pie was safely on a pizza stone. He investigated the dining room and realized he had a bunch of embarrassed, equally pants-less customers.

There was strange stuff going on. This wasn't the issue; there was seldom not strange stuff going on in Mio.

Take, for example, the annual Bigfoot convention. Men, and always men, flocked in by the half dozen early in September to meet and discuss their personal hero: Sasquatch. They believed he lived in the forests of northern Michigan and would stake their wives and children on it. Each had their own story to tell. Rodney saw the creature sulking in the darkness of the deep forest, sad after being rejected by Lady Bigfoot. Earl caught him sipping water from Loud Creek. Igor swore up and down that he saw him reading a 1987 copy of the *New York Times* while squatting behind a bush.

Pinky saw their enthusiasm as an opportunity to make some extra pocket change before the roads became impassable in the winter. He ordered himself a gorilla suit on the Interwebs. When the Footers were on the prowl, he threw it on and took to the woods. His size alone made it believable, especially to a group of people in such desperate need of validation. After evading capture, he met them back at the pizza place to feed them and listen to them regale their tales of near-glory. After a while, he started dressing up and traipsing around the forest for fun. Every time he did, he became less ashamed of himself and more in tune with the Bigfoot within.

What's good for business, he told himself, *is good for Mio. What's good for Mio is good for Pinky. Why not enjoy a new hobby while I'm at it?*

However, the strangeness of the day went well beyond pizza chefs in costumes and middle-aged men living with their mothers after nasty divorces. The entire populace was drunk, amphibians were swarming the town in plague numbers, his walk-in cooler was filled to the rafters with rice— the least useful ingredient for a proprietor of fine pizza pies—and now he couldn't keep his oldest and most trustworthy pair of pants around his waist.

"At least things can't get any worse…" he grumbled to himself as he fought to reclaim his sanity.

He found out how wrong he was as soon as the thought crossed his mind. A yellow Ford Focus, driven by someone he recognized from church, jumped the curb outside his restaurant and barreled through his front door.

***

"Behold," God hiccuped. "The hand of the Lord—hey, that's me!—the hand of the Lord is upon thy cattle which is in the fields of thy realm, upon thy horses, and upon thy asses." She stopped to giggle and take another swig from her golden chalice. "Heh. Ass. Anyway, upon thy camels and oxen and she to morons…no murrain? Wait, what?"

Her muse appeared on her shoulder, whispered something in her ear for clarity, and disappeared into the world of inspiration to mock other would-be writers. She scratched out a few words on the scroll before her.

"Correction, thy dogs shall no longer obey thy command, and thy cats shall scoff in your general direction as they knock your dishes off the counter. Yes, yes. That last verse was a bit archaic. I think this is a fair compromise. Much, much better."

***

Rex, the beloved neighborhood stray, leapt to and fro after frogs, his entire body wagging from the momentum of his tail. They were everywhere, and their presence overwhelmed him. At first, he'd come to drink at his usual watering hole, the drainpipe behind Charlotte's Beauty Salon. He stayed for the entertainment and because everything was blurry and unsteady. His Scooby-Doo demeanor had transformed into a Scrappy-Doo readiness to go a few rounds with any small creature to dare cross his path. He was an Irish setter by blood, emphasis on Irish.

Charlotte came out the back, thus far unaffected by the chaos. The only thing she noticed was the effect of the water, but she was a lady and she'd be damned if anyone saw her lacking composure. All the Natty seltzers had fortified with her tolerance, too.

She propped the door with a woodblock, lit a Capri cigarette, and yacked on a family of newts. Rex eyed her, wagging bodily.

"Shh." She knelt to pet him. He growled. Hunched, the fur near his tail stuck straight up. Rex never growled at anybody. She couldn't believe his first time was at her of all people. "Bad dog. You sit and be nice."

The dog ignored her. He lifted his leg and marked Charlotte as his own before running off the chase more frogs. She screeched and threw her lighter at him as he disappeared around the corner. While she was busy being enraged, a tom cat snuck behind her and pushed at the woodblock propping the door with his paw until it was safely able to sneak inside. The locked door slid shut, and Charlotte began to ugly cry.

**

On top now, the Devil thrust himself deep inside Death. He did so slowly at first, delaying the inevitable, but increased speed as her moans grew louder. She dug her nails into his skin, leaving red marks down his entire back in the wake of where her fingers once were.

"You'll be the first one to master Death, my love," she whispered in his ear. They made eye contact, and he lost himself in the black void of her pupils.

**

"Boils shall break forth with blains upon man and woman, for which no amount of Proactive shall stave."

God leaned back and admired her work so far. She was having the time of her life. She didn't know what possessed her. Nor did she understand why her people must befall such horrors on this day. But she accepted it, relished in it.

"My God—me—you are becoming cleverer with every stroke of the pen. Good show."

Life got boring all alone. The impacts of her creativity were the best company she'd had in centuries. The *only* company, minus her snotty son.

***

To her dismay, the fortune of Charlotte the beautician wasn't turning around anytime soon. Locked out of her own establishment, covered in piss and vomit, she sat leaned against the dumpster to catch her wits. Why not? Her life was in the dumps, anyway.

Any attempt to make herself presentable had failed.

She squeezed her dress out to the best of her abilities and sprayed off with perfume. Charlotte dug in her purse and found her mirror. When she saw her reflection, the pitch of her voice shattered all the glass on Main Street and popped a few straggling toads.

She'd thrown in with the sheriff, throwing away her own dreams at the same time, and had awoken in a nightmare.

Blackheads and pimples covered her face. She took impeccable care of her skin. And her hair. And her nails. And her teeth. And any part someone might notice up close. She had a reputation to uphold, and she was determined to see that she did. Charlotte Vaughn Miller did not get acne. What sort of so-called beauty expert couldn't cleanse her own pores? The Academy wouldn't stand for it. She'd become a laughing stock and would have to hideaway forever.

She found a tube of cream inside the vastness of her purse. Applying it with unsteady hands and no mirror was a challenge. She dabbed it everywhere, missing the spots she needed it the most. On her cheeks and forehead. Around her eyes. Inside of her nose by mistake. After a few minutes, her entire face was covered in white cream.

A warty toad hopped to her side while she worked. It watched her with fascination, unable to comprehend why she'd want to conceal such a beautifully blemished face and croaked to announce its presence.

"Don't judge me, you warty bastard. When's the last time *you* had a facial. Now get out of here. I need to concentrate on *me*."

The toad acquiesced. If the story was true, this was one princess he didn't want turning him into a prince.

***

On all fours, facing the headboard, Death braced herself against the weight of her husband. He stood behind her, arms wrapped around her torso, growing more and more confident in his abilities by the minute. The minutes waned, falling off the clock as the impact of the rocking bed shook the wall.

To slow his release, the Devil thought about everything they'd been through to get here. The image of Dale and Rhonda dancing was helpful. Their movements, gelatinous in their rhythm, did too good of a job. Seeing his wife's face pressed into a pillow gave him the boost he needed to keep going.

Death's voice boomed from the other side of the room. "I'm almost there for you." She was all around him. Everywhere.

***

Looking down at Earth, at the chaos she caused, God reveled in her literary brilliance. The situation in Mio was spiraling out of control, but she wasn't one to take an active interest in the actions of others.

Besides, the situation with the Devil and Death was supposed to have been taken care of. She put her son on it. *Her* son. The son of God, for Christ's sake. How could she know he'd muck it up?

"Joke's on me." She dipped her quill in its inkwell. She didn't need to re-ink, but the mechanical motion helped her think—helped her organize her thoughts. God finally understood where the words came from. They were her own but twisted by the forces of evil on Earth. The union underway, there was no longer anything to do to stop it from happening.

In the past, God opened the sky to wash away her mistakes. For forty days and forty nights it rained, drowning evil from the utopia she'd worked so hard to create. For forty days and forty nights her true might, the full extent of her wrath, reshaped the Earth's surface. If she could wash away the mistakes of humanity, why couldn't she wash away her own?

"Yeah, why not?" God said. "Let it be so."

The sky opened, there was rain, and it was so.

***

The lovers became one. The Devil and Death, entwined in unholy and orgasmic pleasure, ignored reality around them. The world was falling apart by the floorboards, but neither of them bothered to pay attention. They were too far away, lost in the unity of love.

Death spasmed. The lights flickered and popped. Thunder rumbled the hotel, but their own vibrations overpowered the storm. Her muscles tightened, and she closed her eyes before freeing herself. It was the greatest sensation she would ever experience.

The Devil delighted in her pleasure.

"I'm coming for you," Death said.

I'm ready, he thought.

***

God had no choice. As the sun set on Mio, she realized what needed to be done.

She summoned a single lantern with the scrunch of her nose to see if it would work. One of the human's better contributions to the universe was the television sitcom from the 1960s, *I Dream of Jeannie*. God always admired Jeannie in all her womanhood.

Her metaphoric inkwell was running dry, so she had to make the last words count. "Stretch out thine hand towards Heaven, that there may be darkness over the land of Mio and beyond, even a darkness which may be felt."

Lightning and hail, combined with the blackest eternal night in written history, swept over the small town of Mio, Michigan. God put down her quill and shook out the cramp in her hand. The whiskey was dry, and the ink gone. Overall, she was satisfied with the afternoon's work. She reminded herself everything had been done before. That she borrowed their words, making them her own, and that was okay. She might not have been responsible for the humans on Earth anymore, but their fate was written. History was written. It was what appeared on the page, not what happened. Was this what they'd remember her for?

A piece was missing. Her edicts hadn't come full circle. There was one thing left. Since she couldn't write it down, she spoke it out loud.

"I will go out in the midst of Mio, among her people." Her eyes rolled as if possessed by the devil. "And all of thy firstborn in the land of Mio and beyond shall…" She stopped herself in disgust. "No, no, no. I'm not doing that. No way. I'm not a monster."

"Take their firstborns. It is written," a disembodied voice said.

"You can't make me."

"It's the final stage. It is written."

"Absolutely not. That won't do at all. Instead, I shall…uh…I shall give thy firstborns excruciating charley horses. Oh, and migraines. Yes, much better. Don't you agree? Migraines are the worst, and I've never met a horse named Charlie that didn't rub me the wrong way."

"It is written," the voice said. Which was odd because this time it wasn't.

Either way, the final words, driven by the unholy consummation of a fallen angel and Death herself, began the End of Days. Chaos and blackness befell the realm of Mio, stretching out to all corners, er…hemispheres[2] of the world.

Only two unlikely men stood against the tides of apocalypse. But neither had a clue. God was exhausted after the melodrama of it all.

---

[2] This must be clarified because we wouldn't want the flat-earth folks to misinterpret our stance on the subject.

Chapter 24:

An End, but Not "The End"

It was pitch black outside and inside the hotel room. Two sweaty bodies rolled away from one another, satisfied by an unrighteous romp between the sheets. The Devil had a wicked grin on his face. Death held her hands to her heart, feeling the rapidity of its drumming.

She looked at her husband. "That was wonderful, my love."

"Holy shit. Oh my God. Yes. It. Was." Before he could process his mistake, Death slapped him across his face. The handprint she left behind peeled apart the skin. "Baby, I—"

"Screw you. *Holy? God?* I suspected you liked her— of course you do, everyone does—but I thought after what she did to you, you'd be over it by now. This has been a horrible, horrible mistake. They say you never truly know someone... But then, they come back with something that happened almost 60,000 years ago!"

"But, baby, I am—"

"Save it. Death waits for no one." She scrambled to put her clothes on, tripping over an ottoman. "And it wasn't that good. We just tell you it was so your feelings don't get hurt."

Outside, it continued to thunder and hail. The Devil's last glimpse of Death was a shadowy one, shrouded by the tides of apocalypse rolling in from the heavens. The view was nice, but he didn't think he'd be looking at her from this angle so soon. It wasn't as satisfying watching her go as it had been making her come.

***

Naomi walked away from the crystal ball set in the center of the place beyond place, dusting off a hard day's work. He'd gone and done it. More importantly, *she'd* done it.

She was always better than her sisters, but now she had proof. They'd never forget what she pulled off. So subtle. So brilliant. Not even Death herself noticed the genius behind what unfurled.

"That's it?"

"It is done."

"He didn't even say anything...she just freaked out. Besides, won't he just return now?"

"Women hear what they want to hear. Men blurt whatever they're thinking. To be fair, we all have a bit of both trapped inside us."

From atop their throne, the twins Lily and Amelia harmonized, "What about his emanate return?"

"Sisters," Naomi said, "after a shock like that, I'll be surprised if he ever returns."

It was likely true. The male ego was a fragile thing that must be nurtured, coddled even. Stan's had been irreparably damaged. He'd wander the sands of oblivion in search of a panacea until time's end. This, she knew. All as Naomi had planned...

"It is written, sisters. We can rest now."

"It is written," they said in unison.

Chapter 25:

Grace and Chase do some Digging—and Swords

The drive to Mio from the golf course, only twenty miles, seemed to take an eternity. Sheriff Grace mulled a few theories as to why this might've been, none of them even remotely acceptable.

To begin with, she'd rallied the troops to confront Mayor Gunderson. That part went better than expected, despite a few setbacks and stubborn townspeople. Everyone agreed: they needed to hold the mayor accountable for his lack of action. Mio was falling apart, moral fiber by loose moral fiber. Folks were unraveling and needed leadership. The mayor wasn't Mio's face anymore if he'd ever been in the first place.

However, when they arrived at Garland to storm the clubhouse, he wasn't there.

They ran amuck, smashing things and yelling obscenities. The poor young woman behind the desk was flabbergasted. She tried to explain to them Mayor Gunderson hadn't played through for several weeks. It was out of character, and this worried her. He was scheduled to play eighteen holes the day before but never showed. She'd left him a voicemail and everything. The crew couldn't hear her over the smashing of flowerpots and showy grunts of disapproval, so they didn't get the message until the damage was done. That's when they lost steam, but not all of it.

The water turning into booze helped motivate her fury. Sheriff Grace believed in the virtues of staying hydrated. Her mother always used to tell her a well-lubricated mind flowed like the mountain stream, or some such nonsense. It kept the mind sharp, while the booze kept the blades of justice sharp and swinging wildly. A deadly combination, under normal circumstances.

Things got weird on the drive back.

She took it slow, seeing as the two-lane road was now a five-lane. An army of Siamese frogs hopped out of the woods and onto the asphalt. To the police car, they were like sheep behind a fence, fish to the slaughter, or babies for the taking. Whatever they were, they became a messy afterthought, splattering the undercarriage of the car and slicking the treads of the tires. Usually tense, Deputy Lawson laughed until he wet himself; after which, they laughed together.

A ripple in time collided with them after his accident. Space and reality bent around them, contracting and expanding the ebb and flow of their now-false perceptions. Their very existence became a fragile tightrope walk between insanity and, well, lesser insanity. It was like entering a wormhole and coming out in Canada. Or, worse, Wisconsin. After the effects of the time warp calmed, there was one noticeable difference: the ram horns on the center of her steering wheel now simply read *Ford*.

"Blech." She ignored the blatant insult to her family heritage. The Graces had always been Dodge people, ever since The Great Hailstorm of 1912.

But at least it was American-made and equipped with satellite radio *and* navigation. What a time to be alive! Cars took us where we needed to go, even when we didn't have a particular destination.

All of that, along with the current ping-pong balls of hail and constant flashes of blue lightning, made their eventual arrival to Mio a miracle. Someone was looking out for them.

Sheriff Grace slammed on the brakes before running into a familiar face—a divine bonus in her book.

"In my defense, he was standing in the middle of the damn road." She threw the deputy a thumbs-up, then yelled out the window. "The hell you doin'?" It sounded more like a whisper over the storm. "Can't you see I'm diving here?"

"Yeah, I'm trying to stop you *here*," Chase Cross said, approaching the driver side of the car. Big chunks of hails bounced off the mass of his body as he waddled closer. His boots went *squish, squish* as he stepped on a salamander, its guts squelched onto the pavement.

Sheriff Grace reeked of vodka, and Deputy Lawson was clearly intoxicated. To be fair, the whole town reeked of vodka and was clearly intoxicated. Chase wondered why he hadn't been invited to the party.

Sheriff Grace concentrated on the figure before her. She scrunched her eyes together and raised a corner of her upper lip. "Detective? S'that you?"

"Nice car, Sheriff. Not your style, but I dig it." As he said this, a pang of pride swelled inside of him. In all his short time in Mio, no one addressed him by the title he earned without at least a snarky remark or an inflection of sarcasm. And it was *her*. "Move over, I'll drive."

"Like hell you will."

"Sheriff, you're drunk. Now get out of my way."

Deputy Lawson rolled his eyes and climbed into the backseat without being told. With how much effort it took, you'd have thought he was scaling Mount Ararat. With the amount of rain coming down, you wouldn't be too far off. He flipped over the console, face first, and landed with a thud, snoring as soon as he hit leather.

"Where's the mayor's office?"

"S'close to the courtyard. Er, Borehouse. Christ's sake. The courthouse place. It's that-a-away, Detective," Sheriff Grace said, poking herself in the eye in an attempt to point towards town.

"Perfect. First, I've got a quick stop to make."

Sheriff Grace fell into her own lap. Chase shook her back to consciousness. He couldn't do this alone. He needed her in more ways than one.

Find the mayor. Confront the culprit. The climax of the young detective's stay. The fruition of his wildest dreams. No, not those kinds of dreams, you sicko. *I'm almost there...*

They drove to Dietrich Brokerage first. Chase had a score to settle. They rode in silence, the Sheriff fighting the urge to be sick and Chase Cross fearing what he might say. She was vulnerable, and the time was ripe to get everything off his chest without worrying about her reaction. When the effects of the alcohol wore off, she wouldn't remember a thing. Besides, drunk people tended towards honesty. Often brutally so.

"You're beautiful," he wanted to say. "Let's go out. Like *go* out. Not for a drink and a nightcap. But for steak and potatoes. Sweet dessert wine. Wrestling between the sheets. Let's have a hundred children together so at least one of them turns out to be *half* as incredible as you. I'm not a detective, to be honest. Just winging it, but you give me the strength to do it right. I hope you'll forgive me. Please say you'll forgive me."

His stream of consciousness teetered on the tip of his tongue. *Who am I kidding? I'll never have enough courage to say to her half the things I want to say.*

Up the hill and around the bend, passing the motel as it emerged out of the unnatural darkness, they drove on. A shadowy figure wrapped in a cloak stood by the side of the road, hitchhiking, bound to catch cold in this weather. Some several hundred yards away, a woman in a hip-hugging black dress yelled at him, her words audible only between thunderclaps, and then only as garbled nonsense. Chase had been there before, standing out in the rain to catch his death, while some devil of a vixen shouted at him from an unsafe distance.

He double-parked in front of the agency. There was a strut in his step as he trotted around the car to help Sheriff Grace. She curtsied, hitting her head on the mirror. He was quick to grab her arms before she fell into a mud puddle. He planted a gentle kiss on her head where she hit the mirror. To his surprise, the sheriff neither scolded him nor punched him.

A flash of lightning cracked, illuminating the entire town. It struck the base of a tree nearby, and the fire cast shadows all over the place. They were the shadows of the hundreds of frogs and salamanders closing in all around them. A smell in the air, one he couldn't quite place, made his stomach rumble. Suddenly, he found himself craving Mooshoo Pork.

Helping the sheriff along, he ran towards the real estate agency. The door was locked but made of glass, a concept Chase never quite grasped. Why would you build something meant to keep people out with a material so fragile? After even a hairline fracture, all the demons would rush on through.

"I got this, Detective," Sheriff Grace said, slipping out of his arm and grabbing her billy club.

She brought it over her shoulder and swung it forward, following the arc of its trajectory with her entire body. He wasn't fast enough this time. She fell through the door, shattering the glass, and landed on the ground. Chase ran in after her to help her up.

"S'good. These nice shards of glass broke my fall, huh? Very considerate of them. To think Agatha told me they might be too sharp…"

"Uh, yeah. Whatever you say. You okay?"

Chase checked her for cuts and stubborn fragments, breathing a sigh of relief to find her mostly intact. *She's okay…Thank God, she's okay.*

After he cleaned her up, they took inventory of their surroundings. Ficases. Ficases everywhere. Off to one corner of the office, a cheap metal rack displayed the same collection of tourist brochures he'd toppled at the motel. On the wall opposite, the head of a ten-point buck grinned at the unlikely pair. The deer knew they were up to no good, but who was he going to tell, the spider between his antlers?

"Musta been the irony of getting shot by a slob like ole Tony Senior, eh?" the sheriff said, grinning at the deer and fake shooting it with finger guns. "Poor bastard."

"Who?" Chase asked. "The deer or Tony Senior?"

Sheriff Grace laughed. The detective was right. They were both poor bastards; one hid behind stacks of money while the other remained frozen in place. She wanted to say so, but instead she said, "Tony Junior."

They both laughed until they cried, despite the sky falling around them and the sun on the verge of exploding. It wasn't even funny, but when the world was falling apart, it was the small things.

"Always been this funny, Sheriff?"

"Oh, stop."

Chase shoved Sheriff Grace, a wide grin on his face. It wasn't the big, stupid grin she was used to seeing. This one was all dimples and shy, possibly even rosy-cheeked. He shuffled his feet and ventured an awkward wink. She reciprocated the action, then silently reprimanded herself.

"No, seriously. Stop," she said, changing her tune. "We have work to do, Mr. Cross. I plan to play my part with the utmost professionalism and class until the job is done."

"I know another job I'd like to do."

"Mr. Cross!" Out of habit, she slapped him hard across the face. The force knocked him back and echoed through the empty office.

How many times am I gonna get slapped by cops today? Is it something about my face?

Harmful flirting out of the way, their investigation continued. They split up, Chase to search the main office while the sheriff checked out the administrative offices and Tony's private accommodations.

He flipped through pile after pile of paper, crumpling important documents that didn't help their case as he went. He tossed them over his shoulder and moved on. Tax documents? Nope. Client portfolios? No thanks. Bank statements? Burn 'em. Or maybe it was best to keep *those* for later... He rolled them up and stuck them in his back pocket.

He found zilch to implicate the Dietrichs. Nor did he find where they might be hiding. They would pay for their actions, and he needed to erase the doubt rushing back like a flood. It had been them—all of it. If only he could find proof...something concrete to implicate the family ruining Mio.

Sheriff Grace wasn't having much more luck. Contrary to the mustard stains on his suits and his sweaty pits, Tony Senior maintained a pristine office. On the wall, he had mounted three red katanas of varying sizes. Next to them hung a series of framed licenses and awards. Typical. Upon closer inspection, she found his brokerage license, two years expired. He also had another buck mounted behind his desk, giving visitors the stink eye. A price tag dangled in between its antlers.

Nothing jumped out at them saying, "Look at me! Pick me. Pick me. I'm the missing link!" A blank pad of paper, a stapler, pens jammed into a coffee mug, and two stark, empty desk drawers. If the man was hiding something, it wasn't in his office. If Chase was right to expect foul play from Tony Senior, it was happening elsewhere.

The lack of tangible evidence disappointed the sheriff. Chase disappointed her, too. He was a hack. Why had she convinced herself otherwise? Against her better judgment, she'd begun to respect and even admire the man. Right on cue, he walked into the office looking downtrodden and dejected. His sudden presence made her realize she was mostly disappointed in herself.

He frowned. "The cigarette butt had been so promising. I mean, maybe Junior didn't do it on purpose. If he did, I don't think he was acting on his own accord. The kid seems deranged, a bully to boot, but arson? No, this wasn't his fault. Parenting caused this."

"Mr. Cross, we're breaking and entering. There's nothing here. You sure about little Tony?"

He couldn't remember much thanks to his concussion and hangover. A bearded man at the bar who stole his shoes. Talking bushes. Strange shadowy figures dancing about the shrine. In the boonies of Mio, he assumed the samba was a coven or something. The teenagers with their pungent clove cigarettes and mock bravado, their false sense of superiority over a lost drunkard, kept coming back to him. The rest was a blur.

"See any peculiar sconces? Out of place book bindings?" Chase rummaged at random, knocking things on the floor without regard. "Perhaps a small switch in a false drawer?"

"Don't be absurd."

"There's always a small switch in a false drawer. Or a loose brick. Or something. *Anything*."

Chase Cross always did his best to separate reality from fiction. Even as a young man, curled under the covers with a flashlight and a mystery novel, he knew when he pulled those covers that the real world would come rushing back, giving him the fiction bends. It happened like clockwork, no matter how prepared he thought he was.

The stories gave him new perspectives on life, taught him how to deal with the mundanity of everyday disappointment. They taught him to seek fact and piece it together in logical ways. When he learned how to connect two unrelated things, he learned how to cope with a mentally abusive mother. But he drew the distinction between what he wanted and what he actually had. One was filled with excitement and surprise, twists and danger. The other one stunk of boredom.

He noticed the shiny objects hanging on the wall. Second to being a real detective, he always wanted to be a ninja. Hell, he'd even settle for a pirate as long as he could wield a rapier and guzzle rum. The problem with his dream was twofold. Whoever saw a fat, uncoordinated ninja? And there was about a fifty-fifty chance that every swing of his blade would end his own life just as easily as his opponent's. He wasn't a gambling man, and those weren't odds he was willing to risk.

Chase grabbed the top sword off the wall. He held it out in front of him, still sheathed, admiring its craftsmanship. Dragons danced around sailing ships under a blood red sky. Although shoddy and mass-manufactured, the "artistry" was breathtaking. He pulled the blade out, listening for the *shing* as it left the safety of its sheath. Flames rose from the hilt and along the steel blade, ending only when they ran out of room at the tip. Chase drooled a bit but didn't care. He gave the sword a few gentle, clumsy swings.

"Done playing around?" the sheriff asked, unamused.

"Grab one."

"What?"

"Grab one. Fight me," Chase said, squaring off with the sheriff. With the end of the sword pointed in her direction, he beckoned her with his free hand. "Or are ya chicken?"

Sheriff Grace rolled her eyes. She didn't have time for child's play, especially if it could end in someone getting decapitated. But there probably wasn't time for anything given current events. Besides, did she want to miss an opportunity to maim the detective?

As she retrieved her own sword, she noticed a wire connecting it to a metal plate on the wall. It made a *click* sound as the wire snapped. Somewhere further in the wall came the mechanical grinding of a weight dropping and a pulley, well, pulleying. Their eyes followed a new sound; a metallic marble rolled down a track, clicking in place louder than the last. Then, there was silence. Then nothing.

"Try the other one."

She dropped her sword on the ground and grabbed the last one. The effect was immediate. In the middle of the room, the desk slid backwards and revealed a darkened spiral staircase.

"I knew it! Never suspected the swords, but there's always a lever."

"Yeah, yeah, yeah." She rolled her eyes, exaggerating the roll. "Good call, Detective."

Chase beamed. "Tony Senior underestimated my ability to rifle through people's things. Give me enough time, I'm bound to screw something up."

"No argument here."

They followed the stairway into the depths of the real estate agency. The depths turned out to be a crawl space, like an unfinished basement for hobbits; but, in Chase's imagination, they were miles below the surface. In the far corner, there was a man with his arms tied behind him and a safe.

"A man?" Sheriff Grace dry heaved. "Jesus, what is that?"

He was tied with duct tape and gagged, smelling worse than leftover Indian food. Tony Senior hadn't thought about the bodily functions humans do on occasion. Upon closer inspection, she recognized the man at the end of the tunnel.

As soon as he noticed them, he began moaning for help.

"Mayor Gunderson?"

She ripped the tape off his mouth and removed his gag. He grunted a few audible words, *Ouch, Tony, shrine, taking over,* and *Mio,* before passing out.

"Thanks. That's all we needed." She turned to Chase. "Detective, let's ride."

Chapter 26:
Belief

Jesus and Bob—the Prodigal Son and the son of the Prodigal Son. The Chosen One and the Miraculous Accident—sat on the steps of the Our Lady of the Woods shrine. Well, Bob sat while Jesus paced, kicking dirt and mumbling obscenities.

Despite everything going on, Bob stole his focus. Jesus didn't think the Ubiquitous They had considered his situation when they said, "What happens in Atlanta stays in Atlanta." It was hard to leave the past in the past when a peeved-off demoness showed up at your door, carrying a child the spitting image of you in a basket of bones.

Prodding a slimy skink who'd taken up refuge amongst the rocks built around the shrine's creek, Bob processed everything. He was the last flower to bud in spring, the one people all but forgot about as the others grew above and around him, soaking up all his sun. The pressure to open his petals weighed heavier on his shoulders the closer he got to finding answers. Enclosed in a tight bud, safe from knowing and from hurting, life was simple. Now, wide-open, filled with knowledge beyond mortal comprehension, every breath was dangerous.

He was Jesus's prodigal son. God's grandson. That alone was difficult to digest, leaving a rotten melon in the pit of his stomach. Divinity seemed like a lot of work.

Not to mention all the other stuff. He'd been near comatose as he listened to the statues argue. Stone, plaster, and wire wasn't supposed to talk. One of them spoke fluent French, too! It was impossible. The only French in Mio was supposed to be fries.

Jesus—his apparent father, not just his Father—explained the power of belief to him. True, concentrated

264

belief—not the kind people used as a crutch when their lives were falling apart—changed the nature of Earth itself. This wasn't the kind people tapped whenever convenient. Nor the kind they used to condemn other people they didn't understand. It wasn't even the belief that surfaced in a husband for the first time in years as he held his wife's hand at her death bed.

The belief his father explained to him was the kind of belief that pulsed through a person's veins. It breathed life into their heart and helped neurons traverse synaptic gaps in their brain. It was in the air and swimming with the fish. Enunciating every word of every conversation. It was the rising sun and the setting moon. In good times or bad, this belief never waned.

"What makes it so special?" Bob asked.

"Well, son," Jesus said, grasping Bob's shoulder. "High concentrations of belief allow me to be here with you today."

He explained belief—true and unwavering, over long periods of time—weakened the walls between Heaven and Earth. The divine weren't meant to mingle with the mundane. Most people couldn't handle the shock. So, God was kept up there, where she was meant to stay.

Consequently, so was the Devil, demons and angels, and any other deity you'd ever heard about.[1] And the ones you hadn't. Enough belief opened a rift in the wall. This wall, though invisible, was there and thicker than blood.

"Places like these are rare on Earth. People distract themselves with simpler things. Television, mostly, but also all those mind-numbing things television birthed.

---

[1] Rules always have exceptions. Take, for example, Zeus, who reveled in meddling with human affairs. But even Zeus disguised himself. The shock of seeing a god in the flesh would dismantle the entire delicate human ecosystem.

Celebrities. Commercials. Video games. Hero worship. The internet. Each has taken bites out of belief, gorged itself on the piety and devotion of the masses, until becoming its own ineffable entity.

"Because of this, Heaven and Hell drift further and further away in the vastness of space. Only places like the Vatican and a dozen or so small towns like this gap the wall anymore. Places with generations of followers. Of God or Satan. Mio happens to be one of these places. Her people are of a singular mindset. Always have been and, hopefully, always will be."

In Mio, Sunday mornings were times of worship. Every night was time to offer gratitude. Children read the words of God. Parents practiced them. They were a generous and kind people, considerate of their neighbors. Never covetous. Lovers faithful, sinners repentant. Small, everyday displays of piousness breathed life into the statues and allowed Jesus to walk to earth.

"The same applies to places filled with evil. Corruption and greed. Murder and rape. Too many lawyers defending too much scum. A strip club on every block or a working girl on every corner. This type of human behavior has similar, grave consequences. It opens portals to Hell, which are becoming more common as society strays from its belief in God.

"Take, for example, Detroit, Michigan: Motown. The Arsenal of Democracy. Murder Town. The metropolis is only a few hours' drive from Mio and has recently birthed such a portal. People lose their jobs and homes, live under the constant threat of violence, and watch everything they once knew and loved deteriorate. Ultimately, they blame God. In blaming God, they choose a path of wickedness. Neighbors stop helping one another. Lovers stray. Sinners revel in their misdeeds. The world becomes thankless—godless."

"What does this have to do with me, Father?" Bob weighed the consequences of these startling revelations in his mind. The more he thought about it, the more he wondered how he had missed all the signs.

The Devil walked the earth. What's more, he walked the earth with a blushing, pale bride. The couple owned a monopoly on life *and* death. There was no more balance.

The consequences of this union wrote themselves across the fibers of reality. The signs were everywhere. Everyone was drunk as a skunk, even by Mio standards, but no one could explain why. They hopped after frogs and toads, giggling and falling over each other. Rice filled their larders and pantries, and only Gus was excited about this. Belts and buttons failed. Pets ran amuck, doing things pets did when people were no longer involved. And the acne. Oh God, the horrible, pustulant acne. It was as if everyone quit their day jobs, ceased ther personal hygiene rituals, and took up Dungeons and Dragons in their parent's basement.

Then, the signs turned destructive. Ford Focuses crashed through storefronts and narrowly avoided stumbling, zombie-like pedestrians. He never drove, so Bob wasn't sure how different this was from normal. And while these phenomena were confusing and upsetting, none compared to the open sky. A crack in the heavens, trumping even the most glorious plumbers, let loose rains the earth had only seen once before. And the sun—or lack thereof—was certainly cause for concern.

Jesus stopped pacing and sat down. "Big things are happening, son. You still have a part to play. Now, I hasten you to bear witness upon the miracles of my mother, God. Your grandmother, I suppose. See what evil hath wrought upon this world. See how she answers it in kind. It's too late for most, but there's hope. A chance to wash away what we couldn't stop and start anew. Your time will come. The age of Bob will soon dawn."

All Bob had was time. He fancied himself something of an expert at biding his time, hoarding the minutes as they ticked away. Patience was ponderous. Action tiresome. He'd take the former every day.

The first Ford Focus pulled up. Rather, it bit the curb and careened towards them in a déjà vu fashion. It came to a screeching halt in the lawn, only a few feet from the concrete steps. Doors opened, and armed men filed out; lighting struck another tree across the street for dramatic purposes. The Triumvirate of Marys and Trinity of Jesuses stood in the shadows, biding their time. Watching.

Tony Dietrich Senior, trailed by his son and several lackeys, including one turncoat cop armed to the teeth, did his best to strut across the lawn to the robed figure, now standing hip-to-hip with Bob. The fact he tripped coming up the stairs detracted a bit from his swagger, but no one was paying much attention to him anyway. Unaware of who he was talking to, he got in Jesus's face.

"What're you supposed to be? Tony Senior asked.

"Welcome, my son. All will be revealed in due course. Please, join us for the End Times. You are the first to arrive, besides Bob here."

"End Times? Some kind of, er, themed party or somethin? Din't bring the booze, but don't think that will be much of an issue, eh?" He laughed, cupping his hand to catch rain before stumbling towards the shrine. His son caught him and helped him balance.

Three more cars pulled up. Agatha, Gus, Charlotte, and the others got out and stood stage right. Without proper leadership—and with no idea why they'd been compelled to the shrine in the first place—they were lost. Lost and uncomfortable people, especially people holding rifles with little-to-no experience with them, were dangerous. Throw in shot nerves and crackling lightning and you were bound for the perfect disaster.[2]

They stood there, swaying in the heavy wind like the masts of a sinking ship. Everyone expected someone else to make the first move, but no one took up the mantle. The people were more statuesque than the statues (who were hiding, waiting for their cue).

Jesus spoke: "Welcome. It is lovely to see more of my children here. We may yet salvage the night."

"And why are we here?" Agatha demanded.

"Because, my child, I called to you."

Agatha was a woman that got what she wanted but sometimes had to crack a few skulls. The people of Mio learned to hand over whatever she asked for, mostly in fear of their psychological safety. It wasn't often, though, someone got *her* to do something she didn't feel like doing. It had been a long day, and she'd just dried off and sat down for hot cocoa. Cleaning her shop after the amphibian firefight had been a painstaking process, and she wanted nothing more than to relax and watch the sky implode.

Then, she found her serenity interrupted. In her car that wasn't her broom...er, car, Agatha sped towards the void. *Oh, not again*, Agatha had thought, recalling a few of her wilder teenage romps. And thus, she found herself at the shrine, pissed off and wet, being called a child by some robed vagrant.

"What'd you call me, boy? I'm no child, ya hear. I'm Agatha, of Agatha's Eats. You best remember it and respect your elders while you're at it."

"No disrespect intended, *child*. We are all but children in the eyes of God."

---

2 Let's be honest, it's far too late in this story for any more subtle foreshadowing. If you didn't see this coming, here it is.

She raised her rifle a touch but lowered it when a new set of appeared—late, but right on time. This Focus did no careening or curb jumping. Rather, it pulled gracefully off the road and stopped without as much as backfiring. Detective Cross stepped out and waddled to the passenger side. He bowed to her as she slammed the door, giggling from whatever idiotic thing he said.

They let Deputy Lawson sleep it off in the backseat.

The others, besides Tony Dietrich's gang, hooped and hollered as the two joined them. Their leader had arrived. None of the excitement was directed at Chase. He beamed at the group nonetheless, ecstatic at this change of acceptance.

As soon as she noticed Tony Senior, the sheriff drew her revolver and pointed it at his face. In her most authoritative voice she said, "You son of a bi—"

"Welcome," Jesus interrupted, clearing his throat.

The world brightened and raindrops dodged the Messiah. A squadron of slimy creatures retreated into utter darkness. He approached Sheriff Grace, while addressing them all.

"Forgive my interruption, but time is short. I have brought you all here for a reason. Well, most of you." He looked at the Dietrichs, who tried to cower behind one another. "Others have shown up under your own crooked devices, guided by a different master. But no matter, everyone needs to hear what I have to say.

"As you can all see, your mortal trifles no longer matter. Funny thing, they never really did. Your town has fallen into chaos and darkness, as has the world around it. You all seek someone to point a finger at. You all want someone to blame."

No one refuted him. Even Agatha had nothing left to say. Jesus or not, he was very persuasive.

He went on.

"Sheriff Grace. Ah, Sheriff, you wish to see the Dietrichs pay for what happened to your home, and for kidnapping the mayor—though you seem to care less about that. Part of you must know this man sought your power. They wronged you, both personally and professionally. They set fire to the core of what you hold near and dear, at once igniting the fires of your fury. So, there you stand, judge and jury, but only God can judge a man's actions. If you take your vengeance any further, you'll also become their executioner. That's a dark path you don't want to travel.

"And townspeople, my faithful Mio flock, you blindly follow a false messiah in this sheriff. She's always done right by you. Her morals seem to align with your own. She's always protected your town and your loved ones, upheld that which *you* hold near and dear. Admirable, yes, but misguided. You've let your own angers and frustrations get the best of you. I mean, look at yourselves. Sopping wet, out in the middle of a storm—*the* Storm—armed to the teeth. Do you even know how to use those weapons you hold? Do you even want to? If you smite your assumed foe, you will feel no better. Salvation is found in forgiveness, not revenge. Peace comes from mercy. Drop your weapons now and consider yourselves atoned.

"To you, Tony Dietrich, I understand. I do. I don't by any means condone your actions, but I sympathize with the reasoning behind them. You love this town and its people. Almost as much as the sheriff does. For different reasons, of course. Hers out of a sense of duty, yours from enjoying lots of money in your bank accounts. Either way, it's a true and deep love and I cherish it. Seeing Mio hurt, seeing her people afraid and without answers, has been difficult on you, for fear closes the pocketbook. You looked for a scapegoat, finding one in both Mayor Gunderson and Sheriff Grace. The mayor deserves some scorn, to an extent. He hides while the world around him crumbles.

"Again, it is up to God to judge his cowardice. Not you. Not the sheriff. Not even his own mother. How dare you turn your wrath on the sheriff, one of the most unwavering in faith and in dedication? She has been the brightest light in dark times, while you have worked tirelessly to stamp it out."

At this, Sheriff Grace perked up. Any amount of failure she felt, punctuated by the chaos of the last few days, dissipated. She was in the dumps and not acting very sheriffly. The Stillmans. Dale and Rhonda. The police station. She was their safety net and a force beyond her control ripped holes into the ropes binding her together. Nothing she did seemed to come close to sewing them back together. Knowing there were actual divine forces behind some of this—and that Jesus himself praised her efforts—eased the burden of her suffering.

Tony Dietrich Senior returned to his initial hostile stance. He rested his gun against his leg while the Lord spoke, but his finger hovered over the trigger. Then, when Jesus finished, he aimed at Sheriff Grace.

She hunched and cocked her own revolver.

He gritted his teeth, baring them at her and the crowd around him, a frantic animal backed into a corner. The part in the theme song to *The Good, the Bad, and the Ugly*—the one that crescendos as the lowly deputy faced the leader of the bandits—played in his head.

Jesus rolled his eyes and rubbed his temples.

"There'd been no murders for thirty years," Tony said, biting back hysterical tears. He motioned to the sheriff. "Until her. Four dead in less than a week. What else has to happen before we realize she's unfit to protect us? Who else has to die?"

At the last word, *die*, everyone else at the shrine raised their guns.

Chase Cross unsheathed the sword he pilfered from the agency and twirled it around his hand before dropping it on the concrete steps. It clattered down the steps in perfect harmony with a roll of nearby thunder.

At that moment, Riz stepped out from the shadows. The statues had never before been bold enough to reveal themselves to humans. He inhaled and took the plunge. He was sick and tired of all the negativity. Hatred didn't get anybody anywhere.

"Dudes and ladies..." He raised two fingers in peace. Before he could say another word, a loud bang like thunder resonated, but this time it wasn't thunder. Everyone gasped.

Tony Dietrich stood, petrified, as a trail of smoke slinked out of the barrel of his gun. Riz, fingers still held up in peace, touched them to the hole dead center in his forehead. He crumbled to the ground in flaking, uneven pieces until only a pile of dust remained.

"For dust thou art, and unto dust shall thou return," someone said.

The Triumvirate of Marys wept from the shadows, sorrow being the universal translator.

As soon as the dust settled, everyone followed suit, steadying their shooting arms and letting bullets fly.

Tony Junior fired at Sheriff Grace, the sheriff at Tony Senior.

The townspeople shot at one another at random, taking the opportunity to be part of the whole ordeal.

Chase Cross arced the blade of the sword towards Tony Junior, remembering the teenager's fists in vivid detail.

The remaining two Jesuses slid out to protect their Lord and Savior.

Although Death and the Devil had sealed their marriage, gotten into their first and final spat, and left Earth to return to their own, separate lives, their presence loomed over the shrine, burning in the eyes of the townspeople. The

Devil looked out among the others through Tony Senior's eyes. Death reached towards them all, carried on the wings of madness. Their physical presence brought about the end of days, but their metaphoric presence was going to destroy the people of Mio.

Before any of the bullets reached their targets, or Chase's sword cut the flesh of a child, the world came to a standstill. The whole universe stopped. They all saw the hail coming down, heard the crash of thunder, and smelled the fires of the storm as it continued to rage, but no one moved. The air was still, and their death dealers froze in suspended animation.

A voice spoke to the collective. It was a voice without a body, but they all knew it belonged to God, she who needed no body.

"Fools. I leave you to your own devices and this is how you act? I give you earth beneath your feet and sky about your heads and what do you do with? You worship false gods. Gods of money, greed, and laziness. Gods of gluttony and pride. When you should have put your trust in me, you instead put your trust into your own wicked desires. Shame on you all."

She appeared, only not entirely. Rather, the astral outline of God phased into being. The air around her rippled as she made her way through the small crowd. She reached out and, one by one, plucked each bullet out of the air, dropping them harmlessly on the ground. They sizzled, popped, and disappeared into the earth. Next, she ran her palm down the sharp edge of Chase's blade. It dematerialized at her touch until only the handle remained.

She looked Chase dead in the eyes. "Your mother is pleased, Detective. Proud of the man you've become. I am not. Nor would I allow her to see you how you are now."

"How do you know what she is or isn't?" He found he could speak again, if raspingly. "Have you seen her, uh, ma'am? Is she…?"

She caressed his chubby cheek with ghostlike fingers, giving it a couple gentle smacks. Then, she smiled. It wasn't a happy smile. It was filled with sorrow and regret, with tears. It was God's party; she'd cry if she wanted.

"Mrs. Cross came to me after you left her. Her own disappointments in life led her to misjudge you, as parents often do. I've shown her the errors of her ways, though I respect her decisions as a mother. She is proud of you, Detective. But, then again, I didn't show her any of your sins. She can't see you as clearly as I can. I, of course, forgave her her final sin. Times are changing, as you know. "

For the second time in his life, Chase Cross was speechless.

"Now," God continued, addressing everyone, "your world as you know it is ending. Believe or don't, but I'm forced to intervene in the affairs of humankind, though I vowed not to. You have managed an acceptable balance between good and evil for many years. For that, I thank you. Obviously, you can't have one without the other. A lot of my children, though, have left the flock. They've lost their way. Their sacrileges took me a long time to get over, but I've been talking to a professional about it, and I think I'm learning how to cope in healthy ways. A minor plague here. A mysterious disaster there. My therapist reminds me it is not your fault for being the way you are—for being human. I made you and gave you original sin. I created a being with the capacity to make rational—and thus, irrational—decisions. I made you imperfect. You reap what you sow, amirite?

"No, it is not your fault. The blame rests with me for not intervening sooner. Old habits die hard. Call it stubbornness, if you will, but I trusted my son and his followers too much. I thought they would handle things better than they did. I put too much pressure on you, son. For that, I am sorry."

The storm tapered off. Clouds blanketed the entire sky, smothering the smoldering remainder of the sun, and scuttled off in every direction to find somewhere to hide. When touched by the weak rays of the sun, everything returned to the way it once was. Amphibians dispersed, disappearing into various water bodies. Cars transformed back into their different types—Fords, Saturns, Jeeps and the like. Chase's station wagon even returned to its former, rusty self. Water flowed once more. Only Gus's pantry contained even a fleck of rice. Charlotte's face cleared, and she was beautiful once more.

Everything was whole again.

But the wholeness was a fleeting illusion. Earth was broken, never to be mended. The damage was done. Parts were lost, fallen into the ocean of the universe and swept away forever by the seas of change.

Harmony would never exist again. Not after Death's pact with the Devil, not after they'd banged. Only evil remained. Chaos and oblivion. Not even God could change that.

For that reason, there were tears behind her smile.

"There is only one thing to do." God ran her fingers through her hair. "I'll take the righteous to a better place. A place by my side. The pearly gates are open to the chosen few; I embrace you with open arms to join me in my realm. I won't even ask you to take your shoes off at the door, for you are worthy to enter unconditionally.

"For the holy, I will swallow up death forever. I will wipe away the tears from your faces and remove you from all disgrace on Earth."

This time God didn't bother to write down her words. She thought of them often, anticipating the time in which she could say them. As she did, those of the group worthy enough floated into the air and vanished in a wave of pure bliss and bright light. One by one, they made their way to the pearly gates above, never to walk to surface again.

God held up her arm, stopping the progress of Tony Dietrich Senior and his son. They both looked at her, wide-eyed and hopeless.

"Nu uh. No way. Where do you think you're going? You killed the Risen Christ. He died for your sins, rose again, and then you shot him? And you call yourselves Christians? No, not you two. Before, I was going to grant you mercy for your sins, like the others. But I have a special place in Hell reserved for the likes of you two."[3]

Their bodies sizzled away into blue embers, showering ashes to the grass below. The fiery remains burned holes in the soil and sunk into the depths of the earth. They were delivered to the Devil—or to whomever had temporarily taken his place—for their just reward.

In all the confusion, the statues returned to their places, frozen forever in time. Only Chase and Bob remained. They were alone with God and Jesus.

That's when Chase flipped out. Sheriff Grace was gone. He couldn't comprehend what had just happened or where she went, but he knew too truly the pain. She was gone, and he wasn't. He would never see her again.

He dropped to his knees on the wet grass and wailed. It was one of those cries from the movies, arms raised to the heavens, expelled for much longer than any breath humanly possible. It was heard across the world. No one interrupted

---

[3] A circle Dante never found; a circle reserved solely for sleazy businessmen and their constituents where "It's a Small World" plays on repeat, bills pile up day and night, and perpetrators are forced to watch every penny they ever earned melt in barrels behind bullet-proof glass.

him or attempted to calm his fit. Although he might not have earned a first-class ticket to heaven, he had at least earned a moment to mourn the loss of someone he loved.

He wiped snot on his sleeve. "Why am I still here? I should be with her. I think...I love her. I... I've never been in love before."

God rested her astrophysical hand on his shoulder. He greeted her gesture with anger, wanting to lash out and strike her down, but a soothing wave of relief washed over him. The gesture explained everything to him. He saw why he was still alive, why he hadn't followed the others to...wherever they had gone. He saw his past, the horrible sins he'd committed, and understood. Too many women. Too much booze. Too little faith. Besides committing murder, there wasn't a commandment on the books he hadn't broken.

Chase Cross never believed in God. He believed in himself, and only to an extent—on good days. Relying on others always let him down. It left him abandoned and alone, with only his thoughts for company.

Look out for yourself. No one else will.

Despite these truths, he said, "I believe in you, God. Show me what to do next."

"I know, my child. I believe in *you*, too. You'll find your way in time. I'm sure of it. For now, keep on the path. It won't be easy, but you'll be just fine. You'll accomplish so much in the coming days. More than you can imagine. I will send signs and aid to help you along the way, but you have to figure out where to start on your own."

Chase Cross thanked God and walked away. He headed south. This wouldn't be the last time the two met, but somewhere else was calling his name. He felt it on the wind and deep within his blubber. A fire burned in his belly, and it wasn't heartburn. Not this time.

Bob remained at the shrine. Silent. Patient.

"Bob, my only grandson, I am sorry we didn't come to you sooner. I'm sorry to have kept you in the dark for so long. I have a plan, and he is a huge part of it." She pointed at the diminishing figure of Chase Cross on the horizon. "You are, too. He'll need your help soon. This world is going to become such an ugly place. Worse than ever, I'm afraid. But I'm not ready to give up on it entirely. I'm not ready to give up on *you*."

"I know."

"Good. You know what must be done, then?"

"Yes."

Jesus stepped between his mother and his son. "Do we have to? We're just getting to know one another."

She lowered her head, unable to look her son in the eyes, much like Chase was unable to look at her. But God felt no anger towards Jesus—only pity. And regret.

"When sight is dulled, my son, the other senses come to life. Bob needs those more than he needs to see. Especially with what's to come. What he doesn't know only makes him stronger. Do you understand?"

"I do," Jesus said.

"And Bob?"

"Sure." He didn't understand, but Bob had never been one to complain. He'd do what he needed to do, nothing more and nothing less.

"Wonderful," God said. "I will see you again, Bob. Soon, I promise. Until then, stay true to yourself and always follow your instincts. I will never allow them to lead you astray."

God and Jesus disappeared, returning to Heaven, leaving Bob alone. He looked around the shrine one last time, knowing he wouldn't remember the town of Mio, and then picked himself up off the ground.

"South it is," he said, matter-of-factly, and started walking.

His fate was in God's hands. Maybe he would catch up to Chase Cross, maybe he wouldn't. Only time would tell. All he could do was believe.

When everyone was gone, Willy, the groundskeeper, peered out of his shed. The last few days had been far too exciting for his tastes, and he had been too busy sleeping off his first drinks in years to take part in all the excitement. Now, alone with the shrine once more, he had work to do.

He looked around at the mess they'd left. He was used to people leaving messes for him, so it didn't bother him much. Besides, everyone had to play their part. If they didn't, which they all learned the hard way, the whole world fell apart.

"Still," he said, peering around the shrine at a giant, pink elephant toppled over on one of his flower beds. It had a big smile underneath its trunk. "What the heck am I supposed to do with that?"

Epilogue

One of our previous statements was not entirely true. Convenient, yes. We all know a simplification of the truth can *feel* better than the truth. But why?

You don't want to hurt someone, especially someone you love. You aren't equipped with the mental or emotional capacities to do the truth justice. Or, in this case, the simplified truth makes for a convenient, clever little metaphor to wrap-up everything all neat and tidy.

Admittedly, life is never "neat and tidy." Not really. You have to have a little faith. You have to understand that sometimes things happen completely out of your control, that no matter how hard you try, sometimes you fail. But sometimes you win, too. And often at the most unexpected times.

The statement in question regards Stan and Anaya. The Devil and Death did not entirely return to their own separate lives and duties, not as they had been before. What happened, instead, is twofold:

Anaya returned to being Death and was amazed at how quickly people realized she was back. People were getting out of hand. The paperwork and the backlog of emails was hardly worth it after what she'd been through. The whole ordeal seemed like a chore from day one, especially considering only the exceptionally unruly remained on Earth. On the stormy road home, Anaya bumped into a most unlikely traveler: Repugnant Rachel. Rachel's willingness to lead by example helped. Together, her and Death made a grand spectacle of her demise, followed by a wine and cheese girl's night to celebrate. From that day forth, Rachel and Death were inseparable. Everyone needed a friend, and sometimes they're found in the most unlikely places.

Stan grabbed his fanny pack, risked one last glance at the interior of their motel room, and moved on from the whole ordeal. He never thought about Anaya again. It was too painful. He'd been foolish to think he could outpace his subconscious, but instead of wallowing in sorrow, he decided to take a little vacation of his own. He'd never seen much of the world above. Maybe he'd start with Lima, Ohio.[1] It was as suitable a place as any. The Prince of Darkness 2.0 was open to new experiences. From there, he'd follow the ebb and flow of the road. It didn't matter where he was headed, as long as he kept going.[2]

---

[1] Please, please, please, we're begging you. Do not start your mid-life crisis in Lima, Ohio. Buy a Mazda Miata instead, and save yourself the trouble.

[2] While this story doesn't claim superior morality, this is a fine takeaway. We must, no matter the circumstances, keep going. The entire universe depends on it. Feel free to ignore this, however. If you'd rather take away something else, like the importance of frequent cardio and a mindful diet, here's to you. To each his/her/they're own.

ACKNOWLEDGEMENTS

Now that the story is done, thanks are in order. As with everything, the exact order is arbitrary. If I could, I'd put everyone on the same line. But then you, the reader—whom I am so grateful for—would be stuck with the world's most awkwardly shaped book. You'd have a hard time fitting it through doors on your way to the refrigerator. You'd knock over your bedside lamp and put holes in the drywall every time you readjusted your position. And we can't have any distractions. You have more books to read, after all!

Anyway, in normal, easy-to-hold format, I want to thank the following people:

My wife, Danielle, for a number of reasons. Namely, for putting up with me when my mind was focused on nothing but this story. Since 2015, Mio has stolen a lot of my time on more than one occasion. I hope I wasn't too neglectful during those "episodes."

My parents, Beth and Dan, for purchasing their "cabin" in Lewiston, Michigan. Without that first drive up M-33, this novel never would have happened. So, in a sense, this particular apocalypse is your fault. Way to go, guys. You did it.

Mio, Michigan, for being the greatest "unincorporated territory" on the face of this planet.

I'd also like to thank my son, Theodore. If it wasn't for you, Bug, I might have given up on this whole writing thing altogether. I hope as you grow older you too find your "Mio," your place of inspiration. I hope you never give up on what's important to you. And, when you lose your way, always hold tight to humor. Life is too crazy not to laugh about it.

About the Author

Curtis A. Deeter is an author of fantasy, science fiction, and horror. He has published a number of short stories in anthologies and online, including Scout Media's *A Contract of Words* and *A Flash of Words*, Rhetoric Askew's *Anthology Askew, Askew Horizons, Strangely Funny VI,* multiple editions of Fantasia Divinity's elemental drabbles series, and multiple editions of Black Hare Press's Lockdown Fiction series. His first full-length fantasy/science fiction collection, *Catching Lightning*, is available through Of Rust and Glass.

When he isn't writing, he can be found spending time with his wife and son, listening to an eclectic variety of music, working on his local, Northwest Ohio arts and literature magazine, or sampling new brews at the local brewery.

Join Curtis A. Deeter Online

Website: https://curtisadeeter.com/
BookBub: https://www.bookbub.com/authors/curtis-a-deeter
Goodreads:
https://www.goodreads.com/author/show/17795865.Curtis_A_Deeter
Facebook:
https://www.facebook.com/AuthorCurtisADeeter/
Twitter: https://twitter.com/CurtisADeeter
Instagram:
https://www.instagram.com/Curtis_A._Deeter/
Read More of Curtis's Books:
https://www.amazon.com/author/curtisadeeter.com
Check out Of Rust and Glass:
https://ofrustandglass.com/